A WOMAN BEYOND PRICE

Strong-willed and beautiful, Charlotte Forbes is due to inherit her father's fortune on her eighteenth birthday, but even money cannot destroy the scandal lurking in her past. From the moment that Sir James Caraddon, the rising star of Pitt's government, informs Charlotte of her inheritance, both their lives are turned upside down. Time after time, the two are thrown together and, as James is forced to protect Charlotte from the unsavoury characters who have an eye on her wealth, the two find themselves fighting an inevitable attraction.

A WOMAN BEYOND PRICE

A WOMAN BEYOND PRICE

by

Freda Lightfoot

Magna Large Print Books
Long Preston, North Yorkshire,
BD23 4ND, England.

British Library Cataloguing in Publication Data.

Lightfoot, Freda
    A woman beyond price.

    A catalogue record of this book is
    available from the British Library

    ISBN   0-7505-1705-0

First published in Great Britain 1991 in paperback format only
under the pseudonym of *Marion Carr* and title *Outrageous
Fortune*.

Published in Large Print 2001 by arrangement with
Severn House Publishers Ltd.

Magna Large Print is an imprint of Library Magna Books Ltd.

Printed and bound in Great Britain by
T.J. (International) Ltd., Cornwall, PL28 8RW

CHAPTER ONE

Sir James Caraddon allowed his grand-mother's hectoring tone to waft over his head while he unconcernedly studied the antics of a group of strolling players miming and posturing in the square below. It was cold by the window, the leaden December sky filled with the threat of snow, and he would much rather have been warmly ensconced in his study, or better still in his favourite London coffee-house with a good brandy and convivial company. Even the House of Commons, for all its dissension, would be preferable to yet another rendition of this all too familiar lecture. Yet he was fond enough of his grandmother and ready to spend what time he could with her, whenever his political duties permitted.

'What are you now, boy, thirty-four, is it?' the old lady demanded, rapping on the floor with her gold-tipped cane and causing the small mongrel dog curled upon her lap to leap up and start to bark with excitement so that he had to be stroked and petted and persuaded to lie down again before the conversation could continue.

'Thirty-one, Grandmother.'

'Tch. Then it is even more certain that you should be wedded and breeding by now,' she concluded, quite illogically. 'Are we never to have an heir for Brampton?'

James sighed. At sixty-six, Lady Caraddon was perfectly capable of living a further twenty years and had often declared her intention so to do. She would make no concessions to him before that date; therefore James saw no immediate urgency for any heir beyond himself at this stage. Politics were, on the whole, far less trouble than a wife. Several young ladies had caught his eye over the years and he was happy enough to enjoy their company with a little light dalliance here and there. But let them become only slightly possessive and begin to make tentative attempts to lay claim upon him, and Sir James Caraddon would suddenly become mysteriously elusive. Here again he had politics to thank, for it always served as a ready excuse in breaking an engagement without causing offence. When Parliament or perhaps William Pitt, the Prime Minister himself, had demands upon his time, how could any lady presume to dispute it? His grandmother, however, was another matter. She might declare that his presence in Truro at Christmas was not necessary to her happiness, yet if he did not come she would sorely miss him, and he would miss her. Not that either of them would ever say as much. It was all part of the game.

'How do you know that we do not have an heir already?' he teased, lightening his words with a twinkle of humour in his grey eyes.

'Because you have more sense than to land yourself with a scandal when you are angling for a place in Cabinet,' Lady Caraddon declared with telling accuracy. 'You're man enough to enjoy tasting the fruit, I know it, and clever enough to leave it on the table.'

James grimaced. 'You make me sound a rapacious rogue.'

Constance Caraddon threw back her head in a gleeful laugh, almost dislodging the tall powdered wig, much curled and feathered, and already slightly askew. Jabbing her stick in the air at James, she gave particular emphasis to her next words. 'It's time you found a dish you want to savour more fully. I'll not be around forever, though I shall do my best to live till I'm at least one hundred and one and torment the life from you, see if I don't.'

James laughingly parried the thrusting stick to swiftly drop a kiss on the paper-soft cheek. 'I'm heartily glad to hear it. Whatever would I do without you?'

'Now see what you've done. You've woken Bounder again. Do sit down and try to pay heed when I am talking to you. There, there, good dog,' she crooned, but to James, more sternly as he obediently did as he was bid and bestowed himself in the yellow satin chair opposite, 'I know very well what you would do. You'd spend my entire fortune on your political interests, you young rogue. Don't think I don't know it.'

James let out a resigned sigh as he frowned in mock sternness at her. 'Must you always take me for a fool? What little faith you have in me. I care not a jot for your riches, Grandmother. I am not a schoolboy waiting for my pocket-money to be handed out. I am perfectly capable of earning my own crust, and do so very well.'

'Tch. With that rag of yours you dare to call a news-sheet? That's far too staid to make money, my boy. It is scandal which sells papers, tittle-tattle and gossip, not dry-as-dust political comment. It'll lose you a fortune, see if it don't.'

'I am not dependent upon the news-sheet for a living. I do have other investments. Nevertheless it does very well,' James informed her, choosing to largely ignore the nub of her criticism though her point was valid. Gossip sheets sold in vast quantities while his own political tracts performed only moderately well in cash terms. 'Too many politicians seek office these days at any price, for the influence attached to it rather than for policies they believe in, Grandmother. They buy themselves into power, take bribes, carry out favours for their particular friends. Pitt is trying for reform, though not finding it easy. I am not afraid to expose corruption where I find it.' James was leaning forward, large square hands gesticulating the depths of his strong feelings on the matter.

'I can well believe it,' Lady Caraddon conceded with a sigh. 'But why does it have to be you who always points it out? Surely you can see it will win you no friends in the House. If you want a place of note in government, and refuse to buy it as many do, then you are going to have to temper your cavalier spirit a little.'

James's handsome face tightened with a grim determination Lady Caraddon had seen many times before. Stubborn as they come, she thought. Believed he could right every wrong, always did. His father had been just the same. Long on patience and short on tact. If something needed to be said, a Caraddon was the one to say it. There was not a trace of softness in that firm jawline, nor in the way the grey eyes shrewdly assessed every word she said and sometimes, Constance honestly believed, those left unsaid. Yet the caring was there, else why should he voluntarily choose to spend Christmas with an old has-been like herself? Lady Caraddon smiled proudly at her beloved grandson, for she had planned

13

this year to make it a more lively Christmas and she was determined to have her way on the matter. Knowing his perversity on the subject of females, however, she must tread with care. 'One of these days you'll say a word too much or take a step out of line yourself, and they'll roast you alive, mark my words. It don't do to make enemies in high places.'

James uncoiled himself with an easy grace and came to stand behind his grandmother's chair, for she had spoken truer words than she realised and he did not wish her to see his face. 'Have no fear. I take great care.' Bending down he kissed her forehead. 'Besides, you know that I lead an exemplary life, unlike yourself, who I am well aware loses far too much at the gaming tables, drives her carriage too fast and tittle-tattles across half the county.'

It was exactly the opening she had been looking for. 'I like to enjoy life,' she briskly retorted. 'Not that anyone cares how an old woman spends her time. You, my boy, are a very different matter. I know how the gossip sheets love to talk about you.' She sniffed with disdain. 'It is always the way when one rises too high and too fast. Many friends are left behind with nothing but their envy to gnaw upon. The most prudent way for you to avoid trouble and to win your place in the cabinet is to take a wife. One who will be steadfast and loyal, bring you steady respectability and hopefully something of a fortune to lubricate the alliance.'

James cast his grandmother a wary glance. 'And you might just have such a person in mind?'

Lady Caraddon had the grace to flush very slightly and she picked up her needlepoint to distract his piercing gaze, which very nearly unnerved her. She decided to opt for the more oblique route. 'I had hoped the matter would be settled by now, that you would bring me news this Christmas of an engagement between yourself and that lively young widow, Lady Susanna Brimley.' It was the very last thing she wanted to hear but Constance smiled as she arched one fine brow questioningly up at her grandson.

But James chose not to offer a smile in return. The subject was growing too intrusive for comfort. He strode again to the window and stood with hands folded neatly behind his back, glaring down upon the strolling players who now seemed to be giving out hand bills, no doubt advertising their main show to take place later in the week.

'Well?' Lady Caraddon persisted, rapping on the wood floor with her stick.

James let the silence lengthen. There was no doubt that Susanna was quite delicious and more than willing on her part to make a match of it. She had charm, beauty, breeding, money, and her reputation was impeccable. She was perhaps a touch lacking in a sense of humour but would certainly make an excellent wife. Why, then, did he hesitate? He had pondered upon this a good deal lately and, were he not a gentleman and she, in truth, a Lady, he would say she also lacked sincerity. There was a gloss to the charm, a design to the impeccability of her style. In short, he did not entirely trust her.

James sighed. 'I dare say I shall settle for Susanna in the end, but sometimes she seems more ambitious for me than I am for myself. And to be honest, Grandmother, I find that disturbing.'

The silence which followed this confession was rich with understanding. It was finally broken by Lady Caraddon clearing her throat somewhat noisily, giving a little cough, and then clearing her throat again. The old rascal had something up her sleeve; James could sense it. But not for a moment would he make it easy for her to inform him of it, for she was not usually so reticent at revealing her plots and plans. Every visit was the same. She would spirit some poor overlooked female from nowhere and parade her before him like a skinny milk cow at market and expect him to fall upon her with adoration and desire. The last one, a Miss Amelia Devereux, a buck-toothed miss of uncertain

16

age, had fallen hopelessly in love with him and followed him half across England. He'd been forced to marry her off to a friend, fortunately not a close one, in order to be rid of her.

'Oh, James, while I think of it, there is a small favour you could do for me.'

At last. 'No.'

Lady Caraddon started. 'You don't know what it is yet!'

'It is still no.'

Since James had not turned from the window Lady Caraddon could only think that he must be smiling and not at all serious, for he was usually far more amenable to her wishes. 'I'm sure you will change you mind when you know what it is. Besides, it is Christmas and I will not have you grumpy,' Lady Caraddon scolded. 'I simply wished you to escort me to a social gathering, but there, if it would be too profoundly boring for you, I'm sure I would not dream of forcing you.'

James closed his eyes in despair. 'Where is this social gathering, dear Grandmother?' he asked, in a voice filled with self-doom.

'It is a simple country affair and, though I'm not a great lover of the country, particularly at this time of year as you know, since it is given by an old friend and neighbour of mine, Nathan Pierce, I feel I would like to attend.'

James gave an inward sigh of relief. Christmas gatherings over mulled spiced ale, with lively conversation and perhaps a fiddler to tap one's foot to, were not at all unpleasant and far removed from the wickedly contrived match-making ceremonies Constance usually had planned for him. He took little interest in his grandmother's social circle, consisting as it did chiefly of folk of advanced years, but, if he recalled correctly, Nathan Pierce was solid enough, more interested in art and literature than his cows, therefore having some conversation to offer. James swung round upon polished heels and, taking two steps across the room, lifted his grandmother's hand in his own and kissed it. 'Then, Cinderella, you shall go to the ball.'

'Oh, James, what a tease you are,' said Constance Caraddon with a gurgle of girlish laughter. 'There, you see, all you need is some lively company; politics has quite dried up your sense of humour.'

James grinned wickedly at her. 'Never, dear Grandmother, while I have you to tickle it.'

Constance threw her fan at him, which, owing to the fact that James very neatly ducked at the opportune moment, missed him entirely and landed in the fire where the spurting flames consumed it in an instant.

'Now see what you have done,' she pouted.

'I shall buy you another, without delay,' he assured her and strode briskly to the door. He was halfway through it before he thought to enquire, 'And when is this simple country affair? Is it to celebrate Christmas Eve?'

'Oh, my, no. Did I not tell you?' Constance enquired, wide-eyed.

James paused and, coming slowly back into the room, said, 'You know you did not,' suspicion once more rife in his voice.

'It is tomorrow evening.'

'Tomorrow?'

'Yes.'

'Nine days before Christmas? Does it have any particular purpose for being so, this country festivity?'

Lady Caraddon set down her needlepoint with a show of apparent unconcern. 'Ring for Lucy, will you, James? I have a fancy for a dish of chocolate. Would you care for some?'

'Grandmother.' The tone was dangerously low and absolutely uncompromising. 'You are keeping something from me, I know it.'

Constance gave a little squeal. 'Oh, my, how fierce you sound. Just like your dear papa when he was cross. And I was so sure I must have told you.'

'I warn you, Grandmother, I am fast losing my patience.'

'It is merely to celebrate the eighteenth

birthday of Nathan's niece, a delightful girl, quite delightful,' Constance gabbled. 'She comes into quite a fortune, I believe. Why, I was sure I must have mentioned her.'

But James was already striding back to the door, his back stiff with resolution. 'Then you must find another to escort you, Grandmother, for I will not risk being saddled with yet another whey-faced heiress, and if you try to make me I shall return to London upon the instant.'

'As you wish, my dear,' said Constance placidly. 'I have no wish to force you, as I said. I can go to the party with Major Dunskin, perhaps.'

'Major Dunskin? That old roué? Never!' James was shocked and also resigned, for he saw at once that he was trapped. Nothing would induce him to leave his grandmother in the money-grubbing hands of that old skinflint. He'd been courting Lady Caraddon for the last ten years, and if he ever won her James could kiss goodbye to his inheritance for good. And, though James might enjoy a certain degree of independence, the thought of Dunskin passing on the Caraddon fortune to the grasping fingers of his own prolific family was more than James could bear to contemplate.

Sighing quietly to himself, James negotiated a compromise.

'May I at least look her over in advance?'

'By all means,' agreed Lady Caraddon with unseemly enthusiasm. 'You could ride over this very afternoon. Be seated again, my dear boy, for I should very much like to tell you of little Miss Charlotte Forbes.'

Prickling with doubts, yet quite unable to cross his grandmother, James prepared himself to be bored by a list of the dreaded female's attributes, of which no doubt there would be plenty. If not buck teeth, then fat hips or lank yellow hair or even, heaven forbid, a squint. Lady Caraddon's ability to sniff out a fortune was unnerving, but not even her dearest friend and closest ally could bestow upon her the charge of good taste.

'No young lady mindful of her reputation would think of stepping upon a stage, so come down off that stool this instant, Miss Charlotte, and stop making a pantomime of yourself.'

'Oh, Alice, don't be such an old spoil-sport. And it is not pantomime, it is Shakespeare. Listen; it is the speech by Juliet to the friar when she declares she will kill herself rather than marry Paris, whom she does not love.'

Alice Trevail was so startled by this revelation of morbidity in her young charge that the rolling-pin fell from her hand with a clatter and she only just managed to retrieve it before it rolled from the table. 'I'll listen to no such thing,' she flustered in shocked tones. 'You've very soundly proved my point. Such gruesome tales can only turn a young girl's mind.'

Charlotte chuckled with impish glee. 'What nonsense. *Romeo and Juliet* is not a gruesome tale. It is a love story. Only it has a tragic ending since both lovers kill themselves.'

'That is quite enough of that, Charlotte. You know full well your Uncle Nathan would dislike your talking about such matters.' Alice slapped the carefully rolled pastry upon the top of her pie as if it alone were at fault.

Charlotte's green eyes glowed. 'But only think of the great playwrights we have these days: people like Mr Sheridan, and Goldsmith. And the famous actors and actresses – John Kemble, Mrs Siddons and Dorothea Jordan,' Charlotte said.

Alice turned quite pink. 'I'll accept that Mrs Siddons is a properly married lady, although she's chosen an odd way of earning her living, but as for that other madam...' Alice almost snorted her disapproval as she thrust the pie into the oven. 'No good will come of her, mark my words. And what I do hear about the kind of women who frequent such places, let alone those daring enough to perform in them, well...' floundered Alice, at a loss at how to finish her sentence without giving offence to such young, innocent ears '...I wouldn't like to say.'

Stifling her giggles as best she could and wrinkling her nose teasingly at the housekeeper, Charlotte launched into Juliet's speech. Hands clasped to her small bosom, head enchantingly tilted to emphasise the heart-rending quality of the words, she held her audience enraptured by the gently compelling sincerity of her voice.

Despite herself, even Alice stopped her work to listen, enthralled. Ever since this lively, high-spirited girl had come to live with her uncle, Nathan Pierce, on his Cornish farm, there had never, in Alice's own words, been another dull moment. With her nut-brown hair and lively green eyes set in a face of vibrant freshness, for all the pugnacious quality in its square-jawed obstinacy, Charlotte had stolen a place in Alice's heart beside that occupied by her own daughter. But this girl did not have Molly's simplicity of nature. Charlotte Forbes was a paradox. A disturbing mix of practical common sense coupled with a tender loving heart and a marked tendency for dreaming romantic notions which bordered on the reckless. The age-old conflict of birthright against upbringing, Alice supposed, and she could only pray it would not be her undoing.

Charlotte jumped down from the stool, helped herself to a freshly baked piece of gingerbread still piping hot from the oven, ducked beneath Alice's flapping, chastising hand and curled herself into the kitchen rocking-chair. 'But you did promise me some entertainers at my birthday party. Do not deny it, for I remember you gave your word, and I shall keep you to it.'

The wrinkled face creased with laughter. 'Don't scheme with me, little minx, for I have known you too long. I said you might have a fiddler or two for some dancing. That is quite a different matter.'

'Oh, but there are strolling players in the neighbourhood, Alice. I have seen the posters,' cajoled Charlotte, but to no avail. She saw how the lips clamped down in a firm unremitting line and how the plump cheeks dimpled with determination. When the housekeeper adopted such an expression it was best to withdraw and admit defeat, at least for the present. Tactfully Charlotte veered the subject on to more profitable lines.

'And shall you make my favourite cinnamon and apple cake?'

'What do you think I'm about now?' said Alice laconically.

'Oh, and some almond tarts. Yours are the very best.'

Alice chuckled with good humour. No denying that the child had a captivating charm. 'You'll get what you're given and like it, miss.'

Charlotte hugged her knees in delight. 'I'm sure I shall. I can't wait. Uncle Nathan is so kind to give me such a party.'

'Coming out be a special time for a young woman,' said Alice, then added more sombrely. 'Though it sometimes brings with it new responsibilities and changes that a young girl of eighteen summers may not always welcome.'

But Charlotte had already picked up her copy of *Romeo and Juliet* again and, with her head full of poetry and the promise of the celebration to come, she did not notice the warning note in the familiar voice, nor see how Alice cast her a quick glance of compassion. Bouncing from the chair with such vigour that it sent the rocker into a wild dance, Charlotte declared her intention to take the book into the garden and learn Juliet's final soliloquy.

'You will call me if you need me, will you not, Alice?'

'I dare say I might,' sighed Alice, knowing she would not. 'Get along with you, then, before I find some potatoes for you to scrub.'

Popping a kiss on the warm cheek, fragrant with yeast and spices, Charlotte

25

picked up her skirts and ran from the room.

From a shadowed corner of the large kitchen a voice emerged; sulky and resentful, it cut across Alice's thoughts.

'Why does she allus get her own way?'

'I wasn't aware that she did,' Alice replied, sharper than she'd intended.

'She allus do,' Molly grumbled, licking her fingers after dipping them in to the baking-bowl and receiving a resounding slap upon her hand for the act. 'All this fuss 'bout a birthday. Never had no party when I turned eighteen.'

'You weren't an heiress going into her inheritance, so it's hardly surprising, is it?' retorted her mother drily. 'And Miss Charlotte will certainly not get her way, for I can't see Mr Nathan agreeing to have strolling players in this house. It would be tempting fate,' Alice muttered, whipping the cake mixture with more vigour than was called for and sending little spats of creamed sugar on to the scrubbed pine table. 'Where are those apples I asked you to slice for me? I'm nearly ready for them.'

Molly went to fetch the bowl of apples and started to slice them very slowly. 'Mr Nathan might say she can, after all.'

'Can what?'

'Have the strolling players at the party.' Molly secretly hoped that he would, for at present it sounded a very dull affair with

26

only a few of the more upper-crust neighbours invited. 'He lets her have most of what she wants, don't he? And so do you. Here we are, run off our feet with all the extra work for the party on top of the normal chores, with no more pairs of hands but our own to do it. You won't even ask her to help.'

'You mind your manners and call her Miss Charlotte with proper respect,' rebuked Alice, feeling hot and flustered. Her energy and enthusiasm for this wretched affair was fast beginning to flag. So much work still to be got through, and all by tomorrow night, with Christmas only nine days away. It was a most inconvenient time to celebrate a birthday, even such a one as this. And no one could ever accuse Nathan Pierce of enjoying such junketings so there had to be good reason for it. Alice allowed herself a tired sigh as she eased her aching back for a moment. 'Maybe you have a point, Molly. There's little enough help kept in this household for all the work that has to be done, but somehow it don't seem quite right to ask an heiress to peel potatoes. Miss Charlotte is the daughter of a Lord, for all she has been brought up on this simple farm with neither the time nor the money for pampering and fol de rols.'

'What did happen to him – the Lord, I mean – and to Charlotte's mother?' asked

Molly, her curiosity making her quite forget the apples. 'Why will you never tell me?'

'Because it's none of your business.' Alice waggled a wooden spoon at her daughter. 'That all happened long ago and is best forgotten. But, mark my words, the future will be very different. Life for Miss Charlotte is about to change and I'm not sure 'twill be for the best. Not as far as she is concerned, anyway. She's happy enough with the way things are.'

Molly's eyes narrowed consideringly. 'Will she get a lot of money, do you think? And what'll she do with it? D'you reckon she'll go away somewhere, or spend it on the farm? It could do with a bit of money spending on it, could this place.'

Alice looked up in surprise at her daughter, dark head bent over the apple bowl propped upon her skinny knees, and wondered, not for the first time, just how simple Molly really was. Most of the time she quietly drifted along, happy to follow any course her mother set for her. But recently she'd started to balk at the least little thing, and to show petty jealousies quite unlike herself. And some of her questions were growing quite pertinent. At nineteen she'd seemed a child still, but something, or someone, had wrought a change in her. 'Have you been talking to Dickon?'

'Dickon don't want her money.' The dark

head jerked back with the vehemence of the reply and Alice met the fiery gaze with fresh unease in her heart. The child had developed an attachment to Nathan's son, Dickon, far beyond what was right for a mere kitchen-maid. Something would need to be done about that. 'He'm not interested in Miss Charlotte at all, so there. It's only her what says he is.' Molly's dark eyes glittered with malice. 'Dickon has his eyes on quite another, he do.'

'That's enough of such talk, Molly. When the time is right for Master Dickon to take a wife, I dare say Mr Nathan will have some say in the matter. And even if he doesn't it is none of our business.'

Molly's cheeks flushed with self-righteous indignation. 'I never said 'twas. Anyway, Dickon don't intend to marry anyone, not yet. Not till...'

'Till what, Molly?' The question hung in the air between mother and daughter, each aware that much more could be said, but in the end both backing away from the confrontation. 'Get on with those apples. Gossip won't bake cakes.'

And for once Molly readily dipped her head to her work, anxious to break the probing shrewdness of her mother's gaze.

'You can marry me if you like.'

Charlotte almost dropped the precious

29

book from her hand as the low thrumming voice spoke softly in her ear. 'Dickon, don't startle me so,' she scolded, sinking back with relief into the sweet-smelling bed of hay she had made for herself, a warm cocoon in which to savour a half hour's peace with her book before the midday meal. 'What nonsense you do talk.'

Dickon looked downcast. 'Why is it nonsense?'

'Because we are cousins.'

'Cousins do marry.' Dickon eased himself from behind the beam where he had hidden. He loved to watch Charlotte, particularly when she was entirely unaware that he was there. Sometimes she spoke the poetry or whatever she was reading out loud, and it sounded so beautiful coming from her lips that he wanted to keep every word locked in his head so that he could bring them out and listen to them whenever he wanted. But recently he'd started taking more notice of the movement of the lips themselves rather than the words they spoke. They were soft and moist and rosy and from time to time he'd wondered what it would be like to kiss them. Molly let him kiss her often, but Charlotte's lips would be different from Molly's ever-chattering mouth. Now he settled himself beside her in the hay, grinning cheerfully, his large, round, tousled head propped unsteadily upon one rather grubby hand. 'So, why not?' he persisted.

'We are first cousins, Dickon, far too closely related for it to be possible even if we were to consider such a thing as marriage, which of course we will not.' Charlotte had long since grown used to Dickon's crushes, which altered as easily as the waxing and waning of the moon. He was an innocent romantic where young women were concerned, his knowledge of the world stopping abruptly short after the tending of his cows and sheep. 'One day you will find a beautiful young maiden to love. Who knows, perhaps one will come to my party?' Charlotte smiled at him, trying to give Dickon confidence for she felt that this was his chief problem. Riddled with shyness, he held himself in such contempt that he never ventured out into society to meet any young ladies. And, at five and twenty, it was long past time that he did.

But Dickon only looked sulky. 'Don't want anyone else,' he declared, and Charlotte couldn't help giving a little sigh of weariness.

'How can you know till you go out and about and look?'

'You don't like me, do you?' he accused.

'That is quite untrue, Dickon, and you know it,' Charlotte said. 'I like you very much.'

'Molly doesn't.'

31

'Yes, she does.'

'She don't,' he protested, growing agitated. 'She told me to go away and not bother her no more. She said, go to Miss Charlotte if that's what you want, and it is. I do love you, Charlotte, and if you'll only say the word I'll ask Father if we can be wed. Then you won't ever need to leave the farm, will you?'

Charlotte gasped, her heart skipping a beat. 'Leave the farm?' she whispered. It was the only part of his little speech which she really took note of. 'Why should I do that? This is my home.'

'I heard Father telling Alice that you are to go away. But I don't want you to. Don't go, Lottie.' Dickon lay his head upon her lap, and absentmindedly Charlotte smoothed and straightened the rusty coils of his tousled hair, removing the bits of straw which had lodged there, while she considered this new and astounding information.

'Perhaps I am not to have any say in the matter.' Charlotte spoke through lips gone stiff with fear. Never in all her wildest fears had she imagined being made homeless by Uncle Nathan.

Dickon lifted his head to peer closely into her face. 'Are you crying, Lottie?'

'No.'

'You do like me, after all, don't you? You're

32

crying because you'll have to leave me, is that it?'

But Charlotte wasn't listening. 'How can I be sent away? Tomorrow is my birthday. Where would I go? You must be mistaken, Dickon.' The tears shone with her fear, but pride would not let them fall.

'Don't cry, my lovely Lottie. I'll look after you. Kiss me and we will plight our troth.' And, before Charlotte could take evasive action, Dickon had clamped his arms about her and planted his large wet mouth over hers. They rolled together in the hay, locked in an embrace which Charlotte could not break for her arms were trapped between their two bodies. All she could do was to beat her legs in futile despair as the kiss went endlessly on.

'I beg your pardon for interrupting, but the door was open and I am seeking a Mr Nathan Pierce.'

Charlotte found herself released from the punishing grip as Dickon turned to the voice and, as she followed his wondering gaze upwards over shapely booted calves and coat in the finest of blue cloths to the source of it, she let out a little gasp of dismay.

CHAPTER TWO

For the first time in her life Charlotte was struck utterly speechless. If in her fantasies she had ever imagined meeting such a man, it had not been in these circumstances, with Dickon proving more of a nuisance than usual.

The tall, undoubtedly good-looking stranger, most handsomely attired in the very latest many-caped blue coat with matching stock and flat-topped hat, which, she noted, he did not remove, seemed as out of place in the hay barn as a racehorse in a cart-shaft. Charlotte felt suddenly very dusty and decidedly dowdy in her striped poplin overdress tucked up over a faded muslin gown, for all the fineness of the lace kerchief modestly tied about her neck and shoulders. It did not help either that she had covered her only good feature, her mane of nut-brown hair, with a large mob-cap more serviceable than pretty.

With scarcely a scrap of dignity left to cling to, Charlotte scrambled to her feet. Dickon, she noticed, remained sprawled in the hay, mouth a gaping oval of astonishment.

'I did knock. But you were both too busy to notice.' A pair of quizzing charcoal-grey eyes laughed down at her and Charlotte felt her cheeks redden with fresh embarrassment. He took her for a dairy-maid enjoying a frolic.

'I'm sorry. This is only Dickon... It was not...' Her halting explanations came to an abrupt end as she saw only an increase in his amusement.

'I am sure it is none of my business,' he drawled. 'I would not have interrupted you and your lover for the world, had I known. However, on learning I had received an invitation to a celebration here tomorrow night, I was anxious to do the courteous thing and accept personally. The housekeeper believed that Mr Pierce might be here in the yard. Evidently not.' A smile tilted one corner of the wide mouth in an expressive quirk as if by way of apology. And thick silky brows, almost as black as the unpowdered hair drawn into a queue and tied behind his neck, lifted questioningly.

The man was evidently enjoying her discomfiture hugely. His arrogant smile was beginning to kindle an anger within Charlotte she found hard to resist, but he had declared himself to be one of Uncle Nathan's guests so she must curb her tongue whatever it cost her in terms of pride.

She glanced down at Dickon, wishing he would speak, but she saw at once that his shyness had tied him into the familiar knot and with a heartfelt sigh of resignation Charlotte attempted to redeem some of her lost dignity.

'Dickon is not my lover. You have it all wrong. He is my cousin, almost a brother to me.'

If she had hoped that this explanation would resolve the embarrassment she was soon disabused of this notion. Though she had certainly succeeded in dispelling any trace of amusement from the keenly observant eyes, she was astonished to find it replaced by a darkly glowering disapproval.

'Your brother?' The crisply condemning tone sliced through her like sheet-ice.

'N-no, I said he was my cousin. It is only that we have been brought up together as b-brother and sister.' She hated herself for stuttering, but there was something terrible in the appalled expression of disdain upon his cleanly handsome face which set her trembling. Charlotte fully understood his reaction, for their behaviour must have seemed most unseemly. How could she explain about Dickon? Not entirely simpleminded, but certainly naïve in the extreme.

'Can you be the niece?'

He made it sound like an accusation and, feeling she needed more substantial support, she gave Dickon a resounding kick upon his ankle. Far from bringing him to his senses, he simply took to his heels and scampered from the barn. Now Charlotte and this intimidating, censorious stranger were quite alone.

Lifting her chin in defiance, Charlotte acknowledged his accurate guess. 'My name is Charlotte Forbes, and yes, I am the niece of Nathan Pierce. You say my uncle invited you to my party? He said nothing of it to me.' There was the faintest hint of incredulity in her tone, but it did nothing to soften the darkness of his forbidding expression.

'I am Sir James Caraddon and have promised to escort my grandmother, Lady Caraddon, who enjoys such junketings but felt in need of my company. I can fully understand why.' Charlotte watched in helpless horror as his eyes moved impertinently over her body, not simply scanning it, but studying it in intimate detail, removing his hat so that he could adjust his fine head more freely for a better view. Reaching forward, he plucked a piece of straw from a ringlet that lay coiled upon her shoulder. 'I can also understand why your cousin is so besotted. But, if I am any judge in these matters, tomorrow's proposed gathering is as much to find you a husband as celebrate a birthday, and I would say on present evidence that it is not a moment too soon.'

Charlotte's usually fair skin shot with colour and her heartbeat rat-tatted against her ribcage. Worse, her tongue seemed rooted to her teeth and, as she looked up at this giant of a man with his disparaging attitude, she felt like some immoral slut who had crawled out of a bawdy house. 'You go too far, sir,' she said at last in a small choking voice.

'And so, I think, did you.'

Charlotte gasped. 'That is the most scandalous untruth. We did not... Dickon is not quite...' She was floundering for words, lost in her own defence. Desperate to pull herself together, she felt herself sinking in that very desperation.

His disappointment in her made the laugh he gave sound harsh. Determined to be better prepared this time for whatever dreadful female his grandmother had found for him, James's decision to pay a preliminary call to Caperley Farm had evidently been a wise one. Charlotte Forbes was certainly an improvement on her predecessors. Despite the rumpled, dusty dress and that hideous mob-cap, she presented the picture of charming rustic beauty. The eyelashes which fringed the deliciously sparkling green eyes were dark and entrancingly curled. The silky lips took on a sensual pout and she held her body with an

38

unconscious knowledge of its slender beauty. Yet despite this seeming innocence he had found her in an intimate embrace, and with a relative of dismaying closeness – hardly the kind of behaviour one could consider fitting in a young lady of means. 'You need not explain to me,' he said with more than a trace of sarcasm. 'I am used to the acrobatic morals of young ladies, and do not even attempt to understand them.' At the door he paused for a final shot. 'Whatever Dickon's attractions, and I confess I noted none, you could do better for yourself as you no doubt realise. I bid you good hunting.' Replacing his hat at an elegant angle upon his head, he offered her a small bow before leaving.

It was some moments before Charlotte's rage dissolved sufficiently for her to think clearly. What exactly had he been accusing her of? She sat down abruptly upon a clump of hay. His attitude could not have been worse had Dickon indeed been her brother. If only she could have explained properly. Charlotte drew in a deep, steadying breath. The fault of course was Dickon's but he was an innocent and had meant no harm by his kiss. She thought about this for a moment or two. It was what she usually said to herself when Dickon had plagued her with his teasing. But was she correct to go on excusing him in this way? His attitude had grown more and more familiar of late, moving on from childish pranks with frogs and beetles to more familiar teasing. Now, with today's talk of marriage and kissing, she should perhaps deal with him more firmly. But how? She had tried to be firm in the past and Dickon had only laughed at her. But something must certainly be done to distract his thoughts away from herself. She supposed she should mention the problem to Uncle Nathan, but somehow she always backed away from the idea.

Meantime she had the added problem of one of her foremost neighbours and birthday guests believing her to be quite without a scrap of decency. For all that he seemed a fuddy-duddy – after all he was quite old, at least thirty – it was not a situation to be enjoyed. Perhaps tomorrow there would be an opportunity to fully explain the embarrassing consequences of Dickon's foolish fancies. The last thing she wanted was to have her birthday spoilt. Having decided upon a plan of action, she felt instantly better. It was a silly mistake which could quite easily be rectified. Tomorrow, Sir James Caraddon and she could laugh about it. For now she might try once more to persuade Uncle Nathan to invite just a few of the company of strolling players to put on a sketch for her guests. She so desperately wanted to see them and she would never be allowed to visit their little theatre.

Hearing barking in the yard, she jumped to her feet. 'All right, Sam. I'm coming. But it must be a short game today.' Picking up her skirts, she ran from the barn, shaking off her troubles and the wisps of straw that had clung to her gown as easily as only the very young could.

Nathan Pierce had a much more serious problem upon his mind than whether or not his niece should have a group of strolling players to entertain her guests at her eighteenth-birthday party. It was, in his opinion, far too young an age to carry the kind of burden he was about to place upon her slender shoulders. Yet he had his instructions, clear and precise, and there was little he could do to alter them. True, in all the sixteen years he had had care of the child, her father had never been to see her once. For all that gentleman knew, his daughter could well be dead. Ah, but there was the nub of it; in his eyes, Charlotte was not his daughter and never would be. Charlotte had believed her father dead, and Nathan had let her continue to think so, on the basis that it was less painful for her than the truth. But it was not a situation which could be allowed to go on indefinitely.

Nathan leaned back in his worn leather chair, his right hand once more reaching into his waistcoat pocket for his spectacles. Hooking the wire frames upon his bony nose, he read again the letter he held in his hand, his long face pursing with concentration. It was from his old friend Lady Constance Caraddon, delivered by hand from her home in Truro, and he experienced anew the great relief he had felt when he'd first read that she was willing to relieve him of this unpleasant duty. It was one thing to tell a young lady that she was about to inherit a sizeable fortune, and quite another to rob her of her parentage. He owned that the manner in which it should best be done had defeated him and he had written to Constance for help. He was likewise delighted to learn that his timing, as always, had been impeccable and her grandson, James, was indeed at home.

'I am certain James will be delighted to attend Charlotte's coming-out. And we can bring the child back with us for Christmas, if you like, when I will do what needs to be done, dear Nathan. You need have no fear for I am the very epitome of tact, though why you should worry, I do not know, for it is old water under a long-ago bridge and she sounds a sensible enough chit. In any case, I have every faith that James likewise will do what he can for her. You will see for yourself what a fine young man he is.'

Nathan smiled to himself. Constance was

no fool. Though he had made no precise mention of it she would guess his hope that her grandson and his niece might make a match of it. Since Charlotte must take possession of this fortune, a suitable husband would have to be found for her, if only to protect her from the host of predatory males who would inevitably gather and from the tittle-tattle that would follow her. He saw it as no bar that the man was thirteen years her senior, for a mentor of more mature years was considered an advantage. Nor did it worry Nathan unduly that he had, as yet, never met the young man, though he would be pleased enough to have the opportunity to look him over, as Constance had shrewdly guessed.

A flash of colour caught Nathan's eye and, getting stiffly to his feet, he crossed to the window. Charlotte, dressed most unsuitably for this cold day in a red and white striped gown, was throwing a ball for Sam, her small dog, and then in her exuberance running with him to retrieve it. She was laughing and giggling as freely as a happy child and Nathan thought what a great pity it was that such a rare innocence must be quashed.

Taking off his reading-spectacles, he folded them away and stood for a while, watching her. With one hand resting easily inside his half-buttoned waistcoat and the other behind his back, he gave a picture of a man comfortable with life and with himself. His long coat and brown breeches had evidently seen good service and were spotted with small burns from his clay pipe. Upon his bald pate he wore a grey peruke, but not from vanity. He had worn a powdered wig for most of his life, always the same style, with no great regard for fashion. Such considerations made little impression upon him or on the quiet life he led here in the country. Besides which it was more economical not to chop and change. Although by no means a poor man, Nathan Pierce deemed it prudent to be exceedingly careful with his money. He'd disposed of most of the horses he had kept for sporting purposes following the taxation imposed upon them shortly after the election of 1784, more than a year ago. And, though it was a minor irritation to Nathan, he would bear with his decision until common sense prevailed and the government abolished it. As a result he kept only one carriage and grumbled constantly about the tax on those horses. He was now considering having some of his windows bricked in to avoid the iniquitous, increased tax upon his property. Why the government imagined that all people who lived in large country houses were rich quite defeated him. Money was such a worry – he gazed out upon his land and upon his niece and smiled to himself – but not for Charlotte. Money would present no problems for her. And if anyone deserved such good fortune, she did.

Pushing open the window, Nathan leaned out upon the sill and called to Charlotte. It was only fair to warn her of his plans now that he had had them confirmed. She came running to him at once.

'Yes, Uncle Nathan? You wanted me?' Her young face glowed from the fresh air and she was scarcely out of breath despite all the running about she had done. Just looking down at her eager, trusting expression twisted his heart.

'Come inside, Charlotte; there is something I would discuss with you.'

But once Charlotte was seated within the small book-lined study, Nathan felt at a loss as how best to begin. 'Would you care for a glass of wine, Charlotte dear?' he offered, reaching for the bell pull.

'At only quarter after eleven?' asked Charlotte, slightly startled, for her uncle drank little.

'It will sharpen our appetite for lunch. Besides we have your birthday to celebrate.'

'But that is not until tomorrow,' Charlotte laughingly scolded him. 'Oh, very well, if you wish it. Just a small glass of Alice's lovely pansy wine, perhaps.'

When the glasses had been brought and

they had both taken a small appreciative sip, Nathan set his down with excessive care, took out his snuff-box, put it away again, then sat tapping his fingers together as he was wont to do when perplexed.

'Is something troubling you, Uncle?' Charlotte ventured at last into the ensuing silence.

'No, no, not at all,' blustered Nathan, pulling himself together with an effort. It would not do to let the child see his concern; would not do at all. 'Indeed no, the news is all good, my love. My only guilt is in the fact that I have been dilatory in informing you of it, since it concerns you so deeply.'

Charlotte was at once riveted. She had thought she had learned all there was to know about herself.

Charlotte knew that on the death of her parents, when she had just turned two, Uncle Nathan had adopted her, sold his town house in London's fashionable Russell Square and brought her here to his country home to bring her up alongside his own child, Dickon. And whatever this remote farmstead had lacked in physical comfort had been more than compensated for by the lavish degree of care and affection she had received within it. She had felt no lack from not having parents, for dear Alice had been like a mother to her, and she had had Molly and Dickon for playmates. Charlotte had needed nothing more, for she loved her life on the farm.

She enjoyed helping with the animals, though she cried every time one went to market. She loved to walk across the moor and watch the shifting sunlight upon the bracken, to follow the tumbling streams that cut their way through to the main rivers and on to the sea. But most of all she adored walking along the clifftops, gazing out across the crashing surf, pondering on the lands and possible adventures which lay beyond. Sometimes she would feel moved, as if by some mystical force, to call to the gulls that swooped and cried above her head, to add her voice to theirs and pour out the words she had learned from the plays and verses she loved, as if compelled to answer some inner longing she could not fully explain. One day, perhaps, she would see those faraway places – London, Bath, Paris, even Rome or the exotic East – but Charlotte knew that always she would return, for everything in her young life here at Caperley was quite perfect. Everything, that was, except for her growing concern over Dickon.

Mostly he was gentle and kind with a tendency to fawn upon her as if nothing was too much trouble. But at other times his jokes would test the limits of her patience and Charlotte was becoming confused as how best to deal with him without causing offence. A shiver slid down Charlotte's spine as she recalled the feel of his mouth on hers. Though he was her cousin and she was very fond of him, she had not enjoyed the experience one bit. And she couldn't help but think of what might have happened if Sir James Caraddon had not appeared when he did. Dared she mention the episode to Uncle Nathan and ask his advice? Covertly Charlotte studied his face, but before she had time to frame the thought into action her uncle was on his feet, pacing the rug, hands clasped behind his back, and a veritable torrent of words was pouring forth. Charlotte sat up very straight realising that she should try to concentrate upon them, for surely her ears must be playing her false.

'So there you have it, Charlotte, my dear. Your father has made sure you are amply provided for. For my part I think your coming into your fortune at eighteen a mite early, and I suspect his motives for his insistence upon that to be entirely selfish, for the man's a Pharisee and cares not a jot for anyone but himself.'

Nathan pulled himself up, drew breath, and wondered if perhaps he'd gone too far, but Charlotte was sitting quite still, so calm that she looked almost like a model carved from pale wax. Too pale. 'I'm sorry, my dear. I should not have said such a thing. I confess I still feel some bitterness t'wards the man after the way he treated Ella, my beloved sister and your dearest mama of whom you were so abruptly denied.' When Charlotte did not respond, Nathan edged closer, and, fumbling for his spectacles, placed them upon his nose and bent down to peer into her face. 'Are you quite well, m'dear?'

Charlotte tried her voice. 'Yes, Uncle. Quite well.' It came out as an odd little squeak.

Nathan straightened up. 'Ah, good, good.'

'Would you mind, Uncle Nat, repeating the most salient points again? I'm not sure I understood exactly...'

'Ah, quite so, quite so. Too much for a young girl to absorb all at once. I've said as much all along.'

'Are you saying that my father is still alive?' Charlotte stared at Nathan from shocked wide eyes.

'Ahem, yes,' Nathan agreed, as gently as he could. 'In France or Italy or some such place I expect, where he's been these last sixteen years.'

There was a long, appalled silence while Charlotte absorbed the full implications of this news.

'And now he leaves me not a small inherit-

49

ance but a fortune?' she said at last in a small, tremulous voice.

'Indeed.' Nathan whirled about and picked up a paper from among the clutter of books which blotted the desktop. Reading was his favourite occupation and now that Dickon was beginning to show interest in the estate he could indulge his passion more and more. He was enjoying Boswell's *Journal of a Tour to the Hebrides* at the moment, which he found absolutely fascinating, but he must first discharge his duty to his beloved niece before he would have the time to return to it. 'Here it is, plain and simple,' he said, and, picking out a point halfway down the document, Nathan began to read.

'...and when the said child Charlotte Eleanor Forbes should reach a majority of eighteen years she may take into her possession the sum of ten thousand pounds to be paid to her annually on the date of her birth for the remainder of her lifetime. And on receipt of this sum the said child shall lay no further claim either in money or in kind upon myself the said benefactor. Herewith I give my hand on this day the seventeenth of December in the year seventeen hundred and sixty nine.'

Charlotte stared at the paper as if it were not quite real or would burn her fingers should she take a hold of it, which fortun-

50

ately she had no opportunity so to do. 'Signed on your second birthday, only two months before I brought you home to Caperley Farm. Your father mailed the document to me before he left for Italy. I never saw him again. But at least he did the decent thing by you in the end. We should be thankful for that, eh?' Nathan cast his niece an anxious glance.

Charlotte's jade-green eyes brimmed with sudden tears. 'My life would have been nothing without you, dear Uncle Nat. I should have spent it alone in that dreadful cold house, with only servants for company. Instead, I have been given all the love and warmth anyone could wish for. I shall never leave you, never!' Whereupon she burst into tears.

Nathan was appalled, for this was most un-like his Charlotte. 'There, now. Do not take on so. Enough of this.' Pulling a large square of cambric from his capacious coat pocket, he thrust it into her hand. 'Mop up, mop up. This is no way for a young lady to go on.'

Charlotte obediently did as she was bid and was soon able to offer him a return of her smile, albeit a watery one. 'You are quite right, Uncle; there is little point in being over-emotional. It was only that while listening to the legal phrases of that docu-ment it came home to me how very much I owe to you.'

'Tut tut. Stuff and nonsense. You owe me nothing. Haven't I had the pleasure of your company all these years?'

'Ten thousand pounds per annum is a c-considerable fortune and much, much more than I expected.' Charlotte's chin trembled just a little. 'But I feel bound to say that since my-my f-father has not deemed it necessary to care for me throughout these long years, I see no reason why he should do so now. I think I would rather not have it at all. I am strong, and you have educated me better than most young ladies of my age. I could earn my own living if needs be, if–' she faltered over the painful words '–you no longer want me here.'

Nathan looked bleak. 'As long as I live there will be a home for you here, but I am an old man.'

'You are not at all old,' chipped in Charlotte, unable to help herself.

He gave a wry smile. 'But getting older, my dear. We all do, you know. And Dickon is a young man and will soon be taking a wife and it is a sad truth, but a fact none the less, that she would not want a spinster cousin-in-law about the place,' Nathan gently pointed out. 'Nor, do I think, would you wish to stay under those conditions.'

Charlotte felt a reluctance to mention Dickon's own crazed plans for she suddenly saw that perhaps leaving the farm might be her only option. Yet to accept money from a father she'd believed dead was asking too much of her sensibilities. 'May I have time to think about it?'

Nathan lowered himself into his chair, its familiar creaks almost a comfort in his distress, for he felt very tired. Was he being quite fair to Charlotte? Should he tell her the whole of it here and now and get it done with? What a coward he was to leave it to Constance. Yet it was surely better to come from a woman. 'I would not wish you to do anything hasty, Charlotte my dear. I'll concede the amount is a shock, even to myself who was half expecting it, for I had not opened the envelope until the date I was permitted to do so, the day prior to your birthday. And I agree it may well prove to be as much a burden as a blessing; these things often do. But you must not blind yourself to the opportunities it opens up for you.' Nathan cleared his throat. 'You are eighteen years old tomorrow and will soon be looking about you for a husband.' As Charlotte's small face registered fresh shock he hastened to reassure her. 'Oh, pray, do not fret. You shall have a completely free choice. I would not presume... Your happiness is all important to me and there will be no arranged marriages in this house.'

Charlotte went across to put her arms about his neck, placed her overheated cheek upon his collar and hugged him close. 'You are so dear to me that I do not feel the need to look beyond this house for my happiness. I should so like to see that you and Alice and everyone at the farm be the ones to benefit from my good fortune, instead of me.'

Nathan found himself blinking furiously. 'Tush, that is nonsense. We have no need of any more money and it is time you saw something of the world,' he said, firmly seating Charlotte back in the armchair, for sentiment embarrassed him greatly and he was anxious to have this matter over and done with. 'I do not wish you to worry any more about it for the present. There is no need for you to have any contact with your father if you do not wish it, and he has already indicated his own feelings on that score. But you have your future to think of, my dear, and he can well afford the sum mentioned. Now, put it from your mind and enjoy your birthday. I forgot to mention we have a new guest coming, someone I very much wish you to meet. Ah, here he is in person.'

'I am not intruding?'

Charlotte jumped in alarm as she recognised the deep tones of that so familiar voice.

'No, indeed, Sir James, please do come in. May I offer you a glass of wine?' asked Nathan expansively.

'It seems to have become a habit of mine, venturing into places where I am not expected,' said James drily, glaring unsmilingly into Charlotte's ashen face.

'Allow me to introduce my niece, Charlotte Forbes. Sir James Caraddon.'

And, while Charlotte fought for composure, James bowed with excessive courtesy. 'I believe we met just now, in the yard,' he said coolly, and Charlotte held her breath, dreading the inevitable. Uncle Nathan would be desperately upset by such a disclosure, and it was all so unnecessary. Sir James Caraddon's eyes sparkled dangerously at her discomfiture, but at least the brooding frown was gone, and when Uncle Nathan expressed an interest in this first meeting, Sir James merely said that Charlotte had directed him to the house.

Charlotte breathed again, signalling her gratitude with an expression of relief. Perhaps he was not so terrible a man after all.

'You must join us for luncheon,' said Nathan quickly. He suddenly felt a pressing need for a third party to be present. 'It will be but a cold collation since Alice is busy preparing tomorrow's birthday feast, but you are more than welcome to share it with us. Ah, now, Charlotte, and here is the ideal opportunity for you to seek Sir James's advice. He is famous for his acumen with investments, in addition of course to his natural charm. We humble country bumpkins would be glad of your city knowledge, sir.'

'Advice?' queried James, looking from one to the other, for Nathan Pierce was behaving decidedly oddly and Charlotte looked ready to burst into tears. He was more than a little intrigued. Something was amiss here and he couldn't for the life of him make out what it was. Unless, of course, the old man had heard about the frolics in the hay-barn. As his grandmother had indicated, they appeared to be a very odd family indeed. Yet even she, it seemed, had overestimated the girl's innocence.

'I know you mean well, Uncle,' said Charlotte, her voice dangerously high-pitched for she was by now thoroughly agitated, 'but I believe I have already made my feelings on that subject quite plain. I have not as yet decided whether to take up this so-called inheritance. Therefore it follows that advice, no matter how charmingly presented, will not be called for.' Whereupon Charlotte ran from the room, leaving the two gentlemen to make what they might of her behaviour.

CHAPTER THREE

Charlotte sat upon her bed for some time, her body shaking with shock. This was the last news she had expected on the day before her birthday. It hurt so much that she could hardly bear the pain of it. She wished she had never learned the truth, that she still thought her father dead. It would be better that way. Tears ran down her cheeks though she bit hard upon her lower lip in a valiant attempt to stop them. After a while, when Charlotte felt calmer, she began to think more clearly. She was no worse off than she had been before today. Her father, Lord Justin Forbes, whoever and wherever he was, did not want her. So be it. Why he should feel that way she did not know, for how could a child of two have offended him in any way? The only thing she could think of was that perhaps, being a girl, she had reminded him too much of the beloved wife he had lost. Fresh tears of sorrow spurted and her jade eyes brimmed with compassion. Yet sixteen years was a long time, almost a lifetime in Charlotte's case. He might have written to ask after her health, even if he did not wish to see her.

Once more self-pity threatened and Charlotte had to be very firm with herself not to break down again. She drew air into too tight lungs and reminded herself firmly that she had never felt the need of a father in all these long years and did not need one now. She had Uncle Nat and Alice, and Molly and Dickon. Charlotte knew herself to be truly blessed. Going to the porcelain basin, she splashed cold water over her heated face and felt a little better. She would lie down for an hour and rest her sore eyes. Perhaps then she would feel able to face the world. She certainly had had no wish to share a meal with Sir James Caraddon. That would have been too much to endure with him teasing her throughout with his bold assessing stare, particularly with the advantage he now believed he had over her. And to discuss her position with him, this shocking new information which she had not yet come to terms with herself, would have been quite untenable.

There came a light rap upon the bedroom door.

'Miss Charlotte? Are you asleep?'

Charlotte slid from the bed and went to open the door. 'No, Alice, I am not.'

'I have brought you a dish of hot chicken soup. The master said you had a headache and wouldn't want much lunch.'

'Oh, Alice!' The housekeeper's kindness

was too much for Charlotte in her fragile state, and she burst into tears all over again. Later, after they had been mopped up and Charlotte calmed, helped by the delicious soup, she told the silent Alice what she had learned.

'I had never expected such a thing,' Charlotte said. 'And the money, Alice. Can you imagine it? I cannot, nor·do I wish to.' Charlotte was well aware that most young ladies of her age would be delighted by the prospect of ten thousand pounds a year, but she had been brought up not to expect or prize wealth in any way and she certainly could not begin to do so now. Important to her were people to love and to cherish and be loved in return as she was here at Caperley; to respect nature and care about one's family and neighbours; to fill each day with some new challenge and to explore the world of art and literature. These were the beliefs which Uncle Nathan had taught her and these were the things which mattered to her also. Upon these philosophies had been built the foundation of her young life, but now she felt that very security in which she had so firmly believed to be threatened by a future both alien and uncertain. 'What would I do with such a sum?' she asked helplessly.

Alice considered the question quietly for a moment. 'I suppose you could buy yourself

59

a house in town, have pretty gowns to wear and servants to wait upon your every whim. You could attend balls and soirees and look over all the young men who would surely flurry around such a pretty young lady.'

Charlotte had listened with startled attention to all of this, then, catching the twinkle in Alice's eye, she burst out laughing. 'Very well, Alice. You have made your point. Perhaps it is not the worst disaster in the world to be granted such a sum to live on, but it came as a shock to me, on top of everything else.'

Alice patted her cheek with doting gentleness. 'I dare say it did, my lovely. To be honest with you I've mentioned the fact to your uncle more than once that he ought to take you into his complete confidence, but he would have none of it. When she's older, he'd say. Not yet, Alice, he'd say, and I'd shake my head at him and he'd smile in that sheepish way he has. A kind, sweet man he be, but he do avoid unpleasant truths.'

Charlotte gave a little smile of understanding. 'Yes, I can see that.'

Alice looked at her carefully for a long moment, compassion reflected in her kindly eyes. 'You must ever remember, Charlotte, whatever may come about in your life, that you are well loved.'

Charlotte nodded, too full of emotion to speak.

'And from all these fine gentlemen who will come to call, you can choose yourself a husband who will love you to distraction.' Alice beamed. 'You see if I'm not right,' she said, and laughed as Charlotte wrinkled her nose with distaste.

'The idea of being hounded by young gentlemen simply for my fortune is utterly distasteful to me. Besides, I would soon grow bored with such a light-minded social existence. Much as I would like to look pretty, and even fall in love and marry one day, it surely could be achieved in a far less mercenary manner. How would I ever know if they really liked me or simply my money?' It was a cry from the heart and Alice put her arms around Charlotte as she recognised it as such.

'Someone will love you because you deserve to be loved, and it will have nothing to do with your money, lovely. But if you do not want that kind of life, then find another. You could tour the world if you so wished. There are certainly funds enough to pay for companions, luggage, transport, whatever. Or you could give much of it away to worthy causes. The decision is yours, Charlotte, but do not dismiss it quite out of hand. Consider the alternatives very carefully first. A woman has a hard enough way to make through life in this world. Without money it is a hundred times more difficult, believe me. Now, no more weeping. The answer will come to you.'

By the time Alice had left her, Charlotte was feeling cheerful enough to write out the place-cards for the table before taking her nap. It was simply the shock of it all, she decided. Alice and Uncle Nathan were quite right, now was not the moment to make decisions. She was almost laughing at herself by the time sleep claimed her, for if that was the worst news she ever received in her life what did she have to worry about?

Downstairs, in their respective quarters, Nathan and Alice each silently reflected upon Charlotte's reaction to this piece of news and privately wondered what they might expect when she was finally given the whole tale.

The morning of Charlotte's birthday dawned with that kind of silvered ethereal light which often presaged snow. The sky was clotted with creamy cloud and out at sea seemed to melt into the gleaming icy water. Warmly ensconced in the kitchen window-seat as she sipped her morning chocolate, Charlotte shivered. On this day the sun should have shone, the air should have sparkled. Nothing was going according to plan.

'Don't fret over it,' said Alice, pulling the last of the loaves from the oven. She had been up since four, baking them. 'It'll hold off till tomorrow. Old Matthew says so and he'm never wrong.'

There was little time to think of the weather in the hustle and bustle of preparing for the party. The white damask table linen had to be ironed and all the best glasses and china washed and dried with a soft cloth. Then Charlotte and Molly spread the tablecloth over a thick felt mat laid upon the big mahogany table in the eating parlour, and the silver branched candle-sticks were placed one at each end. Molly had spent hours the previous day polishing these along with the silver forks, pepper-pots and salt-cellars. Charlotte trimmed some sprigs of holly with scarlet ribbon for a centrepiece and with the folded napkins and name-cards in place, each one illus-trated with a flower, the table was ready and both girls were pleased with the result.

'Now all I have to do is to get myself ready,' said Charlotte with satisfaction. 'Oh, Molly, it is all so exciting.'

'I wonder what your uncle will have got you for your birthday,' whispered Molly, avid with curiosity. 'He've been planning something, 'cause there've been many secret letters flying back and forth.'

'Then I don't think you should be telling me of it,' said Charlotte with a laugh, only to change it into a small frown. 'But I'm not sure I can take many more surprises. I hope they are pleasant ones.'

'Why shouldn't they be, on your birthday? Everyone have got you a present, even old Matthew.'

'You all thoroughly spoil me.'

'Dickon do,' agreed Molly tactlessly. 'He have been saving for so long and he won't even tell me what he's got you.'

Charlotte passed this off with a slightly shaky laugh. She'd become aware of Molly's affections some time ago and was anxious not to cause unnecessary jealousy. But it served to remind her that she must manage to speak to Dickon most seriously soon. The last thing she wanted was to have to resort to telling Uncle Nat. That would make a mountain out of a very small molehill.

A simple noonday meal of bread, honey and coffee was prepared and, while Molly went to join her mother in the kitchen, Charlotte set a side-table before the fire in the small parlour and sat gazing dreamily into it as she waited for her uncle to join her. But her mind kept playing over the scene in the hay-barn the previous day and a small frown crumpled her smooth brow. She could well understand Sir James Caraddon's taking a high-handed attitude towards such seemingly wanton behaviour, but she had the oddest feeling that there was something more behind his censure, something as yet indefinable.

Even as Charlotte manufactured his face against the background of the leaping flames, her heart began to pound the way it had done when she first saw him. He had the oddest effect upon her and he was certainly not a man to ignore, nor did he seem used to being rebuffed as she had done when she ran from the room rather than share lunch with him. Once again she experienced a deep sadness that they should meet in such a way. Sir James was so intriguing and so very handsome that Charlotte would not have been human had she not wished that their introduction could have been different. Tucking up her knees, she hugged them in a sudden burst of exuberance and her eyes glazed with dreams as she stared into the flames. Perhaps tonight at her party he would be so stunned by her beauty that they would become fast friends and he would forgive her indiscretion. She would dance and smile and show him how very sophisticated she was and not at all the country bumpkin he thought her to be, and he would be entirely captivated by her charm. The sound of the door opening sent the fanciful images shimmering into tiny pieces as she turned, a ready smile for her uncle upon her lips, only to find it was the very incarnation of those dreams.

Sir James looked almost as surprised as

she as he stood in the doorway, his gaze riveted upon the small figure so cosily ensconced before the fire. He saw a picture of appealing innocence, the cheeks flushed rosy from the heat, the eyes lit by a haunting beauty darkly fringed by sweeping lashes. It was hard to equate this sweet girl with the scene in the hay-barn which had done its best to spoil his sleep last night. Even the muslin cap still sensibly in place gave a certain rustic charm to the whole.

'Miss Forbes?' he said at last, then fell silent for he could think of nothing to say to her.

Setting her feet quickly upon the floor and demurely smoothing her skirt, Charlotte could do no more than manage a flicker of her hand, indicting that he take a seat opposite. He was the last person she had expected to see, believing that he had left after lunch yesterday. In a daze, without even asking how he liked it, she poured coffee, added a dash of cream and handed it to him without a word. Her mind was whirling. What was he doing here? Her guests were not expected until four o'clock and it was the height of bad manners to come early, yet nothing on earth would induce her to question him upon it. Small talk was not high on her list of attributes and this seemed not the moment to practise. So she busied herself by cutting thick slices of Alice's fresh bread and passing them to him, together with their own yellow butter and fragrant honey for Sir James to help himself. He did so readily enough and when some moments later they were joined by Uncle Nathan and Dickon it was not perhaps so surprising that the scene was mistakenly interpreted as companionable.

Dickon positively glowered at Sir James as he dropped into a hard chair beside him, but, as Charlotte handed Dickon a plate of bread and butter, he forgot all else for a time in his eagerness to quench his hunger. Sir James watched Dickon load his bread with honey in an almost condemning silence before asking in ironic tones what he'd been doing to produce such a healthy appetite.

'Working,' came the uncompromising reply issued through a mouth as full of venom as it was packed with food. Charlotte was at last forced into speech.

'Dickon does much of the work on the farm, helped by old Matthew and his son Thomas.'

Sir James raised finely sculpted brows at Nathan who stood with his back to the fire, sipping coffee. 'How many acres do you have?'

'No more than a hundred and sixty and much of it rough moorland fit only for sheep.'

'It's still a deal of work for only three men.'

Nathan looked faintly perplexed, not having seriously considered the matter before. 'They manage. We can afford no more.'

'Have you never thought of selling?' Sir James asked with an interested casualness that alighted upon the ears of his listeners with all the force of heavy logs falling.

'Why should we do that?' retorted Dickon, flecks of food spitting from his mouth in agitation. 'The Pierce family have lived here for generations, right back to good Queen Bess and beyond. It might be a sprawling old manor farm none too comfortable in your eyes, but it be our home.'

'I'm sorry; it was only that I thought if money was tight—'

'We don't want no stranger coming here and telling us what to do.' There was money enough in Dickon's opinion, only his father wouldn't spend it. But Nathan was an old man and once he was gone Dickon could use the money how he liked and pay others to labour on the farm. Then he would be the gentleman and if he couldn't have Charlotte he'd maybe marry Molly, of which his father would not approve either. But she was certainly willing enough.

'I'm sure Sir James didn't mean to do any such thing,' Charlotte felt obliged to point out, for she recognised the familiar signs of growing belligerence mounting in Dickon as

68

he fancied himself belittled. But, pushing aside his plate with unnecessary force, he stood up, a stocky figure of sulking, almost childlike demeanour, not much more than head and shoulders taller than the still seated Sir James who stared up at him in cool disdain.

A long awkward silence followed as the two stared at each other with growing antipathy. At length Charlotte could bear it no longer.

'Do sit down, Dickon, and finish your meal. You've not touched your coffee.'

Casting her scarcely a glance, Dickon stumped to the door. 'Nor do I need it. I'll have myself a jug of cider in the barn where I belong, I reckon. Fancy parlour ain't for *working* men.'

With this pointed remark Dickon left, and they listened motionless to the sound of his boots marking a distinct path along the flagged hall and out of the back door.

'I'm not sure how it came about, but I beg your pardon for offending him, sir,' offered Sir James mildly.

Nathan, his attention having been momentarily diverted by the book he held in his hand, seemed unperturbed by the little scene. 'Don't let it trouble you, Sir James. Dickon is too oversensitive for his own good, I fear. It is long past time he grew out of it. You are probably right and I should have sold long since. I confess to the guilt of knowing I have little interest in the place.' Nathan shrugged his shoulders and looked helplessly from one to the other of them. 'But how would Dickon manage were I to do such a thing? His whole life has taken place under this roof and, though he lacks not courage and strength, he has no business acumen, nor, if you'll forgive my saying so, Sir James, your own means to embark upon life as a gentleman. Therefore Caperley, for all its shortcomings, is not only his past, but present and future.'

'Yes, I do see that.' Sir James's tone was thoughtful as his gaze slid once more to rest upon Charlotte. 'Perhaps you should encourage him to seek a fine woman with the means to furnish the farm with fresh capital.'

Nathan laughed good-naturedly. 'I live in hope, but somehow I think it unlikely. He hates leaving the farm for any reason and, for all he is my very dear son, I cannot claim him to be the catch of the month.'

James's gaze was still fastened upon Charlotte and she felt herself flushing hotly beneath his scrutiny as he continued conversationally, 'And what does your own future hold, Miss Forbes?'

'Ah, now, Charlotte is a different story,' offered Nathan, a new pride in his voice. 'We are delighted to find that Charlotte is

70

amply provided for.'

'That is well for a woman,' answered Sir James, bringing a flush of defensive pride to Charlotte's heart.

'So that some man in search of capital may seek *me* out?' she demanded, as haughtily as she was able. 'I'm sure I would very much prefer to remain poor.'

'Poverty, my dear Miss Forbes, has a limited appeal. But it is remarkably easily found.'

Nathan stepped towards his niece to pick up her tiny cold hand and press it warmly between his own. 'I asked Sir James to remain so that we might have the benefit of his advice. He and I had a good long chat last night. I hope you do not mind, Charlotte.'

She looked up into her uncle's face and could say nothing. Of course she minded but knew with a sinking of her heart that to say as much would hurt Uncle Nathan immeasurably, for he only wanted the best for her.

'Sir James has promised to speak with you before the celebrations begin. Lady Caraddon is unfortunately indisposed and reluctant to venture out in this inclement weather, but she has sent word for you to visit her. I beg you to hear it out with equanimity and favour her with a positive response. Now I shall leave you young

71

people in peace.' Collecting a second volume from a chair, Nathan hurried to the sanctity of his study and the delights of biography and literary travel.

Charlotte, her appetite quite gone, gazed bleakly up at the inscrutable Sir James, noting how his broad shoulders more than filled the winged armchair in which he reclined so possessively, long legs stretched out before him in apparent ease. In that moment she very much longed to dislike him, but was far too fascinated by the man to do any such thing. Shrewdly she guessed that the ladies of Sir James's acquaintance would be more likely to suffer the extremes of hate or undying love rather than anything so milk and water as simple dislike. She intended neither of these kindred emotions to touch her own heart where Sir James Caraddon was concerned, and waited with outward unconcern for him to begin.

'Would you care for a stroll, Miss Forbes?'

'My guests will begin to arrive shortly – I doubt I have the time,' she said rather loftily, but Sir James only smiled.

'A breath of fresh air before a party is always beneficial, wouldn't you say? Though you must wrap up warmly, for there is a cold wind. It would not do for the birthday girl to catch a chill.'

Charlotte glanced sharply up at him to check if he mocked her, but could see only polite consideration upon his face, though the grey eyes twinkled suspiciously brightly.

Donning a bonnet, she wrapped a warm shawl over her simple dress and, feeling decidedly frumpish, Charlotte walked with Sir James out of the farm and along a rutted track which brought them to the cliff-top. Far beneath them the sea was a rumpled mat of grey and white flecked wool. It looked cold and forbidding, yet its power and drama was undeniable. Charlotte loved the sea in all its moods – even now, when it skittishly tossed the small fishing-boats, standing at anchor in the distant harbour, with uncaring ease. She had seen whole ships picked up and smashed to driftwood on the rocks in one indrawn breath of its mighty force. And she had seen that same coldness reflected in the grey eyes of the man who now walked beside her. But she had also seen those eyes sparkle like the morning sun forming bright pools of light upon the leaden grey waters. She found him like the sea itself, unfathomable, unpredictable and totally compelling.

Charlotte was still desperately trying to find some way to break the silence when Sir James came bluntly to the point.

'Is it not somewhat reckless of you to refuse so generous an inheritance?'

Charlotte very nearly gasped in her astonishment. 'I should like to know what business it is of yours, sir,' she tartly informed him.

'I'd much rather it were none of my business at all, but your uncle and my grandmother seem bent on making it so. I assure you it is no wish of mine. I have better ways of using my time than dealing with overly dramatic young misses who should still be in the schoolroom.'

It was too much. 'With your fast London set, I suppose?'

'They, at least, are ladies,' Sir James coldly replied, 'and are not to be found rolling in the hay with a ragamuffin.'

Charlotte came abruptly to a halt to glower at him in open rage. 'Will you never let a thing be? I have explained about that. It is only the way Dickon is and he means nothing by it.'

'It looked most meaningful to me. However, you are right in saying that little is to be gained by going over old ground. Your uncle wishes me to advise you on how best to deal with your inheritance, yet, if I understand correctly, you seem bent on refusing it.'

'I know my uncle means well, but sometimes he treats me too much as a child,' Charlotte protested and was mortified to hear Sir James actually laugh out loud at that.

'I wonder why that can be!'

Charlotte pursed her lips on a biting response. She must remember that this was the grandson of an old friend of her uncle and it would not do to cause offence. 'I thank you for your kind offer,' she continued, as blithely as she might. 'And should I ever require advice upon financial matters I shall keep it in mind.'

'In the meantime I would do well to keep my nose out of your affairs; is that the nub of it?'

Charlotte benefited him with her most winning smile and saw with pleasure how his eyes widened in surprise. 'That is exactly it, in a nutshell, as they say.' Feeling at last that she had the advantage, she continued more genuinely, 'though I am sorry that your grandmother is not able to come to our small gathering. I should very much like to meet her. I'm surprised that I have not done so before. Truro is not many miles away to the east of us.'

'Grandmother spends much of her time at her London house these days,' Sir James explained. 'She is no lover of the country and likes to have her friends call, and be taken out to the theatre or, better still, the opera at least once a week. I cannot think where she finds the energy.'

Charlotte clasped her hands together with spontaneous delight. 'Oh, how lucky she is to be able to visit the theatre so frequently. I long to go, but Uncle will not allow me.'

'I should think not indeed,' replied Sir James with a curt laugh as if the very idea was ludicrous. 'The theatre is no place for respectable young ladies unless they are very properly chaperoned.'

'That is the puzzle of it,' said Charlotte frowning. 'One would think that Uncle Nat would be only too happy to take me to Bristol or even Bath, which is very famous, for he loves everything connected with literature and the arts. Yet always when I ask him he gives a categorical refusal and absolutely nothing will coerce him.'

James smiled down at her perplexed face and thought how young and vulnerable she looked in her disappointment. 'Not even one of your delectably captivating smiles, or the lilting beauty of your voice?'

'Not even that,' said Charlotte innocently, then, flushing bright red, glanced up into his smiling face. 'Oh, I-I didn't mean...'

'I'm sure you didn't.' Sir James brushed the fingers of one large hand over his mouth to hide his smile.

They continued on their way in silence for some moments before Charlotte asked softly, 'Do you really think my voice has beauty or were you only funning me?'

'I never make fun of a lady,' Sir James assured her with abject seriousness. 'Even one who has not yet learned all the ins and outs of the job.'

Charlotte gave him a puzzled look and, seeing how his lips twitched at the corners, found her own doing the same in response till it bubbled forth in a delighted gurgle of laughter. 'I don't think I could ever be a lady,' she told him quite seriously when her giggles had abated. 'It simply is not me.'

'What, then, is you?'

They had reached a rickety wooden fence that cut off the end of the cliff path which led down to the shore, and here they paused to lean upon it and gaze out to sea. A fishing-boat was tacking slowly homeward, a fretful wind leaning into its red sail one moment and abandoning it completely the next. Charlotte watched it with half her interest as she considered her reply. How could she tell this stranger of her dream? She had told no one, not even Uncle Nat. Some dreams were reachable if you tried enough, said your prayers and worked hard. Others were too distant ever to be touched, even by the tips of her pleading fingers, and it was foolish to try.

'Does your grandmother visit Drury Lane?' Charlotte asked.

'No doubt.' James put his back against the fence so that he could look down into Charlotte's small face. It was a study of awe, suppressed longing and eager excitement, and somewhere deep inside he found himself moved by it.

'Has she seen the great Sarah Siddons? I believe her Lady Macbeth is so wonderful she cannot get off the stage for curtain calls. Her audiences adore her, is that right?' Charlotte's jade green eyes sparkled with rapture. 'Oh, I should love to see her. It must be so exciting to walk out upon a stage in front of hundreds of people and have them enjoy your acting so much that they cannot bear to part with you.'

Unable to help himself, James Caraddon burst out laughing. 'Is that what you are wanting, to be the new Sarah Siddons? What a child you are.' He saw at once the tactlessness of his words and wished he could bite them off unsaid. The warm flush fled from her face, leaving it white and stiff. The soft moist lips seemed to crumple and shrivel to nothing even as he watched. Then she was running from him, a tiny lone figure along the cliff path, her red shawl billowing out in the wind behind her as forlorn and vulnerable as the fishing-vessel tossed on the heedless sea.

CHAPTER FOUR

Never had Charlotte been so humiliated in all her life. She did not stop running until she had reached the house, where she flew up the stairs past an open-mouthed Molly and ran into her room, slamming the door behind her. Flinging herself back against the panel, she stamped one foot in furious anger upon the wooden floor. It was her own stupid fault. She should never have allowed herself to be lulled into thinking he was truly interested in her, that the smile in his eyes was anything but mockery. She had given away her dearest secret, known to no one but herself. How would she ever face Sir James Caraddon again? Not only had he caught her in a flagrant position of impropriety in a hay-barn, but now he had learned that her dearest wish was to act upon a stage, to be a famous actress like Sarah Siddons. Charlotte cringed at her own naïveté. What a raw country fool she must have appeared. A foolish child with a head stuffed with impossible dreams. No wonder he had laughed at her. She should be thankful that Lady Caraddon was not, after all, coming this evening – Charlotte would feel even more of a laughing stock if she actually met her, which she vehemently hoped she never would.

And after this evening she would make certain that she never saw Lady Caraddon's grandson again either. For some reason, hard to fathom in the circumstances, this afforded Charlotte less pleasure than she'd expected, and when Alice came up later to help her dress that good lady was surprised to find Charlotte sitting bolt upright at her dressing-table, having made no preparations for the evening ahead, not even so much as taking off her outer garments.

'Why, what is this? Mr and Mrs Tregorna are downstairs already, arrived early they have, and with a lovely plum cake for you if I'm not mistaken, and here you are, not even washed.' Alice clicked her tongue in disapproval, at once starting to pull off the damp red shawl and unlace the dress. 'You're shivering, lovely. Master will have to entertain your guests alone for a while; a hot tub is what you need. I've plenty of hot water on the stove. Then we'll dress you up proper pretty in the new dress I've made for you.'

'Oh, Alice, you shouldn't have.'

'Why shouldn't I? 'Tis my present to you. Who has the better right, I'd like to know?'

Less than an hour later, Charlotte stood before her looking-glass a new person, entranced by what she saw. She had bathed and washed her hair and Alice had brushed it dry before the bedroom fire.

'We'll put no powder on it this night,' Alice had firmly declared. ''Twould be wicked to hide the lovely colour of it, and a mite too formal for a simple birthday party. But, Molly, see you do Miss Charlotte's hair well.'

Molly beamed, for she loved to dress Charlotte's hair; it was such a rich glowing colour and so full of life and bounce, unlike her own lank brown locks. Keeping it fairly flat on top, Molly drew the main body of the hair to one side, making sure she allowed some fullness about the face. She then curled the remainder into long ringlets which hung softly over one shoulder.

'Course you should wear a corset if you were a proper lady,' mourned Alice. 'But your waist is so narrow it won't matter none.'

Charlotte giggled. 'And at least I'll be able to eat your delicious food.'

Alice tied on the small bustle pad and Charlotte stepped into a fine lawn petticoat in palest green, deeply flounced at the hem and stopping short of her ankles to reveal matching stockings and leaf-green kid shoes with delicately pointed toes and pink bows. Over this, and with great care, Alice and Molly lowered a cream overdress dotted with roses of pink gauze stitched on individually. The deep square neckline, elbow sleeves and swept-back hem were softly ruffled at the edges and, when the ribbon tapes were tied to loop up the skirt to reveal the petticoat beneath, and every fold carefully arranged, Alice stepped back to survey her handiwork with glowing pride.

'There, quite perfect, though I say it as shouldn't. Queen Charlotte herself couldn't look more handsome for all her silks and satins.'

'It is the most beautiful dress I ever saw.' Charlotte's eyes shone with delight. 'You are the cleverest person on earth, Alice, and the sweetest to make it for me.'

Alice flushed with pleasure and Molly simply breathed, 'Oh, ain't it pretty?' over and over until, laughing, they were forced to hush her.

'I'd kiss you for luck but I'm afeared to spoil the picture,' murmured Alice, a sudden catch in her throat, then more briskly, 'Off with you, Molly. Our job be done here. Get down to the kitchen and check those capons. I'll be down directly. And, Miss Charlotte, hold your head high, for thereby follows the rest of you.'

And with this excellent piece of advice, Charlotte progressed down the wide polished staircase to the main parlour below where a number of her guests were already present and enjoying a convivial glass or two of Uncle Nathan's best Madeira.

She greeted them all. The Tregornas, the Carters, old Mrs Lovelace from Talready, the Holborn family and numerous other friends and neighbours. Several young men were present in the company and each one vied for Charlotte's attention.

The birthday supper was a great success and the capons, game pies, fat roast goose with blackcurrant sauce and other delicacies soon vanished to be followed by a half dozen other courses from cheese-curd tarts to the much revered cinnamon cake. Uncle Nathan bobbed up and down jovially, filling and refilling wine glasses; a rosy-cheeked Molly scurried back and forth with various culinary delights from Alice's seemingly bottomless store, till everyone declared themselves utterly sated and unable to eat another morsel.

At which point the ladies took themselves off to make small repairs before settling in the best parlour for a gossip over the coffee-cups, leaving the gentlemen in peace with their cigars and brandy. Charlotte did her utmost to play her part as solicitous hostess but her mind would keep wandering. She had tried to ignore it – indeed she had inwardly spoken most sternly to herself – but it was of no use. The truth could not be denied. She was disappointed. Perhaps her hopes had been a touch unrealistic although she had not expected him to swoon on sight of her. Nor had she hoped for Sir James Caraddon to fawn upon her as young Tom Carter had insisted upon doing all evening, and greatly annoying her in the process. Nevertheless she had expected some kind of response. A word perhaps, an arm to lead her to the table, even a glance of admiration across it. But no. Nothing. Whenever she looked his way, Sir James Caraddon seemed to stubbornly avert his gaze. What a very disagreeable old man he must be. The good ladies, however, thought otherwise.

'Isn't Sir James an absolute dear? Would that he'd been around when my Katherine had been single,' mourned Mistress Holborn with evident regret.

Old Mrs Lovelace snorted in derision. 'And what be wrong with your new son-in-law, Nancy? Not fancy enough for ye, eh?'

Mistress Holborn leapt quickly to the defence of her daughter's somewhat unexciting husband, anxious to rectify her mistake. 'Nothing at all. He is the very best of sons, ideal for my Kate. You can be sure we are mightily pleased with him. But, in truth, Sir James Caraddon is a rare bird that any mother would welcome, admit it, now,' she coaxed, helping herself to more coffee.

'Aye, rare indeed. He do lead some of

those London ladies a merry dance, I do hear.'

Margaret Holborn's eyes widened in gleeful anticipation. 'Indeed? What do you hear?'

Upon one breath the assembled group of country women leaned closer. There was nothing they loved better than a good tale, and old Mrs Lovelace, who had little better to do than exchange tittle-tattle, was not one to disappoint them.

'I do hear tell that he be as good as engaged to one Lady of Quality but that she'll not have him until he do have a better position in them government circles or some such.' Old Mrs Lovelace wagged her two chins up and down for emphasis. 'Mind, it be unlikely that such a small matter as a ring would keep him the wrong side of her door, I do think. He'm a man, after all.'

All of the ladies agreed that he was indeed.

Charlotte said nothing.

Mrs Lovelace glanced back over her shoulder at the door before edging closer to the conspiratorial circle. 'But then there's some as says that this particular Lady of Quality don't lock it for no one, given the chance.' There was a small shocked silence as they each savoured this delicious piece of news.

Mrs Carter, being the mother of four fine

sons, felt it her place to be the first to voice the opinion of the assembled company. 'Well,' she said. 'Well, I never.'

'That's what widowhood brings you,' finished Mrs Lovelace, as if the Lady had only herself to blame for the condition. ''Tis said that, like the Duchess of Devonshire who exchanged kisses for votes at the last election to get Fox back in, this Lady would do at least as much for Sir James.'

'At least as...' Mrs Carter could not conclude her sentence.

'Quite so. Quite, so. Only it seems that he don't see it. Won't hear a word against her, so besotted is he.' The old lady sank back into her cushioned seat with a sigh, well satisfied that she had entertained her audience most royally.

'More coffee?' Charlotte's quavering voice spoke into the ensuing silence but not a single lady heard her. She refilled her own cup and, forcibly shutting out their chattering voices, pondered on whatever had possessed her to hold a birthday party for the neighbours at all. Though, to be fair to them, they had little enough excitement in this quiet spot so who could blame them if, on being presented with a prime candidate, they took advantage of it? Charlotte wished, not for the first time that evening, that Sir James Caraddon had never entered her life, and that he would just as quickly leave it. A

86

small voice within her told her with perplexing satisfaction that this was unlikely to happen, yet she could not for the life of her have explained why she felt so.

As for the gentleman in question, he was suffering a considerable degree of confusion himself. Ever since James had watched Charlotte walk down those stairs he'd been hard put to it not to stare at her like some besotted youth, and he was certainly not that, was he? There were enough of those here already. First Dickon, then Tom Carter, not to mention at least two of that young man's brothers, all fetching and carrying for her like a pack of pups in training. Yet he could understand their behaviour to a degree. Even when James had walked along the cliff-top with Charlotte he'd been surprised to find himself enjoying her delightful chatter and sorry that he had offended her.

And all through the meal James had felt her eyes upon him, almost willing him to look at her, as if she did not have enough adulation already. The worst of it was that he wanted to look at her – very much. She was not beautiful. He kept telling himself that, though she was fetching enough in a rustic, honest kind of way. No more than a child; how could she hold any attraction for him? James preferred his women more mature and sophisticated, and preferably without any inclination or availability for matrimony. Charlotte Forbes, in his assessment, was the very opposite of all these criteria. He was willing to offer what advice he could for dealing with this windfall of hers, but nothing would induce him to become further embroiled in her problems in any way other than financial.

He watched her now as the gentlemen joined the ladies in the parlour, flitting from one guest to the other, a pink and cream butterfly newly emerged from its chrysalis but still too immature for full flight. Yet how he would love to see her when she was ready to take on the world. Her bright young face was smiling as she listened as if riveted to yet another boring yarn from the Carter boy, and then, as if sensing James's gaze upon her, she looked straight at him and the smile imperceptibly changed in a way he found hard to define. A sensation swept through him, devastatingly close to desire, and he felt the palms of his hands grow sticky with the shock of it. What was he thinking of? She was a child, a difficult, wayward child who had a fondness for kissing cousins.

A glass of hot spiced punch was put into his hands and James almost snatched at it with relief and just as swiftly set it down. He'd do better to get out of this tea party, this house, while he still could. The thought became a decision and then he was striding to the door. Seeing him about to leave, Charlotte half rose from her chair, but before she had fully made up her mind whether or not to follow him the door had burst open and the whole company gave out a loud cheer as Jon the fiddler appeared. The party came at once to life. Women grabbed for their husbands, a tune was selected and soon the room was filled with merry laughter and the thump, thump of pounding feet footing out the steps of a most energetic country dance. Charlotte, still watching James, found herself grasped by Dickon and as he clung fiercely to her she was obliged to skip and swing and side-step and hold up her arms to form an arch for the other dancers to pass beneath at the appropriate moments. Yet her heart was pounding not from the dance but at the thought that James Caraddon was about to leave and she wanted very much to stop him. Her startled mind replayed that glance over and over till she felt dizzy with it.

'Smile, Charlotte. Aren't you enjoying yourself?' Dickon demanded and Charlotte hastened to assure him that she was.

The second time they held up their arms in an arch, James himself passed beneath it with Emily Holborn in the curve of his arm. An odd little pang struck Charlotte and she was astonished by it. Surely it could not be jealousy?

'Play it faster, Jon!' she cried, and everyone squealed, but the fiddler was only too happy to oblige. It was all great fun and Charlotte began to enjoy herself hugely. Certainly she had no intention of letting Sir James Caraddon see how he had affected her or that she minded that he was deliberately ignoring her. She had received presents from every single guest, even Molly who had given her a neatly hemmed new handkerchief. Alice had given the dress, of course, and Uncle Nathan had bought her a new mare, more fitting for her new status than Bella, her old pony whom she still loved and who could now be kept in contented retirement. There had been pomanders and lace kerchiefs, stockings, several books, and from Dickon a tortoiseshell comb. But from Sir James Caraddon not so much as the gift of a word or a smile all evening.

Next came Tom Carter, who swung her round in the foursome reel in a madcap gallop, her feet scarcely touching the ground. This was followed by each of his brothers in turn, then, after several more dances with Charlotte gasping for breath, she laughingly begged to be excused.

'Not tired already?' Charlotte swung round to find her hand being taken by Sir James as he led her back into the dance. 'You have not yet danced with me. Hardly polite, I feel.'

'You have not yet asked me,' she returned, tilting her chin impishly at him.

He proved to be a remarkably skilled dancer for all that the steps were not as familiar to his highly polished town-shoes than to her own soft country slippers, but they moved well together and as their eyes met, danced away and met again Charlotte found her heart pit-patting far more than the exertion merited. Yet after one dance she conceded defeat.

'I must beg you to pardon me, for I am perfectly worn out, not to mention my poor feet. I fear I have gone right through the soles of these slippers.'

'You certainly look heated. Perhaps if we were to step outside for a breath of fresh air? Or would that be considered unacceptable without a chaperon?' He smiled teasingly at her and she could not help but laugh.

Casting him a sideways glance of pure mischief, she flounced over to where Uncle Nathan sat tapping his foot and enjoying the music. 'Sir James has offered to walk a step with me out in the courtyard while I cool down; do you mind, Uncle?'

Delighted by this apparent sign of progress, Nathan adjured her to take her shawl and not to catch cold.

Dickon was at the door when they reached it. Charlotte had noticed that he'd seemed restless for some time, constantly making trips to the door to look out. She now asked him why.

'It's a surprise, Lottie, and you're not to know of it till the moment comes, which I do hope won't be long. They promised they wouldn't be late.'

'Who is late, Dickon?' and then, seeing his frown, laughed. 'All right, I will ask no more questions. Perhaps, by the time I return, the mysterious moment will have arrived.'

Charlotte could feel Dickon's brooding eyes upon her as she and James Caraddon walked out into the courtyard.

'We'll walk a little way along the lane,' she suggested. The top of her head did not quite reach his shoulder and, unused as she was to meeting members of the opposite sex other than those she had known all her life, like Dickon and the Carters, she experienced a sudden rush of shyness. 'If that is agreeable to you.'

He smiled down at her. 'Perfectly agreeable.'

The night air was not so cold as she'd expected, though the stars twinkled gleefully in a canopy of velvet devoid of cloud and her shoes crunched on the icy tufts of grass.

'And which one shall it be?' he asked after they had strolled in silence for a moment or two.

'Which one?' Charlotte frowned up at him.

'Which of your many suitors will win the prize of your hand?'

Charlotte tossed her head, clicking her tongue with disdain. 'And what makes you imagine I would choose any of them?'

'Ah. By that remark do I take it you are considering searching beyond the bounds of Caperley Farm? I believe that would be a wise decision. I see no young man suitable for you in the present company.'

Charlotte almost choked upon instant fury. 'How dare you presume to make judgements for me? I am not searching for a husband either here at Caperley or beyond, and you have no right to suggest otherwise.'

James looked askance at her. 'Are you saying you would rather stay an old maid?'

Charlotte's cheeks flamed. 'I never said any such thing,' she retorted. 'If you knew your Shakespeare you would know that love sought is good, but given unsought is better.'

'So you will wait here at Caperley until some romantic, poetic hero comes to discover you? Is that the sum of it? If so, then I must warn you it could be a long wait. Not many heroes pass this way.'

Charlotte stopped walking and turned to confront him. 'You think this is all highly amusing, don't you? It must be deliciously funny for you to come down from the great city of London and mock the way we country folk behave. Well, let me tell you that we have manners here too, and standards which must be kept. What's more, we care about other people and take no pleasure in mocking them. If and when I choose to consider taking a husband is none of your concern, Sir James Caraddon, so I'll thank you to keep your nose out of my affairs.'

'With pleasure,' said he in the same biting tone. 'But I suggest you make the same point to young Dickon.'

'Dickon?'

'I'm not blind to the way he looks at you, even if you choose to be. But I will say no more upon the subject. Shall we walk?' he said quickly, and, seeing that she was about to refuse, he tucked her arm firmly into his and ignored its wriggling attempt to free itself and they resumed their steady pace along the lane. 'This is delightful. The air is clearing my head; is it yours? It must have been considerably stuffy in your parlour, Charlotte.'

Charlotte had not experienced anything less delightful in her life. The warmth of his large hand clasped firmly over hers was infuriatingly disturbing and she wished he would let go of it. 'I find it rather chilly as a matter of fact,' she said.

'Then we must walk faster. It don't do to

linger. Not at this time of year.' James strode out more briskly and he could feel the sway of her body as she hurried along beside him, hip and thigh brushing against his as she tried to keep pace. It had the most extraordinary effect upon him and made him walk all the faster as if to escape the sensation, then suddenly he clasped her hand in his and cried out, 'Come on, let's run,' and he was off, haring down the lane as carefree as a young schoolboy, and Charlotte was running and skipping beside him, trying to catch her breath and not appear a weakling by falling behind, all at the same time.

They reached a wooden gate and James skidded to a halt. Charlotte's soft shoes slithered on the ice and she catapulted straight into his arms. Far from seeming surprised or objecting to this, he gathered her tightly against his broad chest and upon the instant his lips came down on hers in a warm crushing kiss that banished the last of the breath from her body. She melted against him like a snowflake on warm skin, and if her arms found their way about his neck she told herself it was only to prevent the possibility of falling upon the ice. She held on to him as tightly as she dared and her heart soared with the pleasure of being held tighter, in response. This man wanted her; for all her innocence she could sense it. And for all her sharp words to him a moment ago, she knew she wanted him too. It was the most delightfully satisfying experience in her life so far and she had absolutely no wish for it ever to end. But all too soon, it seemed, the magical moment was over and a cold waft of air separated them as they stood dumbly staring at each other.

'I dare say I should apologise for that,' James said at last, 'though I don't intend to. Perhaps we should have brought a chaperon after all.'

Charlotte gave a soft chuckle, for she could see he was sincere. 'I don't think I was in any danger. Besides, it is my birthday, and everyone is entitled to one kiss on their birthday.'

'Or even two?' he ventured, his grey eyes sparkling, but Charlotte backed away from him.

'I think not. We had better go back now.'

'Perhaps you are right, if you are to stay free from danger.' As she turned to walk back up the lane he caught her hand in his and held it for a moment. 'I never meant that to happen, you know. It wasn't planned.'

She gazed up into his eyes. 'I know,' she said, her voice a soft breath on the night air.

'But I do not at all regret it.'

'Nor do I,' she breathed.

'You have a most extraordinary effect upon a man. Why d'you think that is, Charlotte?' He rolled her name caressingly over his tongue. Charlotte tried to back away along the lane but he kept a very firm hold upon her hand.

'I suspect you are skilled at manufacturing situations such as these, *Sir* James Caraddon, and I'll have you know that you turn my head not at all.'

'Not at all?'

She shook it very decidedly. 'See, it is very firmly in place.' She smiled up at him, for it was really turning out to be quite the most wonderful birthday party she could have imagined. 'Not in the least little bit affected by your pretty words.'

He caught at the ties of her shawl and used them to pull her to him, his other arm going around her once more to hold her fast in a crushing embrace. 'Then it will have no effect if I repeat the exercise.'

Charlotte wriggled and squirmed, pushing against him with her hands, but he was every bit as strong as he looked and her efforts were fruitless. 'If you do not let me go I shall scream,' she cried, not meaning it but hoping he would not call her bluff. She saw the white of his teeth gleam in the darkness as he laughed softly at her.

'Scream away, birthday girl. None shall hear you, for I shall smother your squeals with more and more kisses.'

Whether or not either one of them would have carried out their threats was destined never to be discovered for at that moment a trumpet boomed out of the darkness from somewhere along the lane. It was the very last thing they had expected and both jumped as if they'd been shot.

'Hello, hello, hello. Be there anyone about? Here you see our merry band. The Fosdyke Players, finest in the land. Come to call and bring you pleasure. To offer the finest entertainment for you to treasure.'

Charlotte and James broke hastily apart and watched almost open-mouthed as a motley band of folk in the most fantastic costumes came along the lane, lanterns swinging high on sticks held in their hands. Charlotte came to herself first and ran to open the gate for them.

'Oh, how lovely – it's the strolling players! Uncle must have asked them to call after all.' Her jade eyes shone as she stepped back for them to enter, and with that simple act changed the destiny of her life.

CHAPTER FIVE

Wilfred Clement Fosdyke was a man of bold, swaggering demeanour. Square of frame and face, with a hook nose and eyebrows that bristled roguishly over penetrating blue eyes set exceptionally wide

98

apart, he could as easily have been Shylock as Falstaff and had been known to confuse the two on numerous occasions during his long career. He smiled now upon Charlotte and James, his wide mouth splitting to reveal as perfect a set of teeth as anyone would wish to see. For he was not entirely unhandsome in a waggish sort of way. He hooked his thumbs into the armholes of a bright red and yellow waistcoat plainly visible beneath a long green jacket, and, rocking back and forth on booted heels, let his gaze scan each of them while encompassing the measure of the house beyond. As he seemed satisfied that the occupants would be wealthy enough to pay his bill, his smile grew warmer.

'And what delectation shall we present for you this evening, my good friends? Is it to be *Henry IV* or *Bluebeard?* Or would you prefer a farce, or perhaps a tragedy? We are naturally experts in all styles of theatre so you have only to speak up for we are here to do your bidding.'

Charlotte was so busily engaged in observing each and every detail of the colourful, exotic and in some instances totally outlandish clothes of the company who gathered about him that she was quite unable to answer. She was saved the trouble, for the noise had brought the other guests to door and window, and across the yard strode Uncle Nathan himself, his face set in a grimace of displeasure. Behind him scurried an agitated Dickon.

'What is the meaning of this? Who the devil invited you, you scurrilous crew?'

Injured pride registered upon Fosdyke's face and even Charlotte was startled. Her usually placid uncle was looking beside himself with rage.

'Not you, my good sir, I can assure you of that,' said Fosdyke with scrupulous dignity. 'I believe it was your son who engaged us, if that be he who cowers behind you. An action I do not wonder at.'

'Dickon?' Nathan swirled about to confront the startled miscreant. 'What means this?'

'It means, good sir,' continued Fosdyke unperturbed, while Dickon's pale cheeks turned various shades of puce and scarlet as he sucked upon his lip, wishing himself anywhere but this and plainly unable to speak, 'that we are here, at great inconvenience to ourselves, being as how you live so far from everywhere, to entertain your delightful niece on what we understand to be her special day. Would you have us return those long weary miles with our skills and talents unused?' The great bushy eyebrows rose in mild enquiry as everyone waited in breathless anticipation for Nathan's reply. None came.

A chill breeze scurried across the yard, banging a door of the barn and lifting the skirts of a few hens on their belated progress to bed, tossing them carelessly through the pop-hole of their shelter. Charlotte shivered.

'It was for Charlotte,' mumbled Dickon. 'As a surprise.' He looked about to burst into tears as his father rounded upon him.

'This is no place to be discussing it, Uncle Nathan,' put in Charlotte hurriedly. 'Shall we not all go inside?' She pressed her cheek against his arm. 'It has been the very best of birthdays so far; please do not allow it to be spoiled.'

Nathan looked down upon his niece and his determination weakened. These last weeks he had stood out against this outlandish wish of hers to have the strolling players at her birthday; an innocent enough request, but he had his own reasons for refusing. Of course if he was not such a coward he would have come out with it and told Charlotte from the start that he resented all actors because of their effect upon his beautiful sister. But that might have led to other questions, questions he had not the stomach to answer. He'd long been aware of his niece's love for the theatre and had done his best to squash it. Yet its presence was too strong in the blood to be denied. The only way he could keep her from it would be to chain her to the house. A ridiculous thought. And what was the point of his antipathy, anyway? At some point she would be bound to visit a theatre, but that did not mean she would follow her mother into it. Wasn't he about to settle Charlotte's future most comfortably? Nathan glanced across at James whose interested gaze was fixed directly upon Charlotte, and Nathan at once relaxed. The future did indeed look hopeful.

Nathan slipped an arm about Charlotte's waist and adopted a tone as jovial and light as he could manage. 'You are right, my dear, as always. We shall all catch our deaths out here and we must not spoil this special day. Inside everyone, and we will see what these people of character have to show us.'

Tables were hastily moved back and chairs rearranged. Two screens were brought to serve as sidepieces behind which the actors waiting to appear could conceal themselves. James obligingly helped make the necessary preparations, then sat back with scarcely concealed amusement to view the proceedings.

The orchestra, if it might be termed such, comprised three persons: one old man who sawed valiantly at a violin with more harmony in his exaggerated arm movement than in the music he produced from the instrument – he also turned up later on stage as a second vagabond; another ancient rumbled upon a drum and constantly checked the row of candles he had set across the front of the 'stage', while a third played upon a flute that sounded remarkably like a penny whistle.

Just when the performance was about to begin there came the flurry of hoof-beats in the yard, followed by a loud rapping upon the door. Charlotte ran to open it to find a coachman in purple and gold livery upon the step. It was so unexpected that for a moment she was at a loss for words before her good manners reasserted themselves. 'Can I help you? Are you lost?'

'I believe these people are with me,' said James's voice in her ear and she turned to him in surprise.

'Ah, there you are, my boy,' came a second voice, and this time Charlotte was confronted by a large elderly lady swathed in several shawls over a brilliant gold and green gown, her smiling wrinkled face topped by a grey, much beribboned wig so tall it looked in danger of toppling over at any moment.

'I thought you were unwell, Grandmother, and meant to stay in bed,' said James, adroitly bypassing the astonished Charlotte to lead Lady Caraddon indoors. 'Thank you, Charles,' he said, addressing the coachman. 'Once you have stabled the horses I'm sure you will find refreshment in the kitchen.'

'Oh, but of course,' agreed Charlotte, coming to herself and instantly incensed by this usurping of her authority. She smiled bewitchingly at the coachman. 'But you must come and enjoy the show first of all. It is about to begin.'

'*Show?*' Lady Caraddon's voice boomed out in astonishment. 'What kind of a show are you talking of, girl? It is Charlotte, is it not? What are you doing, answering the door? Have you no servants in this establishment?' She peered at Charlotte through her pince-nez and Charlotte bobbed a deferential curtsy, smiling back, wondering which question to answer first.

'We were about to be entertained by a company of strolling players, ma'am,' Charlotte informed her new guest. 'Or – or would you care for some refreshment first? You must by very cold.'

'I shall be frozen to the spot in a trice if I'm not allowed beyond the hallway.'

A comfortable leather chair was at once procured from Uncle Nathan's study and placed in the centre of the front row so that Lady Caraddon might have a good view of events.

'Thank you, my dear,' she said kindly, squeezing Charlotte's hand in an impulsive display of affection. 'You and I shall talk later. There is much to be said between us.'

Charlotte took her seat beside this most

distinguished of guests and wondered what they could possibly have to talk about. She had met Lady Caraddon only once before and that was many years ago when Charlotte had been quite small. She understood from Sir James Caraddon that his grandmother spent very little time in Cornwall these days, so she couldn't help speculating on what had brought Lady Caraddon on this occasion and why her state of health had been so uncertain and now seemed so heartily wholesome. Had she known that it had all been part of that good lady's grand design to allow her grandson and Charlotte ample opportunity to become acquainted, she might have been less amused.

'Ladies and gentlemen,' boomed Fosdyke, and Charlotte put all thoughts from her mind to fix her attention entirely upon him. 'Kindly be seated, for the play is about to commence. We present to you an extract from that now famous operetta *The Lord of the Manor* in which true love is exalted over rank and wealth, the merits of rural life are emphatically maintained and the foolish pride of the old is overcome by the young. You may laugh at the humour, sob at the tragic and applaud at the end.' With a regal bow in true theatrical tradition, Fosdyke withdrew and, in a space no larger than a goodly sized hearthrug, the half-dozen actors strutted and strolled, declaimed, eulogised and frequently sang at the least provocation with more gusto than tune for a prolonged hour. Whatever the performance lacked in professional expertise was more than compensated for by the enthusiasm of the participants, by the colour of their costumes and by the novelty of the whole affair. The audience sat enraptured throughout, more than willing to obey Fosdyke's instructions by laughing and crying and applauding in all the right places.

Even Lady Caraddon was moved to call, 'Bravo!'

As for Charlotte, she too was enthralled. She sat through the entire performance without speaking a word or taking her eyes for one second from the action. She marvelled at the dancing, was moved by the wistful heroine and convulsed with laughter at Fosdyke's rendition of Moll Flagon. He looked so completely incongruous in women's clothing with his breeches peeping out beneath the tucked-up skirt. And his expressions were so comically lugubrious that she could scarcely contain her giggles. It was only as the small troupe of actors had taken their final bow and were being justifiably regaled with ample helpings of supper and hot punch that she came to herself as if from a trance.

'Did you enjoy it?'

James's deep voice against her ear made

Charlotte jump. 'Oh, yes,' she said, eyes bright as she twisted in her seat to look up at him. 'Didn't you? Such cleverness. So much verve and energy. And how everyone clapped.'

'And what of you, Grandmother?' James enquired, though not taking his eyes from Charlotte.

'Lot of nonsense,' said she. 'But there are worse things in life than enjoying a bit of nonsense now and again. Have to admit I quite enjoyed it. Sharpened my appetite for supper, though.'

'Oh, I'll fetch you some,' cried Charlotte, jumping up.

'Don't bother. I'll find my own.' The old lady gave a sudden grin. 'I'll get more that way. Don't forget, we are to have words later.' She nodded briskly, making the fruit and feathers that decorated her wig lurch quite perilously, and Charlotte held her breath until normal motion had been resumed. She found it almost impossible to stifle her laughter as she returned her attention to the Lady's grandson.

'Might I get you some supper?'

'I have feasted in plenty,' he said, and from the look in his eyes Charlotte had the oddest notion that he meant more by this innocent remark than might at first be evident. Could he be referring to that kiss? She pushed the memory from her mind for fear it would reveal itself in her expressive face.

'It must be the loveliest feeling in the world to please so many people,' said Charlotte, aiming for safer ground.

'Better to please but one,' said James quietly, coming closer, causing her to catch her breath.

'Indeed no, the young lady has it right,' interposed Fosdyke, thrusting himself between them so that James was forced to step back and away from Charlotte, and she felt a piercing disappointment that this moment of intimacy had been broken. 'There is nothing so heart-warming as a spontaneous accolade. I suspect the young lady has talents of her own, were she brave enough to reveal them to us. She certainly lacks nothing by way of charm and beauty.'

Blushing hotly, Charlotte hastily denied any such thing. 'Though I do love to read Shakespeare and Sheridan and was enchanted by this, my first view of live theatre,' she added.

Fosdyke raised the eyebrows along with his booming voice, in shocked surprise. 'Your first viewing? My stars, what a sad indictment upon your education. Had no one the wit to teach you anything of life beyond cows and sheep?'

Charlotte was momentarily nonplussed by this outcry but, gathering her wits, swiftly came to her uncle's defence. 'No, no, that is far from the case. Uncle Nathan has taught me a good deal about art and literature, geography and science. I know nothing of the farm; that is left to Dickon.'

'Ah, science,' said Fosdyke in scoffing tones. 'A passing fancy. And, if you ask my opinion, the sooner it passes, the better.' He chortled with laughter at his own joke and Charlotte attempted to smile with him. 'But there, let us hear some of this education. 'Tis your birthday, after all, and you too must entertain your guests who have come so far to honour you. If you so love poetry and plays then I shall find you a piece to recite to us. Come.'

Not one to listen to protest, Wilfred Fosdyke took Charlotte firmly by the elbow and led her behind the screen.

What followed was to live in her memory for ever after.

'Fanny, Fanny!' called Fosdyke, and the girl who had played the wistful heroine reluctantly returned from the supper-table, a chunk of pie still clasped in her hand. Hair a black tangle, eyes brilliant blue set in a high-cheekboned face, she had an almost gypsy-like appearance. Though probably no more than eight and twenty, she looked considerably older. Her red striped dress failed to quite confine the abundant bosom and Charlotte swiftly averted her eyes from the décolletage. 'Fetch Miss Charlotte a shawl. She is to do a piece from *The Grecian Daughter*.'

'What? Her? Never.'

'Fanny!' The single word slipped silkily off Fosdyke's tongue, but the listener must have recognised a note of chastisement for she vanished in an instant, to return with a cashmere shawl in soft blues and greens which she tossed negligently at Charlotte. Fosdyke arranged it demurely about Charlotte's neck and shoulders and she looked expectantly up at him, thinking inconsequentially that he was not as old as she had at first imagined out in the darkness of the yard.

'Here is the piece. Scan it briefly while I make the usual introduction.' So saying, he thrust a small leatherbound volume into Charlotte's shaking hand before striding out on to the 'stage' once more. Seconds later it was Charlotte's turn to follow him out there.

It was a moment to cherish.

Stepping out to face her audience and drawing a deep breath, she launched herself into the words clenched so tightly in her hand and at once forgot their presence. She recited the piece with all the sensibilities and emotion which came so naturally to her, feeling no shyness, no embarrassment before these people whom she knew so well, and an inner part of her felt surprise at this.

Her confidence grew till she was able to relax and even lift her eyes occasionally from the book and look out over the blur of faces, their rapt attention almost tangible. The speech which she read was that of Euphrasia speaking of her great love for her father who lay weak with starvation in the tyrant's prison. It was a gloomy piece, full of sentiment and tragedy but popular at the time, and when her closing words sank into silence she thought for one breathless moment that she had failed. But then someone sniffed back a tear, she saw a handkerchief employed, and another; then the whole audience was applauding, many people upon their feet and cheering, and Charlotte felt her cheeks burn with pleasure and pride.

Only now did she allow her gaze to come into focus and it centred upon a lean face with grey, almost black eyes that glittered with – she caught at a sob in her throat for the expression was unmistakable – admiration, laced with intoxicating desire. Holding out her skirts between damp palms, Charlotte gave a deep bow as she had seen the other players do, twisted her gaze from James and smiled upon her relatives and friends who smiled back in flushed delight, pleased for her success.

Later, Lady Caraddon came to Charlotte to personally congratulate her. 'Should've known you'd have talent, girl. Just like your mother. Chip off the old block, eh?'

Charlotte felt herself grow still. 'You knew my mother?'

James, coming to join them, noisily cleared his throat. 'Have a care, Grand-mother. Perhaps now is not the time. Take no heed of her, Charlotte. She likes nothing better than to gossip.'

'Tch. Be quiet, boy. Of course I knew her mother. Everyone knew her mother. She was a wonderful girl, sweet and talented, and I for one never believed half of what they said about her.'

James rolled his eyes heavenward, then very firmly took hold of his grandmother's arm and attempted to steer her away with an unusually firm admonition to let things be at the present time. Someone would have to put the child in the picture and, though her uncle evidently hadn't the stomach for it, his grandmother was the last person in the world to exercise any tact. She had even less than himself, which he admitted was not saying a great deal. 'This is Charlotte's birthday party, hardly the moment for revelations of this nature,' he whispered fiercely but, though his grandmother may well have capitulated, he had reckoned without Charlotte.

'What is it you keep from me?' she asked, white-faced. 'I'd much rather know now than worry over it all night.'

James looked at Charlotte and saw how she trembled, and an overwhelming pity for her took a hold of him. Yet he had no wish to become involved. It was not his problem. 'Come, Charlotte,' he said briskly. 'Put the matter aside for now. I'm sure you'll welcome a sip of wine after your recital.'

Constance Caraddon chortled with delight. 'What's this, boy? Stealing her from me already? So that's the way the story goes, eh?' Lady Caraddon smilingly took a step away from them both. 'Perhaps my grandson is right.' Glancing up at him she gave him her most beguiling smile which she used when she had manoeuvred someone exactly into the corner she had chosen. 'It would be far better were he to tell you himself.'

James's look of fury would have shrivelled lesser persons, but Constance Caraddon was made of pure copper plate and impervious to such shafts. The old eyes twinkled knowingly, and she flicked closed her fan to tap her forehead as if indicating that her grandson were not quite right in the head. 'Go ahead, my boy. You will make a much better job of it than I. But Charlotte, my dear, you must not be upset by anything my roguish grandson has to tell you. It all happened a long time ago, and I vow it is of no importance and certainly need not concern you now. Besides, I never did care for pedigrees,' she declared. 'Mongrels are so much more reliable, I've always found.' Following this mystifying statement she swung round upon her fashionably coloured heels and went in search of Alice's delicious pumpkin pie.

Charlotte turned at once to Sir James, green eyes ablaze. 'And what was all that about? I haven't the first idea what either of you are talking of. Why did you send Lady Caraddon away when I most particularly wished to hear about my mother? Uncle Nathan hates to speak of her to me. I don't think he has ever recovered from her death.'

There was a small, almost uncomfortable silence, during which James looked into Charlotte's green eyes, trying to put a name to their unusual shade, and then at the toes of his boots which were dull after their walk along the icy lane. As his gaze returned to her small piquant face, he had an almost irresistible urge to take her in his arms again, to stop her small ears with his hands, her lips with his kisses, and all pain from her heart. But such feelings were madness. She was not a child and it was not his place to protect her. Damn his grandmother for getting him involved in the first place!

'You will have ample opportunity to talk with Lady Caraddon about your mother, but you may, if you wish, follow her this instant. I'm sure I have no wish to detain you.'

Charlotte very nearly stalked off in a high dudgeon but then she remembered. 'Indeed no. There is some mystery here and I would know of it without more ado. Does it have some connection with this fortune I have been left? If so, then I suppose I'd best hear it, though I warn you my mind is quite made up: I shall not accept it.'

'You are a very stubborn young lady,' growled James, his sympathy vanishing in a cloud of fresh anger. 'How can you treat money in such an offhand manner? Do you not know how important it can be? How some people crave the need of a fraction of what you so scornfully toss aside simply to live?'

'It is not important to me,' she retorted. 'I would willingly give it away to anyone who begged for it. I do not deny need, I do assure you,' she finished heatedly, feeling she was being put at fault and unable to work out quite why.

Deciding this was far too public a place for such an argument, which was growing progressively louder, James grasped Charlotte's arm in a punishing grip and marched her out of the best parlour and along the passage. His action, however, had taken place a moment too late, for their conversation had indeed been overheard, and not by a friend. Wilfred Clement Fosdyke now strode among the guests with a thoughtful, if slightly twisted smile upon his rubicund face.

Meanwhile, without even knocking on the door to make sure Nathan was not inside with his books, James propelled Charlotte into the empty study and closed the door.

'How dare you treat me so – so ruthlessly?' she stormed, but the force of her ire was blunted as she shivered in her thin dress in the cold room.

Stepping to the fireplace where Molly had laid a neat pyramid of sticks, paper and logs ready for morning, James set light to it and at once the study burst into life if not instant warmth. Charlotte lit the lamp upon the desk with a taper held in fingers far from steady. The glow from it and from the flickering fire softened the lean hard lines of James's face and lit the already dark skin to a glowing bronze. Once again she felt a slight breathlessness, as if she had been chasing Sam over the cliff-tops, and she was forced to take several quick breaths in order to steady herself.

'What is it you wish to say to me that is of such importance?' she demanded, her small blunt chin tilting upwards as if to declare that nothing he could say would be of the least consequence.

'Perhaps you had better be seated,' said Sir

James considerately. 'I would not have you faint.'

Charlotte stiffened. 'I have never fainted in my life and don't intend starting now.'

James's irritation at having this most unpleasant duty thrust upon him began to fade to be replaced by embarrassment, awkwardness and – dammit all, he felt sorry for the girl. It was not her fault, none of it. Why did she have to know at all? He remembered the large annuity which Nathan Pierce had been at pains to tell him of. Such a sum could take her into the highest echelons of society and there would be plenty in that quarter more than willing to fill in the details. There would be little hope of respectability for Charlotte without a husband, and who would take her on once they had heard the worst of it? He would certainly think twice himself, wouldn't he? James considered this latter thought for a moment longer, then mentally shook himself. Best to get it over with.

'I have to say from the outset that the news is not good, and I am not really the one to break it to you.'

'You seemed more than willing a moment ago,' quipped Charlotte in biting tone. 'You couldn't wait to take over the unpleasant duty, if that is what it is, from your grandmother.'

James almost gaped at her. 'I tried to stop

Grandmother speaking of it this evening, on your birthday celebration. It was *your* idea to have the whole thing brought into the open now.'

'Then what are you waiting for? Have done with it. I'm sure you cannot wait for the pleasure of seeing me suffer.' Charlotte could scarcely think what she was saying, but instinct made her keep up her defences in preparation for this unpleasant piece of gossip about to be revealed to her, which had evidently been to her mother's cost. No doubt it was some tittle-tattle that she had taken a lover or some such, a common enough tale and one which Charlotte meant not to allow to concern her in the least. She strode to the window and stared miserably out into the icy blackness, tapping her fingers upon the glass. 'I am still waiting,' she said coldly, and strode back to the fire to warm her now frost-tipped fingers against the blaze.

'Damn you, Charlotte. Will you be seated! I cannot talk to you if you are skitting about like a demented kitten.'

'Indeed I am not.' But she sat none the less, her legs suddenly feeling weak and tired. How very bad-tempered he was. If this was an example of town manners, she'd do best to remain in the country. 'I do wish you would come out with it at once before I scream. What is this gossip and how does it

118

concern me?' If she were the kind of girl prone to hysterics, she would certainly be having them by now. As it was, she remained calmly seated upon the hard-backed chair, almost smiling up at James, however insincerely, with every sign of patience.

'That you are not your father's child.'

Charlotte continued to stare at him for a long, silent moment as even her own breathing seemed to stop. So she'd been right; her mother had had a lover. It explained a great deal. She examined her own feelings on the matter and found them fairly uninjured. 'I can see that such a prospect would worry you, an aristocrat. It does not trouble me in the least. I have never known my father – at least, the man I thought was my father. I believed him to be dead. Therefore it is of no real consequence if it should turn out that he was not my father at all.' With a small smile she got to her feet. 'If there is nothing else I will return to my guests. It is cold in here.'

She had her hand on the brass doorknob before he spoke again. 'Don't you want to know who your real father is?'

Until he had suggested it, she was astonished to realise, she had not even considered the matter. The idea caught her off guard. 'I'm not sure. Is it important?'

James walked towards her and there was a strange compassion in his gaze as, reaching out, he took her small cold hands between his own and led her back to the chair by the fire. 'I think it may be. The fact is, Charlotte, your mother, Eleanor Pierce, was an actress when she married the man you believed to be your father, Lord Justin Forbes. He was rich and titled and absolutely besotted by her. But he was a jealous and possessive man. It is not known whether he and Eleanor were lovers before their marriage but—' James stopped abruptly to glance at the pale face across from him. 'If I must speak of matters not normally discussed with young girls of your age, you must forgive me. I see no benefit in dressing things up. You are old enough now to learn the truth.'

'I am not a child, I do understand about such things,' said Charlotte rather primly, and, apparently satisfied, James continued.

'Little more than four months into the marriage, you were born.'

Charlotte swallowed the hard lump that had risen in her throat. 'That is not so unusual.'

'Indeed not. Many full-term babies are passed off as premature. Nevertheless, Lord Justin did not like it. He claimed the child was not his.' James sucked upon his lower lip and wished himself a hundred miles away, regarding Charlotte with eyes grown bleak but surprisingly kind. 'Gossip can be cruel, and in this case ran like fire. Justin's rabid jealousy convinced him the child was not his and gossip supplied the answers your mother would not give. The scandalmongers decided that Eleanor had truly known only one man before her husband. A man with whom she had ever shown a marked affection, and who was always to be found at her side. That man was her brother, Nathan Pierce.'

Charlotte stared in disbelief and mounting horror at James. Then she was on her feet, trembling as if with the ague. 'It isn't true, it isn't true,' she kept repeating over and over.

James had hold of her arms and was desperately trying to return her to her seat as if he were afraid for her sanity and that that would in some way restore it. 'Of course it is not true. It was pure vindictiveness. I dare say some person, for their own malicious purposes, wanted to hurt Justin Forbes. There are many would be glad enough of the opportunity to twist their knives into me. Justin's jealousy and foolish behaviour gave them the angle they sought. After almost two years of such whisperings your poor mother, not surprisingly, could endure it no longer and fled back to the people she had known and loved before she met your father. So far as anyone is aware she may still be with them, still acting, still–'

'You mean my mother didn't die either?'

James could scarcely bear to meet the

121

agony of her gaze. 'No, Charlotte, she did not die. She returned to the stage where she hoped to find some remnant of happiness, no doubt.'

'And left me?' The soft voice was pitiable and James's heart tugged painfully in response to it.

'I expect she thought it would be for the best. How could she manage, a woman alone with a child, and an actress at that? At least Lord Justin could feed you.'

A light exploded in Charlotte's brain. It was as if everything had slipped into place. She could understand it all now. The reason why her so-called father had gone abroad and never contacted her, why her uncle had sold up everything to bury himself in the country, why no one at Caperley liked to speak of the past. She did not understand why Lord Justin should decide to bestow a fortune upon her, but perhaps it was simply to prevent her trying to find him. So be it. He was the last person she wanted to see. Her mother, however, was a different matter. Not for one moment did Charlotte believe this dreadful story. But, apart from any other consideration, only her mother could reveal the truth of it, and if Charlotte was to have any hope of happiness or even sanity she must find her.

She was pushing away James's restraining hands, heedless of his soft placating words.

'I won't believe it, I won't! I'll *prove* that it isn't true. I swear I will!' She ran to the door. Charlotte knew what she must do and intended to waste no time in putting her plan into immediate effect.

CHAPTER SIX

Most of Charlotte's guests had already left. Some were in the process of taking their leave and her progress was impeded by the need to exchange pleasantries. Her present state of shock meant that she did so with lips which bent only stiffly to her will and many goodbyes were terminated more abruptly than good manners demanded. She saw the look of puzzlement enter her uncle's face, but she could not meet his gaze. Nor did she have any wish to approach him on the subject. Only too clearly did she understand how much a confrontation would embarrass him. She loved him dearly, despite this most human failing, and would continue to believe in him. But she would discover nothing further here at Caperley. She must go elsewhere to discover the truth.

'Please forgive me, Uncle, but I am quite tired after all the excitement. If you will excuse me, I will go to bed at once.' She gave him a sweeter, more lingering kiss than usual, then hurried away before he could see her tears.

'Of course, my dear.' Nathan watched her go, ignorant of the turmoil in her heart.

In her room, Charlotte changed out of her beautiful new dress into a simple lawn gown in coral and mauve stripe and tied her favourite lace kerchief about her neck. Next she put on her warmest cloak and stoutest boots. Finding a small leather satchel, she packed in a few essential items, then sat herself down to wait with as much patience as she could muster for the house to quieten. She dared not wait more than an hour or so, or the players would get too much of a lead on her. When she felt it safe, she crept down the back stairs to the kitchen where she found Alice snoring with exhaustion in the big rocking-chair. Creeping stealthily past her, Charlotte managed to unlatch the back door and was halfway across the yard, thinking herself free, when she heard a door bang and a familiar voice call out.

'That you, Miss Charlotte?'

Charlotte turned, heart beating slow and hard in her breast. She had to get away. Nothing and no one must be allowed to prevent that. 'Yes, Molly,' she answered as calmly as she could. 'Did you by any chance see which direction the strolling players

124

took? I forgot to return the shawl they lent me, so I thought if I hastened after them I could give it back before they got too far.'

Molly considered this point, painfully slowly. 'The left fork, I reckon. But I ain't certain. Would you like me to fetch Dickon? He could run faster 'n you.'

'No, no. Dickon is no doubt busy shutting up the animals for the night. They can't have got far and I'll be glad of a little fresh air before I retire for the night. Leave the kitchen door on the latch, Molly. I won't be long.'

'Right you are. I'm near dropping on my feet, I can tell you.' Molly ambled off about her late duties, sighing of how beautiful the play had been and what a fine feast they had had.

Charlotte did not stop to listen to her rambling. She was running on winged feet, stumbling over the icy ruts but determined to catch up with the players before they got too far. If she was any judge, they would be making for a new town tomorrow and, if she was lucky, eventually for London. She wondered where they would be spending the night and was thankful that Uncle Nathan had not offered them the use of his barn. The further she got from Caperley this night, the better.

She ran until her sides ached and she was forced to slow to a walk. A mile or two after that her heart skipped a beat as she glimpsed a light penetrating the darkness ahead.

She found them huddled together around a tiny fire in the shelter of an old disused barn. It was only as she approached that she began to consider what she would say.

'Who goes there?' The dramatic tones of the booming voice rang out in the gloom and Charlotte jumped, crying out in terror as a hand grasped her arm. A lantern was swung in her face, blinding her for a second, and she heard an oath of surprise as she was recognised. 'Can it be our talented Miss Birthday Girl herself?' Wilfred Clement Fosdyke almost licked his lips in delight. This was an unexpected piece of good fortune. Ever since he'd overheard that most interesting piece of information between herself and Sir James he'd been frantic to think how it could best be applied to his own benefit. The old man had obstinately refused to offer them lodging, paid them the price quoted to the penny with not a groat extra as tip. Such miserliness had only served to make Fosdyke wrestle all the harder with the problem. Now here was the solution, standing dewy-eyed before him. 'My dearest girl, you look quite worn out, and more than a little frozen.' Resting his arm protectively across her shoulders, he led Charlotte closer to the fire. 'Put on more logs, get a blaze going; the lass is pinched with the cold. Make room there.' He cuffed and booted one or two recalcitrant members of the orchestra from the choicest positions and settled Charlotte into the space they vacated.

She gazed about her at the assembled company and wondered at her own daring. There was Fanny, rubbing sleep from her eyes and already glowering curiously at her. A cup of scalding tea was placed in her hands and she sipped it gratefully. Fosdyke introduced the two younger men as Carl and Phil.

'Carl, being so handsome, does the romantic leads and Phil plays the villain. Ain't that right, Phil?' chortled Fosdyke.

'Aye,' agreed the grinning Phil, looking far from villainous. 'I'm a brilliant actor, Miss Forbes, but I never get the girl.'

Charlotte laughed out loud, beginning to feel more relaxed now that she had her breath and her toes were thawing out.

'And this here is Sally Drew. She plays some good character parts, does Sal. You should see her Mrs Malaprop – a proper treat. And this is her terror of a son, young Peter. He plays page-boy roles and such like. Does all the errands, helps put up the scenery and cooks the meals if necessary. What would we do without him? Say hello to the lady, Peter.' Fosdyke stuck his face close to the boy, who briefly nodded at Charlotte then closed his eyes and went back to sleep, his dusty blond head resting upon his mother's ample lap.

Sally Drew smiled lovingly as she stroked his hair. 'He'll talk plenty tomorrow. You see if he don't.'

'And you've met Fanny already, of course.' Fosdyke raised his bushy brows at the black-haired Fanny as if to ask if she meant to greet their new guest. Fanny merely sniffed, rubbed her eyes and lay down beside the warmth of the glowing embers. 'Bit tired just now, she is. Been a long day, as I expect you have found too.' Fosdyke was avid with curiosity about why Charlotte had followed them, but knew better than to startle this fragile wide-eyed fawn. 'Was there something special you wanted us for? Your uncle has paid our account, you can rest assured,' he said, adopting a polite smile.

'Oh, I'm so glad. N-no. I forgot to return the shawl,' Charlotte said, handing over the small neatly packed parcel.

'Dear Lord, you needn't have run after us just for that fleabitten thing,' put in Sally.

'I didn't. I mean, there was another matter.' She turned to Fosdyke and her jade eyes, darkly starred by thick lashes, had never looked more appealing. Yet he would have agreed to her request if she had been as ugly as a cow and twice as stupid. Fosdyke was not a man to be won over simply by a pretty face. They were two a penny, as he was often wont to say, and didn't give half as good service. 'I wished to ask a favour of you.'

'A favour.' Fosdyke stuffed his chest with air so that it bellied grandly out like a pigeon's, though he would have preferred to think himself a swan, and smiled beatific-ally, revealing the perfect white teeth. 'You have only to name it and it is yours. How could anyone refuse so charming a young lady?'

Charlotte had meant only to ask if she might travel with them to London where she intended to search out the whereabouts of her mother. But a wild thought had catapulted into her head and before she could stop herself she asked, 'Might I join you?'

Even Fosdyke was surprised. It was the last thing he'd expected. Yet, when he thought about it, why should she not wish to join them? The girl had talent – that much was certain. She'd read the piece which she'd never set eyes on before with the skill and ease of a professional. There was no question but that he could make something of her. 'Now, why would you want to do that?' he probed. 'Not fallen out with your uncle, have you?' This thought alarmed him for a moment. What use a fortune if it was cut off? But Charlotte hastened to reassure him.

'Oh, no, not at all. Only...' And here for the first time in her fife she decided that some form of a lie might be safer. She had no wish at this stage, or to these people, kindly though they seemed, to relate the full sordidness of her problem. '...I have relatives in London, and if you should be going in that direction I wondered if I might accompany you. I have always longed to act and it would be so much more fun than taking the coach. I do so love an adventure.' Her smile vanished. 'But if I'd be a nuisance you have only to say. However, I do assure you I would work hard.'

Fosdyke decided that the gods must be pleased with him this day. The teeth positively glittered in the darkness as he smiled upon Charlotte. 'Nothing would give us greater pleasure than to have you become a member of the Fosdyke Players.'

James awoke later than usual and at once became aware of a great hubbub of noise outside his room. Running footsteps, banging doors and the loud clamour of voices. Hastily pulling on his shirt and breeches, he went to investigate. Alice and Molly were hurrying in confusing and alternating circles up and down stairs, along passages and into and out of various rooms. He watched this odd performance for a second or two before managing to catch a hold of Molly and halt her madcap dash.

'What on earth is going on, Molly? You all seem quite demented.'

'Oh, sir! 'Tis Miss Charlotte,' Molly gasped, heaving great gulps of air into her flat chest.

James felt a prickle of foreboding. 'What of Miss Charlotte?' He gripped tighter upon Molly's arm and she winced.

'She have gone. Leastways we can find no trace of her either in the house or in the yard. Please don't squeeze my arm so, sir, I 'ad a drop too much cider last night and I do hurt all over.'

James lessened his grip only to shake Molly as if she were in some way to blame when he knew it was himself. 'You're sure she isn't out riding the new horse?'

Molly groaned as the headache worsened. There was something she kept trying to remember but she couldn't quite get to grips with it. What with Alice's shouting and scolding and now this gentleman shaking the life out of her she doubted she ever would. 'No, we've checked and the mare is eating her head off in the stable, sweet as you please. No sign of Miss Charlotte. Oh, where can she have got to? My head, sir.'

James relented sufficiently to release the girl's arm and, brushing her to one side, went in search of more alert members of the household. He found Alice on her way into Nathan's study, her old face a wrinkle of anxiety.

'She's nowhere to be found, master. If you ask me she's taken off somewhere.'

James did not miss the long look which passed between them. 'Do you think you can guess where that is, Alice?' he asked.

'I can, sir,' Molly said as she hurtled into the room, her thin face wreathed in smiles, and James felt his heart give an odd jolt, which surprised him more than a little.

'Have you found her?'

'No, sir, only I've remembered something. I saw Miss Charlotte go out last night.'

'You *saw* her go?' gasped Nathan, white-faced.

'That's right, sir. I was just seeing to the ashes, from the fire you know, and I saw her crossing the yard – off to return a shawl to the players, she was. Said to leave the kitchen door on the latch for she wouldn't be long.'

A heavy silence fell upon the room.

Alice was the first to recover. 'I knew it. Never any other thought in her silly head but play-acting.' Turning to Nathan, who sat ashen-faded and strangely silent at his desk, she continued. 'But why now? On her birthday? She hasn't even ridden the new mare yet. I could understand it better if something had upset her ... if she'd heard ... if you had told her, master...'

'I told her.' James had never felt so sick in his entire life as each pair of eyes swivelled to look at him in open incredulity. Nathan got slowly to his feet, suddenly looking a very old man, and leaned across the desk.

'*You* told her?'

James inclined his head. 'Yes.'

'I meant her to hear it from a woman.' His voice was a cracked whisper.

'I know you asked my grandmother to do it, but she is not the most – well the fact is...' James fumbled for words... 'the conversation came round to Charlotte's mother quite by accident last evening and before I knew what was happening my grandmother had elected me for the task of enlightening Charlotte. Possibly she thought I would employ more tact,' James finished miserably.

'It seems that you failed, boy,' came a voice from the door. Lady Caraddon sailed into the room, swathed in her favourite pink and purple house-robe. She surveyed the assembled company with a critical eye. 'What long faces! Good heavens, the girl has only run off with a tom-tiddle band of players. Anyone would think she'd been clapped in Newgate. She can easily be found and brought back. Charlotte Forbes is not the first young lady to have done a runner, nor will she be the last. It's the shock of learning she may not be who she thinks she is, I dare swear. But that'll pass. A day or two with that bizarre crew and she'll be begging to come home. James shall set off at once, won't you, boy?' She smiled confidently at her grandson but he felt no inclination to return her smile.

'This is none of my concern,' he told her through narrowed lips. Then, turning back to Nathan Pierce, continued, 'I am sorry, sir, that your family matters have alarmed and upset Charlotte, but I did no more than inform her of them because no one else seemed willing to take on the task.' There was the very slightest hint of reproach in his tone. 'If she has indeed gone off with the players, it would be my guess that she'll head for London, and you would do as well to try to catch up with her there. I'm afraid I can be of no further assistance to you, and have more than enough problems of my own to attend to.' Instructing Lady Carad-don to dress as quickly as may be while he got the carriage ready, James turned to go.

'You would leave us in this pretty pickle?' Nathan called out, finally abandoning the security of his desk to hasten to James's side. 'I accept my part of the blame. I confess I should have told Charlotte myself but it was difficult and embarrassing. I believed it would be best for her were it to come from a woman. For that, sir, I hold you equally responsible. You have indeed upset and embarrassed my niece over a subject which needed handling with the utmost delicacy. You can hardly walk out on the result of your bumbling. Your grandmother is quite right. You must go after her with all speed.'

James was speechless with rage as he looked from one face to the next. Alice's creased with loving anxiety, Molly's a wreck of guilt and anguish, Nathan's concern and on his grandmother's placid acceptance. Perhaps it was this last which exasperated him the most, for she had played tricks upon him all his life and for all he knew Constance Caraddon could well have engineered the whole thing, making absolutely sure that he was put into this impossible position.

'I doubt they'll have got further than Plymouth by the time you catch up with them, boy,' she said, in mild tones. 'Unless you delay your departure too long, that is.'

James sighed and closed his eyes. He could see no way of refusing this admittedly reasonable request without seeming totally churlish. 'Have my horse saddled. I'll try Plymouth. If she has gone much beyond that, sir, you must make other arrangements.' James took a step closer to Nathan to issue a piece of advice in a low hoarse voice. 'And no matter your embarrassment,

135

sir, when she returns be prepared to discuss the whole matter through with her and answer all her damned questions without demur.'

'Thank you,' said Nathan, 'for your action, and your advice. I will think on it.'

Less than ten minutes later James was on the road and he still couldn't work out how his quiet Christmas in Cornwall had gone so badly wrong.

That first morning, as the players trudged along the road, Charlotte was happy to talk with Sally Drew and her son, Peter. They proved to be both friendly and informative and Charlotte gleaned all she could from them. The first thing Charlotte learned was that there was little done by way of rehearsal. Fosdyke as actor-manager issued a few instructions to which the cast listened with varying degrees of attention. Everyone was then expected to write out their words from the one book, if the play was new to them, and be word perfect by the first performance, often with only hours' notice. The second thing Charlotte learned was that everyone was expected to perform at least two parts in the larger cast plays and since Fosdyke was fond of doing Shakespeare, Sheridan and Goldsmith this was quite often. The reason, she discovered, was not so much artistic preference as Fosdyke liking to get value for money. He paid a weekly wage to his players and he meant them to work hard for it.

'We'll be doing *Othello* this evening, at Plymouth Dock,' Fosdyke informed them as they stopped by the wayside to eat a meagre lunch of bread and cheese and drink water from a nearby stream. 'The main part played by myself, of course. Phil, you will be Iago and Carl will play Cassio as usual. Fanny can be Desdemona and Sal will be Iago's wife. As for our new member here,' Fosdyke smiled expansively, 'you can play Bianca, mistress to Cassio. What d'you think of that, eh?'

'I usually play Bianca as well as Desdemona,' grumbled Fanny, her lip trembling in a sullen pout.

'Well, then, you'll have an easy night of it for once, won't you?' retorted Fosdyke unfeelingly.

'I don't mind simply watching, for the first night,' put in Charlotte hastily, quickly disguising her instant flush of delight at being handed such a part, but equally anxious not to cause offence to Fanny.

'Poppycock. Everyone here has to do their bit. We don't carry passengers in the Fosdyke Players,' declared Fosdyke forcibly. 'Sal will find the words for you and fill you in on the moves. And there's no more to be said about it,' he finished, giving Fanny's

137

thigh what might have passed for an affectionate squeeze had he not looked so unsmilingly at her. Fosdyke then proceeded to hand out the rest of the parts. Much to Charlotte's relief, there were few female roles in *Othello* so she had just the one part to remember. She spent the rest of the journey saying over the words and desperately memorising Sally Drew's instructions.

Yet it was like no Shakespeare she had ever read. Sally told her that in order to accommodate the fact that each actor was playing several roles and could not be in two places at once, and to liven up 'the dull bits' for the audience, the great playwright's famous words naturally needed a bit of alternation here and there. Whole chunks were cut out and in parts the story rewritten to such an extent that Charlotte found it hard to equate it with the tragic love story of the Moor and his doomed wife. She was appalled to find that at times it fell almost into farce, certainly painfully close to melodrama. But she dared say nothing. She learned her lines and vowed to do exactly as she was bid. As they drew closer to Plymouth the nut of excitement deep in her stomach grew and she could scarcely wait for the performance to begin. Wasn't this exactly what she had longed for? And it was infinitely preferable to dwelling on the unpleasant news Sir James Caraddon had so bluntly revealed to her, or on the gentleman himself. And if her mind kept returning to him more than she cared to admit, that was purely a temporary state of affairs which would soon pass.

If she had imagined a pretty little theatre at Plymouth Dock, Charlotte was soon disenchanted. The Fosdyke Players assembled their makeshift stage by way of deal planks upon boxes in the corner of a warehouse smelling strongly of fish. A row of candles was stuck across the front and it was Peter's task to make sure that they did not set light to the curtains; a prospect not to be contemplated in such a confined space. Nor did the audience prove to be particularly salubrious either, consisting as it did mainly of sailors passing bottles of rum back and forth and making ribald jokes at a group of women penned slightly apart in a roped-off section of the shed, but making their calling more than plain.

They'd arrived early and embarked upon a series of hallooing, catcalling, shrieks and shouting, not to mention the popular pastime of tossing nuts and orange peel at the respectable persons who had happened along and taken the trouble to pay for a seat at the back where they had believed themselves safe from such abominations. None of this did anything for Charlotte's nerves.

'Is it always like this?' Charlotte asked

Sally, as she peeped through the makeshift curtains, strung across a piece of rope, to view her first audience. She felt more than a little alarmed by the sight of them.

'Sometimes it's worse. This lot look quite civilised, considering. Mind you, it's early yet. Wait till the rum goes down.'

Fanny was at Charlotte's elbow. 'Not worried, are you? If you think yourself a bit too fancy for all this you should get back home before it's too late. Young ladies such as yerself ain't usually seen on a stage and they might not like the looks of yer at all. Then 'oo knows what they might do?'

Charlotte gazed at Fanny in horror. 'I never thought. You don't mean they might actually attack me?' Charlotte's eyes grew wide, and dark with dismay. Until now she had not considered any possibility of being actually disliked. Her mind had been firmly fixed upon learning her lines and preparing to give of her best so as not to let anyone down. Now it seemed that that might not be enough.

'I've known 'em throw rotten eggs, stinking vegetables and all sorts at folk they take a dislike to. We'll just have to hope for the best, won't we?' said Fanny and strolled away, hands on hips, swaying in the long Desdemona gown, the trailing hem more grey than white.

'Jealous cat. Take no notice of her,' muttered Sally. 'Only I wouldn't recommend you audition for the heroine's role while you're with us, not if you value your eyesight. That's always belonged to Fanny and it wouldn't be healthy to dispute it. Not that it mightn't do her a bit of good to be brought down off her high horse.' Chuckling softly, Sally moved off to get herself ready, for the performance was about to begin.

Before she went on Charlotte knew a moment of terror but, as with her performance in the parlour at Caperley, once she was on stage she found that the tight breathlessness faded and to her delight the lines came out clear and strong, word perfect. And as the evening progressed she began, very surely, to enjoy herself.

'I can do this, Sal,' Charlotte told her new friend during the interval, her delight bubbling over.

'Course you can. Who said you couldn't? You're a natural, my dear. Perfect timing and impeccable diction. But don't let old Fosdyke work you too hard. He will if you give him half a chance.'

'But I must earn my keep, and my fare to London,' said Charlotte.

'Aye, well, that's as may be,' continued Sally with some doubt in her voice. 'But mind what I say.'

Fosdyke clasped Charlotte to him in an effusive display of emotion. 'Lottie, Lottie, what a delight you are! Can you not tell how they love you?'

Charlotte blushingly thanked him, pulling herself swiftly free from his rotund and rather crushing embrace. He smelled of greasepaint, candle-wax and brandy. He certainly issued forth a pleasant aura of contentment far from in keeping with the character he was playing. His nose positively glowed scarlet in startling contrast to the white of his teeth. Aware of Fanny only a step away, Charlotte denied any skill in her performance.

'You must thank Sally, for she has tutored me all along the way. I could not have gone on without her.'

'Well, they certainly seem a merry audience,' said Fosdyke with beaming satisfaction, 'and enough of them to cover our expenses for once.'

The trouble began in the last act. The seamen became so engrossed with the play that they took it to their hearts in deadly earnest. And when Othello, after a suitably shortened dialogue with the ill-fated Desdemona, covered her face with a pillow, pandemonium broke out.

'Leave her be!' cried one. 'She be innocent!'

'Kill Iago!' cried another.

And, before anyone could prevent it, one of the sailors had leapt upon the stage and,

142

grabbing Othello by the throat, flung him sprawling across the floor. From the pit below a veritable roar broke out and soon there were a dozen or more sailors all milling upon the narrow, makeshift stage, some crying for Iago's blood so that poor Phil had to flee out into the night if he was not to be murdered in very truth himself. Others grew a mite too familiar with Desdemona even for Fanny, who was no innocent where men the worse for drink were concerned. Fights broke out, knives appeared and the air was filled with the screams and squeals of the women fleeing for their lives if not their virtue up the congested aisles and falling out on to the dockside in a ferment of stinking humanity.

The tattered green curtains fell to the ground, covering a dozen sprawling, unidentifiable figures, and had it not been for the unruffled and incredibly quick thinking of young Peter, who had snatched up the candles at the first sign of trouble, the situation might well have been worse. But it was bad enough as far as Charlotte was concerned. One moment she was watching the riot in a daze of disbelief, the next she'd been swept from her feet by an evil-smelling hairy individual and was being carried off, her fate most surely sealed. Then she was pitched forward, and the sound of shrill whistles were all about her. Hands were

143

pulling at her and in desperation she tried to fight them off.

'Have done, Charlotte. It is I.' She looked up into a pair of familiar and, at this moment, beloved grey eyes. She cried his name once before blackness closed in upon her.

CHAPTER SEVEN

James Caraddon had been the last person Charlotte had expected to see, but when consciousness returned a moment later she found herself clinging very tightly to his hand none the less.

'I thought you said you never fainted?' He sounded amused, and Charlotte thrust his hand away in disgust.

'Must you score points at a time like this?' Heartless monster, she thought. 'Where are the others? What has happened to Sally, and young Peter?' The building seemed deserted. Broken chairs lay everywhere. The homemade stage, divested of its candles and green curtains, was nothing but a sad collection of fish-crates and planks of wood. Suddenly anxious, she tried to scramble to her feet, but James put out a hand to restrain her.

144

'Don't hurry. You've had a nasty crack on the head. You'll have to take things quietly for a while.'

'There is no need to tell me what to do!' retaliated Charlotte, pushing his arm away and then having to grasp it again as she wobbled uncertainly.

'There is every need,' he said, placing his arm very firmly about her slender waist. It was surprisingly pleasant leaning against him, drawing in the scents of the outdoors and the horse he had ridden. When the room had stopped spinning she focused more steadily upon his blue coat and then upon the lean lines of his face, which looked so strong and suddenly so dear to her that she had a most dreadful urge to weep. 'And what on earth are you doing here?' she asked crossly, though she rather thought she could guess.

'I've come to take you home, Charlotte.'

The sound of her name so softly spoken upon his lips was almost her undoing. In truth the rabble had terrified her and her first night on stage had not been at all as she had imagined. Nevertheless she managed to suppress her fears, for home was no longer the haven it had once been: it was filled with dark secrets and threatened insecurity. She broke away from him in an instant. 'I won't go. Nothing you can say will make me. I have things to do in London and Mr Fosdyke has kindly agreed to take me there.'

'Then what are you doing in a fish-shed in Plymouth?' He was standing, arms akimbo, glaring at her and she had forgotten how very angry he could look.

'I'm paying for my fare. I have no wish to be beholden to anyone and if Mr Fosdyke is kind enough to allow me to accompany him the least I can do is to work for my keep. Fosdyke Players carry no passengers,' she repeated.

'I'll warrant they don't,' said James caustically. 'And what exactly does this work consist of? And why are you so ill dressed?'

Charlotte leaned over to dust down her dress, or at least the dress she had borrowed from Sally for the part of Bianca. Guessing that Sir James would disapprove, she was toying with the idea of finding some way to avoid telling the truth. But she had forgotten that the dress was slightly too large for her, since Sally was not so petite as she. It was a gown of cheap blue satin with a wide neckline far lower than she usually wore, and this imprudent action afforded James an enticing view of a pair of firm rounded breasts. He made no effort to disguise his interest, and as Charlotte became aware of his gaze she clapped her hand to her bosom and flushed scarlet to the roots of her disordered hair.

She met his wickedly gleaming gaze with

as much injured fury in her own as she could muster. 'I was acting the part of Bianca, if you must know,' she said with a large measure of defiance. 'The play was *Othello* and I loved every minute of it.'

'Evidently the audience did not agree with you.'

'That is not true. It was because they became so involved—'

'That they wrecked the place?' James swept out one hand in a condemning arc, encompassing the scene of total destruction.

'They were only defending Desdemona,' said Charlotte miserably, knowing he would not understand.

'Whatever the reason, this is not the place for you.' Taking a firm grip upon Charlotte's wrist, he set off for the door, heedless to her protests as she staggered behind him.

The door opened just as they reached it. 'Ah, Charlotte. There you are, my dear. I was wondering what had become of you.'

'Mr Fosdyke, you are all right?' Charlotte gabbled thankfully. 'What about the others? Sally, Fanny, little Peter?'

Fosdyke beamed at Charlotte while shooting a speculative glance in James's direction. 'All well. All well, and enjoying a pint of porter in the Drunken Duck. But we missed you and I elected to search you out.'

'Charlotte banged her head when she was

dropped to the floor by a ruffian who was attempting to carry her off. Have you only now thought to look for her?' asked James pointedly.

The white teeth gleamed. 'As a matter of fact I was told that a fine young gentleman was assisting our Lottie in her moment of need, so I had no wish to intrude upon what might have proved to be a tender scene.'

'Or in point of fact the very opposite,' replied James stonily, and Charlotte began to squirm with embarrassment.

'Really, there is no need to champion me in quite such a high-handed manner. I am perfectly well able to take care of myself. And I am sure Sally and the others would never have left me if they'd thought for one moment that I was in any danger.' Charlotte tugged at his arm. 'Perhaps a glass of something would make you feel better too,' she suggested.

'Indeed yes, young sir. The hostelry serves a most excellent French brandy.' Fosdyke tapped his nose. 'Though how they come by it none dares ask.'

Later, when James had confirmed Fosdyke's opinion on the brandy, he began to consider how he might succeed in extracting Charlotte from the players. Already she seemed to be a part of them, laughing and joking, and accepting food and drink without paying a penny piece. The silly girl might well have set out without money, so upset had she been. James sighed with fresh exasperation. If he returned without her no one would be at all pleased with him, and his grandmother had a way of making her displeasure most strongly felt. Up to her old tricks of trying to match him off under threat of running off with that old reprobate Major Dunskin herself, she'd embroiled him in a convolution of family skeletons he'd much rather not inspect and landed him with the responsibility of a wayward innocent he'd much rather not have. But he could only do his best. If the child refused to accompany him that was the end of the matter. He had better things to do with his time than chase foolish females half across the West Country. In his opinion it only made the matter all the more annoying that she held such a bewitching charm about her. But it would take more than charm to move him.

Worst of all, there was no knowing how long this state of affairs would go on. It was rumoured that Pitt was thinking of changing one or two positions in his Cabinet and if James was away too long he might well be forgotten. Though he had friends to speak up for him. A vision of Lady Susanna in the cream lace ballgown she had worn on their last outing came to mind. He could not for the life of him describe the gown but he remembered it paid considerable tribute to Susanna's shapely figure with its incredibly small waist and high rounded bosom. She had worn it to indicate how she was at last out of mourning for her little-lamented husband, and James had to admit that she was not a woman one easily overlooked. The balls she held at Courtly Place were readily attended by everyone who could procure themselves an invitation, for, as well as all her other attributes and a title in her own right, Susanna had all the right connections. When the time came she would make him an excellent wife should he so choose, and a willing bed-mate. What more could a man ask?

He found himself gazing at Charlotte's animated face. He'd forgotten how very pretty and appealing it was. She was describing, in loquacious detail, her feelings when the audience had applauded her first efforts on stage. What a child she was. She might well have some talent in that direction for all he knew, and he felt a tinge of regret that he had missed her performance. The piece she had done at Caperley had been pleasing enough, but those ruffians watching tonight had been more interested in her physical attributes, he was sure of it, than the expression she put into her blank verse.

'Though I did dry up at one point, and would have gone to pieces completely had not Carl rescued me,' Charlotte was saying. 'And I felt far too wooden in places – as if I had three hands!'

'We all feel that way at first, m'dear,' chortled Sally. 'It'll pass. Just relax and enjoy yourself.'

Then, turning to Fosdyke, Charlotte continued more urgently. 'I shall work on the part so that I can do better next time.'

'No need,' he said. 'We'll be doing *Much Ado About Nothing* when we get to Exeter. You can play the part of Hero, the much maligned daughter of Leonato and cousin to Beatrice, who will of course be our own dear Fanny.' He pinched Fanny's cheek since she sat so close beside him and for the first time Charlotte saw her smile. 'Now, that play requires lightness of touch, and though it is not as bawdy as some of Will's plays we have our own ways of livening it up a little, eh, Fanny dear? Particularly since it will be Christmas.'

'Charlotte will not be with you in Exeter, I'm afraid,' interposed James coldly. 'So you must make alternative arrangements.'

The smile positively froze upon Fosdyke's face. 'Not with us? Why ever not? She ain't ill. Not that sickness is allowed to interfere. Rain or storm, packed house or one flea-bitten boy, sick or healthy, alive or near dead, the show, as they say, must go on.' Satisfied that these platitudes had made his point, Fosdyke called for another brandy. But James was not so easily put off.

'Nevertheless she will not be there. Charlotte will be accompanying me back to her home where her uncle waits most anxiously for her return.' Not accustomed to being crossed, James took it for granted that his decision would be accepted without question and, getting up from the table, spoke across it to Charlotte. 'If you will gather your things together we'll be on our way. I'd like to be home before morning.'

Charlotte was struck momentarily speechless with astonishment, then, as all eyes turned upon her, she fired up with indignation. 'I'll not go home. Nor will I be spoken to in such a manner. I have already told you that I have important matters to attend to in London. Matters of a most delicate and personal nature and I'll not return until I've dealt with them, so there,' she said, acutely aware that her voice had grown petulant at the finish but determined not to be browbeaten.

'In the meantime you intend to demean yourself before half the louts in England when it is not at all necessary. If you must go to London, do so, but after Christmas and in a civilised manner.'

The cold reasonableness of his voice made her feel instantly very foolish, as she guessed it was designed to do, and stoked her ire even more. The assembled company held their collective breath in fascinated anticipation. But she was nothing if not stubborn. Charlotte raised her small blunt chin, green eyes glinting with feline ferocity. 'I do assure you that I have never demeaned myself in front of anyone and I take great exception to the implication, as I am sure do these good people here.' There were grunts of approval around the table as they realised they too were being slighted. 'Shakespeare is one of the greatest playwrights the world has ever known, and will no doubt remain so. I see nothing to be ashamed of in performing in his plays; indeed I deem it an honour so to do. I only hope I can do them justice.'

'Bravo! Bravo!' cheered Fosdyke and began to applaud, bringing a flush of embarrassment to Charlotte's cheeks.

'It showed a poor resemblance to the Shakespeare I know, from the little I saw of it,' growled James, pressing his fists upon the table as he leaned ominously closer. Charlotte was forced to push herself back in her chair, looking anywhere but into his eyes, which had the strangest weakening effect upon her resolve. 'Now get your cloak and we will leave this instant. I'll not have you lose all your character.'

'How dare you suggest such a thing?' cried Charlotte, jumping to her feet at last. There was one bright spot of feverish scarlet upon each pale cheek. 'I have not at all lost my good character as you are implying. Nor will I meekly go with you like some naughty child who must be taken back to the schoolroom. You can return without me.'

'I'll not.'

Fosdyke looked from one to the other, glaring across the table. An awful, unquenchable silence was growing between them as neither would back down. An interesting situation. The young man was evidently chivalrous and taking his responsibilities to that old skinflint uncle most seriously. Fosdyke realised that he would not get rid of James easily, certainly not until he was content over Charlotte's well-being. Yet little Lottie had spirit, there was no denying it, and was more than anxious to stay. Pity he couldn't turn this most piquant stand-off to his own advantage. After scratching his chin thoughtfully for some seconds, Fosdyke hooked his thumbs in his yellow waistcoat and beamed up at them. 'I believe I have the solution.'

Both James and Charlotte looked down at him in surprise. They had both been so engrossed in staring so fiercely at one another that they had quite forgotten Fosdyke's presence, and anyone else's for that matter. And almost, in Charlotte's case, the point of her argument. There had been a brief second in that long-held gaze when at a word she would have gone with James anywhere. But as she dropped back into her seat to listen to Fosdyke's suggestion she was relieved that that hadn't happened, for she surely would have regretted it. Sir James Caraddon was far too bombastic to allow her a moment's consideration, and she was quite determined to find the mother she'd so long believed to be dead and put an end to a pernicious piece of scandal at the same time.

'What is it?' she asked.

'Sir James could accompany us, at least as far as Exeter, and act as your chaperon since he seems to think you need one. After our performance at Exeter the matter can be reconsidered. He may well feel that his fears are allayed by that time. There, is not that the perfect answer?'

James stared at Fosdyke in grim silence. The last thing he wanted was to prolong this journey further or he would miss Christmas entirely, the weather would close in and the roads would become impassable, even on horseback. Yet he could hardly bring himself to abandon Charlotte to the clutches of this rapacious hog.

'Naturally, since Sir James would not be a performing member, it would be necessary for him to pay for his keep.'

Ah, so that was it, thought James. Money. If there was a way of making more, Fosdyke knew of it.

'I need no chaperon,' said Charlotte, frustrated at being haggled over as if she were a piece of property. 'Sally will stay by me, will you not, Sal? I shall be perfectly safe.'

Sally cackled with laughter, her merry eyes twinkling. 'I've never refused the protection of a handsome young gentleman yet and I wouldn't commend you to do so either, little one. Not without very careful thought. Aw; let him stay. He can afford it, I'll warrant. Besides which, there's plenty of work I can find him to do. With shoulders like that he'll be a wonder at lugging scenery back and forth.' She grinned disarmingly at James, and despite a gap in her teeth showed herself still to be an attractive woman for James smiled back. The matter, it seemed, was settled.

The only person to be less than satisfied with the whole arrangement was Fanny, though since no one asked her opinion she did not offer it. But that was not to say that she did not have one.

The walk to Exeter was long, wet, and immensely tiring. Charlotte's legs ached so much that she was sure they would collapse beneath her. She had not known there was so much mud in the whole world. It took three long, tedious days before their first sight of the city and, were it not for Charlotte's resolute determination to complete

156

her quest, and a desire not to appear beaten in front of Sir James, she would have given up long since and begged a lift of any passing cart, had there been one, to take her home at once. The players did own a cart, pulled by a scraggy, nondescript pony, but none was allowed to use it as it was piled high with scenery and props. As it was they saw nothing but ponies, deer and rabbits, several of which latter ended up in the communal pot, doing little for Charlotte's waning appetite.

James made one more attempt to persuade Charlotte to return. He was not successful, so contented himself with staying close beside her as a protection against Fosdyke, whom he did not trust. His gallantry was not particularly well received, for whenever he walked too close or took her arm to help her over a rut or through a bog he could feel her quiver as if with revulsion.

It was with relief all round that they came at last to their lodgings, which comprised three rooms over a milliner's shop. Charlotte was to share with Sal and Fanny and, though the room contained nothing beyond three narrow beds and a jug and basin on a rickety table, they welcomed it as if it were a palace.

'You all make yourselves at home,' instructed Fosdyke, 'while I investigate the location of the Temple of Muse. Adieu, fellow thespians.'

Charlotte couldn't help but giggle at his pompous rhetoric. 'What does he mean by that?'

'By Temple of Muse he means the theatre where we are to perform,' said Fanny, an unwilling interpreter. 'And a thespian is an actor, which includes all of us, except you a'course.'

Charlotte tried not to feel slighted for it was a fair enough comment, yet somehow Fanny said it with such satisfaction that it made Charlotte feel uncomfortable. 'I shall learn to be better,' she said with a smile. 'Perhaps you will help me.'

''Taint my job to teach you,' retorted Fanny and flounced away to give her face a perfunctory scrub with cold water before lying down on a bed to sleep.

'Then I shall watch you all and learn that way,' declared Charlotte.

The 'Temple of Muse' turned out to be the stable-yard behind the Black Boar Inn and by six o'clock the planked stage had been assembled, the green curtains lifted into place and the candles set ready in their tins. The dressing-room left much to be desired, being a draughty corner of a beer cellar, a double row of barrels forming a division between the men's and the ladies' section. There was a deal table and one cracked mirror on each side and a few pegs stuck in the whitewashed wall. It was all very primitive, yet everyone set out their costumes and greasepaints with scarcely a glance about them. The smell of stale beer was almost overpowering but Charlotte resolutely closed her mind, if not her nose, to it and got on with the task in hand.

Sally did her make-up for her, applying deep carmine to her lips, a touch to her cheeks and black kohl around her eyes to highlight them. Then powder was applied and the excess brushed away with a hare's foot. 'Always use this,' said Sal, 'for luck.' Charlotte's hair was brushed until it shone and a blue ribbon tied about it. 'We'll let it hang loose, for effect,' said Sally, smoothing the ripples with her hand. 'You've lovely hair; 'tis a pity to cover it. 'Twill give the young gents something to ogle at, eh?'

'What is she to wear?' asked Fanny sharply, coming over at last to take an interest.

'Well, since she can't provide no costumes of her own, which is what we usually do,' explained Sally to Charlotte, 'she'll have to borrow one out of the props box. Not of the most salubrious, you understand, and archaic in origin, but it's the only way.'

'She can wear this yellow satin,' suggested Fanny, pulling a grubby-looking dress with torn lace from the box. Charlotte could scarcely disguise a shudder. She was perfectly sure it would have fleas.

'Can't I stay in my own dress, or wear the blue one again which you lent me at Plymouth, Sal?'

Sally looked doubtful. 'Wouldn't be right for the part, duck. But I don't much care for that sickly yeller one either. Here, let me have a look, Fanny. We must have something fit to wear.' Fanny tossed down the yellow dress and went to finish her own dressing while Sally delved deep in the old trunk, pulling out all manner of costumes, none of which looked less than fifty years old. 'Got to be simple,' Sally puffed, heaving her ample frame into a kneeling position for a better look. 'I know fashion is for the spectacular on stage, but in this case I maintain simple is most effective. Hero is an innocent, much disgraced by malicious gossip. Aw, now, what about this grey?'

Clad in the grey stuff gown which, though it clung well enough to Charlotte's trim figure and belled out beautifully at the back into a long train, had not a trace of colour to it, Charlotte felt a twinge of disappointment. Surely half the fun of appearing on stage was the delight of wearing pretty costumes? And when she saw Fanny's gown, for the part of Beatrice, Charlotte felt even worse. It was bright scarlet and encrusted with spangles and tinsel, and edged with

160

gold lace and silken tassels. In contrast to the girl's black mass of hair it looked magnificent and made Charlotte feel even more insignificant. It was evident as Fanny's blue eyes scanned Charlotte from head to toe that that was her own opinion exactly.

But on stage it was a different story and Sally was proved to be right. Whenever Charlotte made an appearance, despite her hedge-sparrow dress, or perhaps because its very simplicity emphasised her own innocent beauty, she was greeted with so many admiring whistles and bold comments that the dialogue was often blotted out and she was forced to say her lines over again. Everyone was delighted with this reaction, except, of course, Fanny, who glared furiously at Charlotte throughout. Once she almost tripped Charlotte up and would have sent her spinning off the stage had she not managed to snatch at James's hand where he watched from the wings and be pulled to safety.

'Take care,' he whispered in her ear, 'of the green-eyed monster.'

She knew not what he meant, blaming herself for her clumsiness, and with fast-beating heart vowed to take more care in future. Sally, busily playing both the parts of Ursula and Margaret, noticed nothing untoward but found odd moments to wink or smile reassuringly at Charlotte to confirm that she was doing fine. And on one occasion when they were on stage together Fosdyke himself whispered in her ear, 'You'll top the bill yet, my sweet one. Fanny must watch out.'

There was no doubt that the play was a success for there was a good deal of fun in it even as Shakespeare wrote it. Fosdyke 'enlivened' it even more in his own way by breaking into popular songs at any opportune moment, though this involved drastic rewriting in order to fit in such melodies as 'Greensleeves' or 'Love Lies Bleeding'. Particularly popular was the verbal combat between Benedict, played by Fosdyke himself, and Fanny's interpretation of Beatrice. But at the conclusion, when Hero's virtue was proved, the delight of the audience was so excessive that it almost drowned the coming together of the main protagonists and Charlotte kept well to the rear of the stage, her cheeks flushed with pleasure and embarrassment.

In the interval, which allowed ample opportunity for the audience to replenish their dryness before the performance of the farce, Fanny gave full vent to her jealousy. Seeing both James and Fosdyke congratulate Charlotte on her performance, she stormed into the dressing-room and with one flick of her hand swept the table clear of all the make-up sticks, mirror, brushes and tacky jewellery. Staring at the mess upon the floor, she ground the broken shards of glass to dust with her heel. Everything had been perfect until little Miss Wonderful had joined them. Any week now Fanny had fully expected to become Mrs Fosdyke, but ever since that prissy miss had appeared Wilfred had hardly glanced Fanny's way. And damn her, but she could act and was not half bad-looking neither in an insipid sort of way. Fanny pressed her scarlet lips together in a tight line of rage, and the blue eyes narrowed thoughtfully. But if Fosdyke fancied Charlotte Forbes there must be more to it than liking her missy good looks. Wilfred preferred his women to be more inviting, if you could put it that way, than a young country wench fresh from the schoolroom. Charlotte Forbes might well have the winsome smiles, the soft tendrils of warm brown hair about her pretty face, and those mysterious green eyes so darkly fringed and enchantingly slanted, but that was not enough to entice Wilfred Fosdyke, as Fanny well knew. She must have some other more tangible charm, well hidden but present for those with the patience to root it out. And if Fanny had a virtue, it was surely that. Patience. Hadn't she waited for Fosdyke these past four years? But he'd grown decidedly warmer of late and she'd not risk losing out now that she was so near victory.

Smiling softly to herself, Fanny bent down and began to restore the fallen items to the table.

Had Charlotte been aware of these thoughts she might have been less happy. As it was she skipped from the stage and the adulation of her audience to accept a cup of wine from the hand of, and admiration in the eyes of, Sir James Caraddon, an occurrence as exhilarating as it was unexpected.

'I have to admit, Charlotte, that you were good,' he said, making no attempt to disguise the admiration in his tone for all it was tempered with surprise.

'Did you think I would not be?' she said. 'Whatever I do, I make sure it is my best. Whatever I give, I put in everything I have to offer. I can be no other way.'

'In this instance it worked,' agreed James. 'In some cases, I suspect that is an attitude which could prove dangerous. Sometimes it is safer to retain a part of oneself and keep it untouched.'

'Oh, no,' replied Charlotte, eyes wide as she disagreed. 'I could never do that.' And, as she looked up into his interested gaze, her heart gave an odd little leap and she wondered if perhaps he might have a point after all.

CHAPTER EIGHT

Fanny confronted Fosdyke and the fire in her eyes should have warned him that she was serious. But his head was filled with the profits he could expect for this night's performance, the long-term improvement to his future fortune if his plans went right. And his belly was warm with brandy. And so he chucked Fanny under the chin, squeezed her nicely rounded buttocks and asked her why she looked so glum.

They were in a dark corner of the beer cellar, the others having gone into the kitchen for a cup of wine before the farce, and she took advantage of their solitude to press herself against Fosdyke and plead with all the charms she undoubtedly had. 'What d'you want that whey-faced child hanging around for?' she murmured, running a finger along Fosdyke's jaw and skittering across his lips with a sensual movement that did not fail to arouse him. 'We don't need her. We never have. Sal and I can manage and young Peter don't mind dressing up now and again.'

'Yes, he does,' said Fosdyke. 'He's getting too old to play girl's parts. He doesn't like it.

165

We need another actress but you know well enough I can't afford to pay one. Would you work for nothing? At least Lottie is prepared to.'

'I reckon I give good service,' murmured Fanny hotly, trailing her lips in the wake of her fingers. But the moment of erotic desire had been fleeting. Business always came first with Wilfred Clement Fosdyke. Grasping her hands, he pushed her from him. 'Leave be, Fanny. While she wants to stay we'll use her. What harm can it do?'

'I never see you alone any more, that's what harm it does,' Fanny sulked. 'And you and me was getting on so well.' She flickered her long lashes, blackly stuck with charcoal and grease to make them look longer. 'Shall I come to you tonight?' she whispered. 'We can make up for lost time. Not much chance on the road, eh?' She kissed him lingeringly, reminding him of the pleasure they'd enjoyed between the sheets. But Fosdyke had his mind on more important matters for once and he was short with her.

'Be done, Fanny. Can you think of naught else? There's work to be done; now get in your costume and open the performance with a smile and not sulks.'

'I don't sulk.'

Fosdyke laughed, and it was not a kindly sound. Taking a hold of her arm, he twisted it up her back, jerking her close. 'Make no mistake, Fanny, my love, no one is indispensable. Not even you, m'dear. So do as you're told and mind what you say or you might be sorry.'

As he walked away she swore softly to herself, but the battle, as far as Fanny was concerned, had only just begun.

'What would you normally pay an actress to play Hero?' James enquired as soon as Fosdyke walked into the kitchen. Everyone was present, except the members of the orchestra, who were entertaining the audience with a selection of their favourite pieces, being the only ones they could play.

'Is there any particular reason that you ask?' Fosdyke was instantly suspicious, for Sir James had a nasty predilection for asking pertinent questions.

James did not reply. Instead he asked, 'How many towns will you perform in before you reach London? And for how long in each?'

'Avaunt, sir. Questions, questions, questions. What motivates them, I ask?' Fosdyke cloaked his words in jocularity but James was not deceived. The man was displeased at being so probed. James glanced across at Charlotte and, despite her look of uncertainty or perhaps because of it, continued with his theme.

'It has occurred to me that if Charlotte were to accompany you all the way to

London, she would more than pay her fare. Indeed she might very well be out of pocket.'

Now Fosdyke positively glowered. 'You are surely not accusing me of theft?'

'No,' replied James. 'Of usury, perhaps.'

'James,' interjected Charlotte in shocked tones. 'How can you suggest such a thing?'

James lifted his fine eyebrows a fraction as he acknowledged her comment before turning again to Fosdyke, a wry smile upon his lips. 'If that is not so then I am sure you will be happy enough to answer my original question. We might then add up the sum you owe to Charlotte for her performances, which, if tonight is any judge, will undoubtedly draw the crowds for the rest of your week here. Add to that all the other towns you have mentioned, such as Bristol, Bath, Weymouth and so on, till we have an idea of the total sum involved and from it we can deduct the cost of a standard coach fare from Truro to London. How would that serve? Do you not consider that to be fair?' James waited unsmilingly for Fosdyke's reply, and, breathless with surprise, Charlotte waited also.

She wasn't sure whether to be pleased or not by James's interference. Could it mean that he'd changed his mind about her continuing on to London with the Fosdyke Players, or could it merely be another example of his pernickety morals? Though she had to confess that a part of her quite liked being championed by him, and she certainly had no wish to be exploited by Fosdyke or anyone.

'I'm afraid you have a quite fallacious idea of the profitability of running such an operation as this,' Fosdyke smilingly told him. 'We are not made of money, Sir James – far from it – and take very little in terms of salary. Why, on some wet nights when we have no audience at all we actually make a loss. Now, I'm sure young Lottie here has been delighted to have had your company for this early part of our tour, as we ourselves have, but once this week is over I am sure you will be happy to leave her in our very capable care. It was, I think, what we agreed.'

Before James had the opportunity to express his opinion upon that debatable point, the inn-keeper appeared in the doorway to inform Fosdyke that it was past time for the second half to commence and the orchestra had played the overture five times already.

'Then where is Fanny? We cannot begin without her. Fetch her, Sal, and scold her for being dilatory. Do not fret, my good man,' said Fosdyke, pouring himself another glass of brandy. 'We will be with you directly.'

Fanny, however, was in no fit state to go on. Sally found her flat on her back beneath the deal table, an empty bottle of brandy still clutched in her hand.

The inn-keeper became quite demented as he thought of the profits he'd so satisfactorily made upon his beer and porter sales disappearing in a trice if he had to refund half the ticket money.

'Fear not, my good man,' said Fosdyke expansively. 'The Fosdyke Players are nothing if not flexible. For every part we have an understudy and the part of Lydia Languish in *The Rivals*, which Fanny was to do, will instead be performed by our newly born star, Miss Lottie Forbes.'

The inn-keeper looked doubtfully at Charlotte, as well he might, for she had gone quite green with fear. 'They won't like it,' he stated flatly. 'They're used to Fanny's, well – er – special characteristics which she brings to the part.'

'Not another word. I shall make that announcement to the audience myself,' maintained Fosdyke, clapping the inn-keeper on the shoulder as he ushered him out of the door. When he had gone Charlotte was beside Fosdyke in an instant.

'How shall I manage? I don't know the words.'

'You have read the play?'

'Yes.'

Fosdyke waved a hand airily. 'What more do you need? Someone will have the words around somewhere which you can read on stage since you are a stand-in at short notice. We can cover any blunders you might make with a quick song or dance routine. You will love every moment of it, dear girl.'

Seconds later Charlotte heard him making the announcement of a change in programme to the audience, who did not greet the information with joy. For all Fanny was a bit brash, she was a fine figure of a woman and many were content enough to ogle her without having a clue as to what she was actually saying. Playing the sweetly demure Hero was one thing, Charlotte thought; playing comedy unprepared was quite another. But there was no time to dwell upon the horror of it as Sal, stepping over Fanny's prostrate form, pulled the dress she would have worn over Charlotte's head, talking to her all the while. After a moment of blind shock, Charlotte began to listen most earnestly to what Sally had to say. If anyone could save her, Sal could. A book was thrust into Charlotte's hand and then she was on stage, the faces of the audience a pink blur before her stunned eyes, inwardly praying that the cast would keep fairly close to the script this time.

Through slitted lids Fanny watched them

all go, then began to get softly to her feet. Perfectly sober, for she had touched no more than one glass of the brandy, she meant to watch the undoing of Mistress Forbes with some pleasure. 'Now we'll see what a fine mess you get yourself into, Miss Prissy,' she muttered vindictively. 'When the audience pepper you with peas and sour plums, Fosdyke will be begging me to return, and then your moment of glory will be over sooner than it's begun.'

As Charlotte stepped out on stage for her first scene a voice rang out, 'Where's Fanny? You're not Fanny.'

Her mouth went ash-dry and her limbs started to shake. She could not do it. She must have been mad to have agreed. The book trembled in Charlotte's hand and the words danced before her eyes. She found herself quite unable to take another step.

'Go and fetch our Fanny,' came another voice, harsh and demanding, and Charlotte took a step backwards. Could Fanny be sobered up and brought on stage? She very much doubted it.

There were whistles now from the audience, a loud hallooing and bellowing of protests, their earlier benevolence towards Charlotte quite gone. More and more voices called for Fanny Watkins. In their suspicion of being cheated, Fanny had become their darling sweetheart, and no counterfeit was acceptable in her place. How Fanny would smile, Charlotte thought, if she could see her about to make a complete fool of herself and be laughed at for her vanity of thinking she could act. These people knew her for a fake, and so she was.

Charlotte met Fosdyke's patient stare as once more he repeated her cue, buying some time for her by elaborating on Sheridan's words. She licked dry lips, opened her mouth and prayed that the words would come. But nothing more than a squeak emerged and Charlotte knew that she could not continue. She half turned as if to run from the sea of resentful faces, but then she caught a glimpse of a white shirt and a maroon waistcoat and above it a face grown dearly familiar. James's eyes were watching her with their steady grey gaze from the wings. Did he expect her to fail? Was he saying, 'I told you this was no place for you, Charlotte Forbes'? She saw him give an imperceptible nod, scarcely more than a jerk of his head, and the dark eyes grew compelling, willing her to continue, filling her with a vibrant energy. Joy soared through Charlotte as she realised that James believed in her. And in that instant she learned two important facts. The most pressing was that she could cope with this night's performance, after all. The second she would examine later, when she had the leisure to do so.

For now she knew only a kind of wonder as her nerves miraculously steadied, the shaking in her limbs stopped, the words upon the page became clear and Charlotte found herself able to pick them up easily, even carry a few in her head. And she felt more alive than ever she had in her life before. As her voice rang out clear and true Charlotte sensed the collective sigh of relief which rippled through the rest of the cast, brought new colour to the wretched cheeks of the inn-keeper and held the audience spellbound. Oddly enough, as the play progressed it was the audience who helped her most by their very silence, for in some strange way Charlotte felt them draw to her side, willing her to do well. And not for a moment did she forget that in the wings Sir James Caraddon was watching every move she made. If she failed in this he would sure as eggs take her straight home and she would have no argument left. But more than anything she found she needed his approbation.

Had she glanced again to the side where James stood, hidden by the curtain, she might well have faltered. For, watching her as she turned to the audience, James suddenly caught his breath at the radiance upon her face. For a second he envied the people who sat on upturned beer barrels since it was they to whom she spoke and

174

smiled, whom she teased with the witty words of Mr Sheridan's play. She did not strut or paw at the air with awkward jabs as did many actors he had seen in better theatres than this. She moved naturally about the stage, using every inch, turning instinctively in just the right way so as never to leave her back to the audience for more than was absolutely necessary. And her sense of timing was superb. Undoubtedly in one of the best parts in the play, she played it for all she was worth, not missing a single twist of comic irony in the situation or wit. James did not stir from his place until the green curtains swung to after the seventh and final curtain call.

After supper, and to Charlotte's great surprise, James came straight to her and, raising her hands to his lips, kissed them first on the backs and then in the soft palms.

'May I congratulate you on a superb performance. I confess it made me quite proud.'

'Proud?' Charlotte flushed, astonished. This was carrying proprietorial concern a bit far, or was he mocking her again? She searched his face for insincerity but found none.

'It took immense courage to face that hostile crowd, which could well have turned nasty.'

'I-I never thought they would actually

harm me,' Charlotte responded. 'But I did feel so inadequate. Then I thought of everyone depending on me–' she mentioned nothing of her desire to please him, as startling as it had been intense '–and knew that whatever mess I made of it, however foolish I might look, I had to try. Poor Fanny. I wonder if she has recovered yet. She must feel awful for letting Mr Fosdyke down, since he would have lost a good deal of money if the rest of the show had been cancelled.'

'I wouldn't waste too much sympathy on Fanny Watkins if I were you,' said James, tucking Charlotte's hand into the crook of his arm. 'Come on, I'll walk you to the digs.' They strolled almost companionably along the road and Charlotte, suddenly drooping with tiredness, could scarcely keep her head from slipping down against his shoulder where it so longed to be. The stars blinked and silently watched, interested compatriots of all would-be lovers. 'Fanny didn't miss one word of your performance tonight. She watched through a peep-hole in the cellar door.'

'Watched? But I thought–'

'That she had passed out? So did we all. But she'd recovered sufficiently to hear the audience call out her name. It was her chuckles which alerted me to her presence.' Frowning, James gave Charlotte's hand a tiny squeeze. 'I should take care with Mistress Watkins if I were you. She doesn't take kindly to being upstaged.'

Charlotte was thoughtful. She realised that she had already experienced signs of Fanny's jealousy which she'd tried to ignore. 'You're right. I'll keep an eye on it. But in the last resort, Mr Fosdyke is in charge and if he says I am to play a certain part how can I refuse? I owe him so much.'

'You owe him nothing.'

Charlotte jerked to a halt to gaze up at James with entreaty in her jade eyes. 'I understand all you say and I'm grateful, really I am, for your trying to protect me. But I have come on this quest with very little money in my purse and have no wish to borrow, neither from Uncle Nathan, my inheritance from an uncaring father, nor from you, James.' It was the first time she had used his name, except to herself, and it made her heart jump.

James found himself not unmoved by it either. He rather enjoyed the sound of it upon her tongue; somehow softer, less shrill than when Susanna uttered it. 'All the more reason why you should receive proper reward for the work you do. Otherwise Fosdyke will simply exploit you for all his worth and, whatever I may think of you, Charlotte, you are no fool.'

She was still standing looking up at him,

her head tilted slightly back for he was a good foot taller than she. The moonlight slanted across his face, throwing his dark eyes into shadow. 'What is it that you think of me?' The words seemed to speak themselves without any bidding from her and she held her breath as she awaited his response.

'I think,' he said slowly, his eyes moving over the lines of her lovely face, 'that you are a sweet, innocent—'

'Child?' she interrupted.

James smiled and tucked back a curl that fluttered across her flushed cheek. 'I did not say that.'

'But you were going to, and I am not a child, James Caraddon. I am eighteen years old.' She pulled herself up with dignity as tall as she was able, which was not impressive, and he smiled.

'And a woman grown.'

'Yes.'

Taking her firmly by the shoulders he held her at arm's length away from him while he let his gaze travel slowly down over her firm young figure. And as his eyes lingered and acknowledged the undeniable beauty of the rounded breasts and the slender waist, a hot flush rose in Charlotte's cheeks. 'If that is so, then I shall offer my approbation in a manner more interesting to both of us, certainly to myself.' And before Charlotte had any idea of his intentions his hands had slipped down her back to pull her into his arms and his mouth had closed upon hers.

His skin felt cold from the night wind but it smelt fresh and masculine and set her heart pounding. Nor did she resist. Her own hands crept up to smooth his cheeks, to curl about his neck, and as desire leapt between them she felt his hold upon her tighten. It was not the first kiss he had given her but somehow this one was different, more possessive, yet gentler. As the kiss deepened, Charlotte was afire with her need and came at last face to face with that second revelation she had experienced this night. And when James finally put her from him with a half-laugh her heart plummeted, for she was no fool and did not need to be told that this kiss did not mean that her feelings were reciprocated.

James repeated his request that Charlotte be put on the proper payroll as soon as Fosdyke arrived back at the digs that night, believing that there would not be a better time to touch him for money than when his pockets were filled from a good performance.

Fosdyke nevertheless frowned his displeasure. 'I dare say you'll not let me be till I agree, but I'll tell you things ain't good, they ain't good at all. We've had a shocking season all round. In some places we counted ourselves lucky if there were a half-dozen in the audience. Sometimes after days on the road the town's mayor or magistrates would refuse us permission to perform and we must needs continue on our way, unpaid and unfed. It is not an easy life by a long chalk. Whatever little we make we share, after the pony has been fed, the damage to properties repaired, and board and lodging paid for. Sometimes it is no more than a miserable pittance, I can tell you.'

'I understand all that,' agreed James with some sympathy, though if he guessed correctly Fosdyke would be the one to suffer least. Nevertheless James could see that Charlotte's burning need to have her fling in the theatre was almost as strong as this hare-brained scheme to find her mother. Perhaps if she succeeded she would be satisfied and return home, an obedient niece to her longsuffering uncle. Yet James wanted to be sure that she remained as sweetly innocent as on the day she had left that home. Only if she had money, earned independently as she so wished, could she have the freedom to leave the Fosdyke Players if it should prove necessary to do so. What other precautions could he take for her except to follow her about indefinitely, and he could hardly do that, could he?

'I see no reason why Charlotte should not have her share, less the agreed sum for your trouble of allowing her to accompany you.' And even then Fosdyke was making a profit out of her, thought James, for the other actors did not pay their fares. But he had no wish to risk losing the argument entirely so let that point remain unspoken.

Fosdyke sighed in an exaggerated fashion. 'If you insist then I must agree, but I would have thought that a man as well-placed as yourself could have seen his way to assisting young Lottie and not left her security to the vagaries of the strolling life.'

'It's not my choice, damn you,' said James through gritted teeth. The man was a boor and any moment now James would lose his patience with him entirely.

'There is no necessity for foulness, sir. The English language is equipped with words for every occasion,' Fosdyke stated portentously, and James held his rage in check with difficulty. Fosdyke moved to the door of his bedroom and then, almost as an afterthought, continued casually, 'Does little Lottie have no means of her own, then?'

A prickle of alarm crawled down James's spine. There was something in the manner in which the question was asked which put him instantly on guard. As a politician James was used to hearing people say the very opposite to what they meant. And he could not help feeling that it was as if Fosdyke already knew Charlotte's situation and was feigning ignorance. But how could he know? Perhaps he was being over-suspicious and seeing problems where they did not exist. All the same, it would be as well to take care.

'Not that I am aware of,' James said with commendable self-composure. 'I am glad we have settled this matter. Goodnight to you, Mr Fosdyke.' James turned to go, but Fosdyke now seemed as ready to linger over the conversation as a moment ago he had been to conclude it.

'I dare swear you'll be eager to return to your lady love in London.'

'My lady I...?' James almost gaped in his astonishment.

'Lady Susanna Brimley, ain't it?' Fosdyke asked, a satisfied smirk puffing out his round cheeks still further. 'Of Courtly Place.'

'How did you–?'

'Know her name? I hear the gossip. Rampant for you, they do say, and warm in the pocket herself.'

If James had been angry before, he could scarcely contain his fury at this. He might not yet have properly made up his mind over Lady Susanna, but she did not deserve to have her name bandied about by any street ruffian. James took a step towards Fosdyke and, gathering a fistful of his coat in one hand, backed him against the doorframe. The difference in the two men's heights was now very much apparent, and if pound for pound Fosdyke were greater, his fat did not carry the power of James's undoubted muscle. 'Say Lady Susanna's name once more in such a derogatory manner, or Charlotte's for that matter, and you'll find yourself unable to speak the lines in your next production. Do you understand what I am saying?'

There was no question but that Fosdyke understood. Only too well. And he was bully enough to be a proper coward. The very thought of pain made him feel ill. He attempted a conciliatory smile which flickered nervously over his thick lips, and only risked a long-held sigh of relief when, swinging on his heel, James stalked to the door of his room and after one last menacing glance in Fosdyke's direction went inside and flung closed the door behind him with a resounding thud.

As Fosdyke turned to enter his own room, his fingers on the knob trembling just a little, a figure emerged from the shadows of a doorway opposite and startled him.

'Oh, my God, Fanny! You half scared the life out of me,' he muttered, angry that she should see him under threat.

'What was all that about?' she asked, jerking her head to where James had departed.

'Naught to do with you,' Fosdyke sourly

informed her, pushing open his bedroom door. He glanced back at Fanny. She was dressed in a flimsy wrap that had seen better days and left little to the imagination. She didn't have a bad body though, for all she was now fast approaching thirty. Not to be compared with the delicacy of Lottie's enticing little body, admittedly, but as yet that was not available to him.

'Get inside,' he ordered, and, smirking with satisfaction, Fanny readily did so. Fosdyke closed the door and locked it. Until he had everything neatly worked out he'd just have to make do with what Fanny had to offer.

CHAPTER NINE

Christmas was celebrated with a joint of pork and a bottle or two of good wine at their digs in between the matinee and evening performances which marked the end of the Exeter run. It was a poor Christmas – not at all what Charlotte had planned for this, her nineteenth year. And she felt some guilt that Sir James had had his spoiled likewise by her impulsive flight. Charlotte did not quite understand why James had not returned home to Truro to his grandmother, who must surely be expecting him, and had once questioned him upon the subject.

'She can manage well enough without me for once,' he had said. 'At least, she is always telling me she can.'

'You need not remain with the players on my account. I can manage perfectly well on my own,' declared Charlotte.

'I dare say you can,' said James, but he stayed none the less and secretly Charlotte was glad. Despite her declaration of independence she felt safer with him close at hand.

As for James, he had found it quite impossible to turn his back upon Charlotte, mount his horse and ride away. He made several excuses to himself: the roads were unfit, which was not strictly true, or that Christmas was too close. After that, as they moved on to Bristol and Bath, he was always going to leave following this or that performance. But he never did. In the end Fosdyke had come to him for an explanation and a protestation that he could not afford to keep Sir James indefinitely.

'I'll make an agreement with you,' said James, pouring Fosdyke more brandy one freezing cold night in a village hall. He was always more amenable after a glass or two. 'I have no intention of leaving just yet for reasons of my own.' Reasons he could not explain, even to himself. 'But I'll pay for my keep and more in return for a share in the profits.'

'A share?' Fosdyke paled.

'I'll invest in the Fosdyke Players. It will give you some ready cash to purchase new properties or costume, even rent your own theatre somewhere if that is what you wish. We can agree a sum, but I want a fair return on my investment. Shall we say a twenty-five-per-cent holding initially, with an option to increase it later?'

Fosdyke was tempted by the prospect of cash in hand. He was getting older and the months on the road grew harder each year. A theatre of his own was an enticing prospect and with both Lottie's talent and Fanny's natural attributes pulling in the crowds he couldn't go wrong. All the same he had no wish to hand over his hard-earned profits. 'I'll not deny my interest in your proposal, but how would this dividend be paid. I'd need time to get established.'

James smiled. Time was what he needed; time to help Charlotte do whatever she felt she must. He was willing enough to pay for it, particularly if it kept Fosdyke toeing the line. James guessed he'd be less likely to risk offending Charlotte if an investment of cash were involved. 'That's fair enough. Shall we say the first payment of the dividend in twelve months?'

Fosdyke's blue eyes gleamed. Who knew what could happen in twelve months? He'd find some way to postpone payment still further when the time came. 'That would be most agreeable,' he said, and in no time at all a figure had been mentioned and accepted, and an agreement made to visit a lawyer at the very next town and have it all tied up neatly and legally.

'Let us drink to our new partnership, then,' said James, lifting his glass. And as he downed the brandy in one swallow he wondered what exactly he had let himself in for and if perhaps his brain was quite unhinged, for this must be the worst investment he had ever made in his life.

Never again was Charlotte allowed to play Lydia Languish. Fanny reclaimed her place in the company and, realising her mistake, meant not to repeat it. She would bide her time. An opportunity would present itself in due course, she was sure.

But there were plenty of other good parts and Charlotte became a firm favourite with the audiences who nightly came to view this new star with the pretty voice and natural grace. She rapidly learned all her lines and remembered to keep a close eye on Fanny's movements on stage, several times adroitly circumnavigating a potential hazard.

As for Fosdyke, his self-importance knew no bounds. So far as he could tell he was well set for a prosperous future; even more prosperous than the naïvely generous Sir James Caraddon might imagine. As soon as his current list of engagements were completed and they reached London, he meant to look about for a place to establish himself a permanent theatre. And, if he could but win Fanny round to it, with Lottie as top billing. He'd discovered, quite by chance, that Charlotte also had the sweetest of singing voices, albeit untrained. He meant to change all that the moment they reached the capital. His fortune lay in that young girl's voice, and if he was not mistaken there was still more to be had through her bed-chamber. But he must tread softly there. Never panic a young filly or she would bolt. Fosdyke's arrogance had led him to believe that he could handle a woman as well he could any horse.

Unaware of all these machinations on her behalf, Charlotte felt filled with unaccountable optimism. She just knew everything would work out right. In London she would find her mother, probably famous by now, who would fully explain to her the circumstances of her birth and reasons for abandoning her. And when all that was cleared up who knew what doors might be opened to Charlotte? She could not have explained why she felt so, but her heart was filled with hope. If it had anything at all to do with a certain kiss by a certain gentleman she did not for a moment allow herself to consider it. It was simply that she was at last doing what she most enjoyed and had always longed to do – acting. What other reason could there possibly be for this glorious sense of happiness?

In view of these feelings, everything should have been quite perfect. And for a while it was. But then one evening, just as they were about to go on to play *The Recruiting Officer*, Carl, struggling to mend the curtain from a precarious perch on a wooden stool, slipped and fell, badly twisting his ankle. It was quite evident that he could not go on.

'What were you thinking of, to do such a thing?' stormed Fosdyke, beside himself with rage. 'Haven't I enough problems with everyone taking more parts than they should, without losing yet another valuable actor? You imbecile!' He had the greatest urge to knock the stupid boy's head but there were people watching, not least a grim-faced Sir James, so Fosdyke managed, with difficulty, to control himself.

'I am sure someone else can be found to step in for him,' said James, but even as he spoke he knew it to be a faint hope. Who else was there? Phil was the only other male besides Fosdyke, and already doing two parts so he could hardly be expected to conduct a dialogue with himself. It was then that he noticed everyone looking at him. 'Oh, no. I'm no actor.' He stepped hastily back. 'I will take Carl to a doctor, pay for his treatment, pull the curtains to and fro and help lift scenery and props back and forth. But as for acting... No. Never.'

'But there is no one else, James,' said Charlotte in a voice he found seriously hard to ignore. 'And the audience is impatient for the play to begin – listen. If we do not start soon there could well be a riot.'

'I'm afraid that's true,' came the pained voice of Carl from the floor. 'My ankle can wait if someone can strap it up for me. But the show can't. I've seen an audience tear a theatre apart and the actors with it when they felt they'd been cheated.'

If this were not enough to sway James, the look of impassioned pleading in Charlotte's jade eyes would have done it. 'I must be turning into a sentimental weakling,' he barked. 'Find me a costume and a book, then. The sooner it's started, the sooner it's done with.'

'Oh, James, thank you!' Charlotte couldn't help herself. She flung her arms about his neck and kissed him, right in front of everyone.

'Well, well,' muttered Fosdyke, noting the possessive way James's hands lingered upon

Charlotte's waist as he put her from him. This won't do at all, he thought.

James knew he was by no means the greatest actor to have trod the boards, but to his great relief he got through the part without mishap, spoke his words in his strong, full-bodied voice and did not, as they say, trip over the furniture. Charlotte seemed to find the whole thing deliciously amusing and teased him unmercifully for a while.

'We shall have you playing in *King Lear* next week,' she chortled, 'with a full beard, and winning rave reviews.'

'Have done. Once is enough to last a lifetime. I shall happily leave the acting to you from now on.'

Charlotte's eyes grew entrancingly wide. 'Oh, does that mean that you have abandoned your disapproval of my wayward style of living?'

'No, it does not,' James retorted sternly. 'I'd take you home tomorrow if you would allow me.'

'But I won't.'

'So you say.' James glowered at her, and for once Charlotte did not shake in her shoes but only laughed all the more for she saw that a twinkle lurked in those grey depths, however carefully he might try to hide it. 'Perhaps I should just pick you up and carry you off,' he said.

191

'Like a maiden in an Arthurian legend?' she teased. 'Admit it, James, you are really quite enjoying this life. You could very easily have gone home without me. It is an adventure and I'm sure far more exciting than politics.' She wrinkled her small nose and James had the sudden and intoxicating desire to kiss her. Yet again. He really must curb these moments of weakness.

Charlotte saw the expression in his eyes, a fleeting unexplainable change which was there for a moment and then swiftly hooded. In any other person, at any other time, she might have thought that that look had meant something more than simple desire. But how could it? This was Sir James Caraddon, an interfering busybody who seemed set on spoiling her plans and her fun. And this was no society ball. They were sitting in a chophouse eating supper with a group of actors neither of them had known until a few weeks ago. Nevertheless, throughout the meal Charlotte's eyes strayed constantly back to James's and every time she experienced a small shock to find him looking at her.

'I'm tired,' said Charlotte at last, getting to her feet. 'I shall go to my room.'

'I'll take you,' said James.

'There is no need–' she began, but then Fosdyke started to laugh and the sound somehow chilled her.

'The chivalrous knight of the road. Sir Galahad James Caraddon. What can happen to Lottie between here and the corner of the street? Does he carry your silk stockings, Lottie, tied upon his sword for a favour like the knights of old?'

Charlotte made no reply to the teasing, noting how a muscle quivered in James's cheek as he held his anger in check. But then, as she turned to go, she heard Sal speaking up for her.

'Leave her be, Wilfred. She ain't like one of us, nor should be. If Sir James feels himself responsible for her care at least it saves you a job. Keep your mind on your supper. That was a good show tonight but I'm ready for a change. What are we doing next?'

Charlotte cast Sally a look of gratitude for so adroitly turning the conversation and, tugging at James's arm to prevent him expressing the anger that boiled just below the surface, she hurried him from the room. 'Take no notice of Fosdyke. He loves to plague people. I've seen him do it even with Fanny and she's his–' Charlotte stopped, a flood of embarrassment colouring her face.

'His mistress?' James smiled. 'I dare say. I like the man not one bit and I wish you would not place so much trust in him, Charlotte.'

Charlotte looked at James in surprise. 'Why should I not? He has done nothing

193

untoward, nothing to deserve my mistrust.'

'Nevertheless I would recommend you keep your family matters to yourself and not discuss them with Fosdyke,' said James with a severity so earnest Charlotte felt bound to acquiesce, though she secretly considered James to be overly suspicious. Perhaps it was because he was a politician. They fell silent for a while and, as they walked arm in arm to their lodgings on the corner, snow started to fall. They both looked up at the dancing flakes and the peace of the night settled upon them, filling Charlotte with a rare and beautiful contentment.

'I have nothing particularly against the theatre, you understand,' said James unexpectedly, and Charlotte glanced at him in surprise. 'It is only the seediness of Fosdyke's variety which I dislike. If you are going to do Shakespeare, then why not do it as Shakespeare wrote it, and not an adulterated version?'

Charlotte sighed. 'If only we could, but Fosdyke says it wouldn't pay. No one would come to see true Shakespeare. It is simply not in fashion.'

James growled his contempt. 'Fashion! Theatre could become every bit as *fashionable* as the opera if it were presented with intelligence.'

Charlotte gave a gurgle of laughter. 'Listen to the new expert!' And James had the grace to join in her laughter, acknowledging her teasing.

'No reason why Fosdyke should have exclusive rights on the theatre. Or on anything, for that matter,' he said, wiping a snowflake from the tip of her nose. They climbed the stairs in companionable silence to the top floor where the Fosdyke Players had rented rooms, and Charlotte wished life could go on this way forever. But they were drawing nearer to London and soon James would be gone from her life entirely.

James, in fact, was thinking similar thoughts. To his growing astonishment he had found himself enjoying the tour. The company of players was quite talented – even Fosdyke, though it galled him to say it. But the greatest source of his pleasure, he had to admit, came from the developing relationship with Charlotte. Even now he tried not to own to the directions of his feelings, but he knew that he could not simply bid her goodbye when the tour was done. And, oddly enough, he had quite lost his appetite for urging her to return to Cornwall.

He told himself that it was simply her plight that had moved him, that she was undoubtedly sweet and gentle with unbounded courage. What man would not want her? It meant nothing; nothing at all. He did not want it to mean anything. Didn't he enjoy his life just the way it was? Yet the recollections of the rooms in his townhouse standing empty, and all the times he had gone out rather than spend another night alone in them, arose to taunt his mind. For he knew that after these weeks spent with Charlotte they would seem even more empty than before.

At the door of the room which Charlotte was sharing with Fanny – not that she saw much of her since she spent her nights chiefly next door with Fosdyke – she turned to bid James goodnight.

'Have you considered what you will do when we reach London?' he asked, somewhat abruptly. 'It is a big city and it will not be easy to find your mother, even if she is still there. And I have to say that she may not be. Sixteen years is a long time.'

Charlotte lifted her chin obstinately. What was he saying? Was he trying yet again to make her go home? Well, she would not. 'None the less, I intend to try. I shall make my way around all the theatres asking if they know her. I'm sure I shall find her. I feel it.' She smiled bravely at him, not wanting him to see her own doubts. 'Thank you for walking me home. Goodnight, James.'

But as she would have closed her bedroom door he pushed it open and followed her into the room. 'No matter what you say, Charlotte, it will not be as simple as you think. Your mother is an actress and actresses have a habit of changing their names for use on the stage. How will you know what she calls herself now? Do you have a picture of her?'

Charlotte shook her head. The idea that her mother might have a different name had never occurred to her. But she could see now that that would create a problem.

'Do you even know what she looks like?' he persisted.

'No.'

'Do you have any other relatives that you are aware of in London? Did your mother have any family besides your Uncle Nathan, for instance?'

Charlotte, annoyed by his pessimistic warnings and guessing them to be very likely true, merely shook her head, her throat too full of emotion to trust herself to speak.

'What about your father, Lord Justin? He must have some family.'

'He had a brother, I believe,' said Charlotte tautly, 'but he died in a tragic accident. Something about a mock duel going wrong. There is no one else that I know of. I am quite alone but I assure you that does not worry me in the least.' But it did, now that she thought about it. A feeling of quiet desperation swept over Charlotte and her eyes glanced wildly about the room as if seeking a solution, an escape from her troubles.

'Then the answer is obvious,' he said crisply. 'It is absolute madness for you to trek around London on your own. I shall certainly not permit it.'

Charlotte gasped. '*You* will not permit it?'

'Certainly not. The streets of London are riddled with dangers for a woman alone. You must come and stay at my house and I shall make the necessary enquiries.'

Charlotte's heart turned over in her breast. 'N-no, I could not do that,' she said, knowing instinctively that it would be bad for her. Knowing the strength of her own feelings for him, how could she bear to be near him and not have them returned?

'Don't be stubborn, Charlotte. For once in your life do as you are told.'

'By you?'

'Yes, dammit! Why not by me? Have you made any better plans?'

The truth was that she had not thought it through at all. She had simply set off on what was obviously a wildgoose chase with no idea how or where to start looking. He must think her a complete fool. Indeed, she was a fool. Charlotte could feel the tears sting the backs of her eyelids, but not for the world would she meet his gaze, which seemed to be searing right through her, reading the very words scarred upon her soul.

But James saw how the eyes stared like

dark hollows from an ashen face. 'Charlotte, you are unwell. What a fool I am to be lecturing you when you are clearly exhausted.' He led her over to the bed and, making her sit down, began to unlace her boots. 'You've been overdoing it. I told Fosdyke he was working you too hard and now you look absolutely all in. I'll speak to him.'

She could not bear him to touch her. If he did not go, she would burst into tears and beg him to make love to her. Her frozen limbs were shaking yet she was on fire. 'No, don't do that.' Charlotte thrust out a hand and it caught accidentally in his tangled curls as he knelt before her. She pulled it away to clasp it in her lap out of harm's way.

James looked up, saw the feverish flush upon her cheeks and felt his own throat tighten. He wanted her. There was no possible doubt in his mind now. With equal certainty he knew it would be a mistake to take advantage of this unusual situation. Yet he could not let her go. Not until he had explored his own feelings with greater care. Perhaps later he could persuade her to agree to come home with him. He knew better than to push her obstinacy too much when she was in this mood. 'Charlotte, you must take better care of yourself. And if you will not, then someone else must.'

'Do you realise how dreadful it has all

been?' she burst out.

'I can imagine,' James said softly.

'You cannot imagine,' she said. 'You cannot imagine at all. For the last sixteen years of my life I have believed that both my parents were dead, that I was an orphan. Then I am told that no, my father is still alive somewhere, but he has no wish to see me. Instead he leaves me a large sum of money on the proviso that I do not ever attempt to contact him. It is quite outrageous that I should be expected meekly to accept it. Then as if that were not enough I learn that my mother too is alive and well, and apparently wants me no more than my father does. Why? What is wrong with me?' The traitorous tears spilled gently over trembling lids to slide down her cheeks. 'I can think of no reason why I should be so treated, unless those dreadful rumours are true.'

'They are not,' said James, his teeth gritted so tightly they hurt. If he could lay his hands on Lord Justin Forbes he knew exactly what he would do to him. How could a man of such standing treat his family so abominably? 'They cannot possibly be true and you must not for one moment think so.' He was shaking her, wiping the tears from her eyes, trying to calm her and scolding her all at the same time. He saw how the beauty of her eyes was blurred almost to silver by those tears. 'However fond your mother may have been of her brother, I cannot imagine for one moment her taking it further.'

'But if...' Charlotte swallowed the hard lump that had risen in her throat. 'No one would ever wish to marry me, would they? If I were the child of...' She could not go on. She could not say that hideous word, and James was hurting her hands fearsomely. 'What man would want me for a wife with such a doubtful inheritance?'

His arms came around her then and he was stroking her cheek, laying his own against hers, pulling her into the shelter of his warm body. 'Any man would be a fool not to want you,' he murmured against her ear, sending shafts of longing racing through her veins. 'Hush; no more tears. Have done. You will be safe with me.' His lips were caressing her mouth with a purring softness, setting a burning desire aflame inside her. Then, moving on to the small hollows in her neck, James could feel the thud of her pulse beating hard upon them. Desire was no less strong in him and his control was fast slipping away.

Lost in their private worlds of wonder and discovery, neither of them heard the click of the latch or the first steps into the room.

'Well, well. Begging your pardon, I'm sure. Shall I go away and come back later when you're done?'

They leapt apart, each stung with quite unnecessary guilt. Fanny was standing in the doorway, hands on hips, lips twisted in wry amusement, her whole expression ablaze with curiosity.

'So that's how the land lies, eh? Does Wilfred know? He don't much care for fraternising 'twixt his cast.'

James was the first to recover. 'It is not at all what you might think, Fanny.'

'I'm sure it is not,' she murmured, eyes brilliant with delight. This was exactly what she wanted, for little Miss Prissy to become involved with the handsome Sir James. That way she might leave Fosdyke alone; with luck, even leave the company altogether and run off with him, then things could get back to the way they were. Fosdyke had always been generous with Fanny, and most attentive in the bedroom department until *she* had happened along. Now he scarcely noticed her, and there was somehow a lack of warmth and enthusiasm in his love-making these days. She didn't like that, not one bit. She was getting too old to start looking for a new man. And if she didn't watch out she'd miss the boat altogether. 'It's none of my concern what you get up to, or why. I'll leave you to it.' Shrugging her shoulders, Fanny turned to go, but James strode quickly across the bedroom to catch her by the arm.

'Fanny. I promise you that I was merely commiserating with Charlotte over a family problem she has. There is nothing between us, nothing at all. I would not for a moment have Charlotte's reputation besmirched in any way by unkind, and in this case untrue, gossip, you understand?'

Listening, Charlotte felt no sense of relief. She found that she wouldn't have minded in the least if Fanny did think there was something between them. She wished very much that there were. But the idea was plainly so horrific to Sir James Caraddon that he was making an absolute meal of explaining away their innocence.

'I think so, sir,' said Fanny, evidently puzzled. 'I think I understand.'

Charlotte wished that she could say the same herself but she rather thought she would never learn to fully understand Sir James Caraddon, not in a thousand years.

Later that same night Fosdyke decided that their next and final production of the tour was to be *Hamlet*. He had saved this play until Carl was fit enough to take part, and until he had his plans carefully made. Even so, it would be difficult enough to cast. Yet he was determined to do so. It was essential. Fanny, however, was proving difficult.

'I'll not do it,' she reiterated, not for the first time that night. She would have stormed out of bed and scratched Fosdyke's eyes out, only she hadn't a stitch on and he was not a man to take kindly to histrionics. 'Let *her* play the man; I'll not.'

Fosdyke smiled his frosty, white-toothed smile that was almost a leer and Fanny took pause for thought. It wouldn't do to alienate him too much, she thought, and manufactured a pout. 'You know I hate parts where I must wear breeches. Why cannot *she* play Horatio and I Ophelia? It is not fair.'

'Because, my sweet one, as well as making a finer-looking Horatio since you are taller and probably have better legs than young Lottie, you are by far the better actress.' This was totally untrue. The truth was that Lottie would play Ophelia with greater sincerity than the brash efforts of Fanny, who was in Fosdyke's estimation getting too old to play the part in any case. But Fanny preened herself with pleasure at the praise, which was ever more scarce in coming. 'Any foolish female can simper and drape herself about a stage as Ophelia,' Fosdyke said.

'And die,' recalled Fanny, remembering that Ophelia drowned in act four.

'Quite so. Horatio is a much bolder part and lasts right through to the end of the play. He is in fact one of the few persons left alive.'

Fanny was slightly mollified by this prospect. She loved endings when the audience applauded her at the closing curtain. 'And you will play Hamlet, of course.'

'Naturally. Carl will play Laertes, Ophelia's brother. Phil can be King Claudius, Hamlet's stepfather, and Sally will make an excellent Queen Gertrude, Hamlet's poor foolish mother. Which leaves us with Polonius, father to Laertes and traitor to Hamlet.' Fosdyke smiled again and the teeth positively glittered in the darkness of the bedroom. 'It is a small part and I intend to inveigle our young friend Sir James to step upon the boards again.'

Fanny was aghast, and flopped back against the pillows in exasperation. 'You must be mad. Caraddon can't act for toffee. If you must give him a part let him be Fortinbras, who only comes in at the end.'

'No,' said Fosdyke with soft emphasis. 'It is essential that he play Polonius.' He moved over to the bed and looked down at Fanny. She was a particularly stupid woman, and even her much vaunted charms were fading. But she still had her uses. He must keep her sweet for a while longer.

Meeting his blue gaze, Fanny shivered. 'You got some scheme afoot?' she daringly asked. She always found Fosdyke at his most exciting when he was planning something.

Fosdyke pulled back the sheets and got in beside Fanny with scarcely a glance at her

205

voluptuous charms, his mind on other things. 'It may become necessary for you to make a short trip for me, into London. We ain't far away now.'

Fanny was all agog. 'What sort of trip?'

'To call upon a lady. I feel she may be able to rid us of our nuisance. Her name is Lady Susanna Brimley and she and Sir James have an understanding of sorts. I think it would be useful if you were to inform her that he was growing a mite too attached to a certain young miss. You can point out the danger of losing her lover and future husband if she does not call him to heel, as I am sure she is well able to do. She must be worth a pretty fortune.' Fosdyke was so engrossed with his plans and his own view of the situation that he paid no heed to Fanny's reaction. She too was anxious to be rid of a nuisance, but not the same nuisance. Nevertheless she listened avidly to Fosdyke's instructions. There might be some way she could twist it to her own advantage and rid themselves of both Charlotte and James.

Later that night, as she returned to the bedroom she shared with Charlotte, she dropped her first dose of acid in her room-mate's ear.

'Sorry I interrupted you earlier, when you were – y'know,' she said as she climbed into bed.

Charlotte had been asleep until Fanny woke her and it must have been well past midnight. 'There was nothing in it, I do assure you. What Sir James said was quite true. I have a family problem which has upset me, that's all. There is absolutely nothing between us,' Charlotte repeated, though it pained her to do so. 'Nothing at all.'

'Just as well,' said Fanny pulling the covers up over her head and adding, 'God, it's perishing in here!' before continuing, 'Since he's betrothed to a lady already, or so I do hear tell. You'd be bound to get hurt, then, wouldn't you?'

CHAPTER TEN

Charlotte was devastated. She should have realised of course. A man of Sir James Caraddon's calibre naturally looked for a wife in the higher echelons of society. And one would not be difficult to find, for he was undeniably good-looking, and no doubt with those he loved his domineering ways would be termed chivalry. If she was honest she'd been glad enough of his presence on numerous occasions. A wild hope had been born in her and nurtured by his lovemaking. Hadn't he said that any man would want her? Now she had to accept that what he had told Fanny yester-evening had been no less than the truth. There could be nothing between them because he already had a betrothed, in London. He might want her as a woman, but that did not mean that he loved her, or that he thought of her as a possible wife. Charlotte told herself that the pain she felt below her heart was no more than hurt pride. But she knew that to be false.

She lay on her back, staring into the darkness. She was in love with him. She had loved him from the first moment she had seen him – so tall and strong, his dark eyes challenging her in that hay-barn – which seemed a lifetime ago. But what could she do about it? A single tear fell from the corner of one eye and slid down her cheek. Charlotte angrily brushed it away. He must never know. She would keep her dignity at least.

Tomorrow they would be within easy distance of London and she would have no further need of his nursemaiding. She would be her own person again and make it perfectly plain to Sir James Caraddon that she needed no help from him at all. To stay at his townhouse would do nothing for her peace of mind whatsoever, an offer he had no doubt made out of pity or an odd sense of duty, neither of which she needed.

Nothing would induce her to accept.

The theatre where they were to play *Hamlet* was the largest they had visited to date. It belonged to a Mr Levenstam and, though still very much a small amateur theatre, situated as it was between a fish-shop and a public house, most convenient for the clientele, it was none the less better fitted-out than any they had performed in previously. For once there was a proper stage, albeit a small one, with oil lamps instead of candles across the apron. The traditional green curtains were already in place, and flats and side-screens could be slid into place along grooves set in the stage floor. Charlotte could see that the advantages were great, for the scenes could not only be quickly and smoothly changed but also give a whole new dramatic dimension to the play in that an actor could enter as if from another room, or between trees in a woodland grotto. The prospect was exciting.

Mr Levenstam, a reed-thin gentleman with long fair hair and a gentle voice, welcomed them in the green room with tea and coffee as soon as they had finished unloading their wagon. This small courtesy was a new experience for the Fosdyke Players and they revelled in it.

It was in this room, with its traditional green baize carpet, damask walls and full-length mirror for checking the drape of one's dress before going on stage, that Fosdyke handed out the parts for the next night's performance.

'But I don't want to be a ghost,' protested thirteen-year-old Peter. 'He hardly says anything. It's time I had a proper part.'

'This is a proper part, my boy,' said Fosdyke expansively. 'Most proper. The ghost may not say a great deal but think of the costume and the status of the part. You are the dead king upon whom the whole play hinges. And it will also leave you ample time to act as call-boy and prompt, for which valuable service, Peter, we are ever indebted to you.'

Peter's eyes lit up. 'Will that mean I'll be getting more pay, then, for doing three jobs?'

Fosdyke chortled with laughter. 'What a wag! We'll have to see, eh? We'll have to see. Fanny has volunteered to play Horatio since she looks so well in breeches,' he continued blithely, and grinned at Fanny who attempted a weak smile in response.

Charlotte was surprised, and delighted, to find herself given the important part of Ophelia, but not half so startled as James was to find himself included yet again. It took considerable pressure from everyone, though this time not from Charlotte, to persuade him to agree, though against his

210

better judgement.

'It is not at all onerous, good sir,' Fosdyke assured him, 'though you will need to wear a small beard, for Polonius is an old man. But it is over by the third act.' As you will discover, thought Fosdyke.

They walked through the moves, though no one cared much for rehearsals and avoided them wherever possible. Charlotte spent the intervening period before the opening night learning her lines and persuading any actors willing to humour her to go over pieces with her.

She did not see Fosdyke or Fanny again until the performance was about to begin, when they both swept in, fully costumed and made-up, Fosdyke looking mighty pleased with himself and Fanny more disgruntled than ever.

'Whatever can be the matter with her?' whispered Charlotte to Sally. 'Is she blaming me for playing Ophelia, do you think?'

'Don't you worry over her, my love,' scoffed Sally. 'She'd be jealous if a crow walked over the stage before her.'

Fanny in fact was smarting from a recent conversation with Fosdyke in which he had told her that she needn't return immediately after she'd made her trip to Lady Susanna's house the next day. 'You settle yourself in our usual quarters and I'll meet up with you there as soon as I can,' Fosdyke had told her.

'Why must I go tomorrow?' Fanny was appalled. 'I thought you needed me here to play Horatio. We are booked for four nights.'

'I know it, I know it. But once young Peter has watched you perform Horatio this evening I intend to give him the chance. His big moment, eh, which he so longs for?' Fosdyke took her casually by the throat, stroking it with his fingers and thumb, and smiled down into her darkly shadowed eyes. 'And what you have to do is of far greater importance. Besides, Lady Susanna may not be at home the first time you call. Society ladies lead a busy life. Besides which she'll not be panting to let you in. You'll have to use some of this great acting talent of yours, Fanny, and pretend to be a lady of note yourself, even of mystery, so that she feels compelled to see you. Can you do that, do you think?' The hand had tightened slightly and, not risking her voice, Fanny had managed a slight nod.

But now, looking at Charlotte in her flowing white gown that draped her slender figure so beguilingly, Fanny entertained grave misgivings about leaving Fosdyke even for one night, let alone four. But if she got to see Lady Susanna right away, dared she defy him and return? She thought not. If he said wait for him in London, she had little choice but to obey. If only Miss Prissy had injured her ankle instead of Carl, who still walked with a limp except on stage when he suffered his pain in silence as all good actors did. She glared across at Charlotte, noting how her cheeks glowed pink and how she coyly turned her gaze from Sir James Caraddon who was attempting to talk with her. Hatred and jealousy fired Fanny's breast. Why should she have all the men kowtowing to her? She wished the girl could break her damned neck, or really and truly drown just as the crazed Ophelia did. It was a pity the scene took place off stage or she might well be tempted to help her to it.

'Are you ready, Horatio?' called Fosdyke brightly.

'Aye,' grumbled Fanny, tugging at her hose with peevish fingers. 'I'm ready as I'll ever be.'

'Then let the play proceed.'

The orchestra was playing the overture; the bell for the opening scene was rung and three chords from the orchestra answered. The first scene began. James, watching from the wings, found himself grudgingly admiring Fosdyke's portrayal of Prince Hamlet. The actor-manager's voice was potent, with a resonance which reached every corner of the theatre and held even those who usually fidgeted in the pits spellbound. His large square hands, with their thick bony knuckles

were yet eloquent and expressive, trans-
mitting the message of grief and melancholy
felt by the Danish prince at the recent death
of his father and the swift remarriage of his
mother to his uncle, King Claudius.

Looking about him, James could see no
sign of Charlotte. He'd been puzzled by her
behaviour since the night Fanny had en-
countered them chaste but guilty at being so
caught upon Charlotte's bed. James got the
feeling that Charlotte was avoiding him. Did
she object to his kisses so very much? At the
time she had accepted them readily enough
– even passionately, he had thought. But
now she had gone cold on him and would
scarcely look him in the eye. Could she not
see that he was here only because of her? He
didn't know why he'd stayed so long. It was
plainly a mistake. Yet he could not bring
himself to leave. Why was that? It didn't
even seem to matter if some of his old
friends saw him here. There was no denying
that Charlotte Forbes had had a most
dramatic, if he might use the word, effect
upon him. Even his remembered vision of
Lady Susanna was growing dim; he could
barely summon up her face for it kept
getting confused with that of a very different
person: one who wore her natural brown
hair curling softly about her gentle face with
no sign of the fashionably powdered formal
styles, nor of any rouge upon her rosy

cheeks. And he had discovered that he far preferred this natural look. But where was Charlotte? He would look for her; make sure she was all right.

As he quietly moved away from the wings Sal appeared from the green room ready for her entrance.

'Have you seen Charlotte?' James asked her.

'She's sitting in the green room,' said Sal. 'Looking a bit peaky, I thought. But naught to worry about,' she said with a laugh on seeing James's sudden expression of anxiety. 'Only first-night nerves.'

Not satisfied, James went in search of her. She wasn't in the green room. He tapped quietly on the dressing-room door but there was no answer. Peter, coming off stage after his first scene, saw James and came over. 'Miss Charlotte says she don't want to be disturbed till it's time for her call,' Peter told him.

James glowered at the boy.

''Taint my fault. No need to look so fierce. Said she wanted to rest. And you'll be on in a minute yerself.'

James knocked again but when there was still no reply he gave up. He could hardly force himself upon her.

He did manage to snatch a brief word with Charlotte between Scene Two and Scene Three, just before she went on. She had

215

come to sit in the green room to wait for her call and he found her there, head hung low, hands clasped loosely in her lap, when he came off stage. His heart turned over for she looked a picture of absolute misery.

'Charlotte, aren't you well?'

She looked up at him in surprise. 'I'm perfectly well, thank you,' she said stiffly, getting up and walking away from him. This tactic baffled James so much that he strode after her and, catching her wrist, spun her round to face him.

'What in damnation is the matter with you? You've hardly spoken a word these last two days.'

Charlotte resolutely drew in her breath, not wanting to be caught out by the way her heart pitter-patted when he touched her. 'I've been learning my lines. I've had no time for chat,' she said rather pertly.

He softened slightly, knowing how important it was to her to perform to the very highest standard. 'And you are not angry with me?'

She looked at him wide-eyed as if she had not the least idea what he meant, though she knew very well. 'Why should I be?'

He was still holding her wrist and he slid his hand up her arm, wanting very badly to pull her into his arms. She looked so soft, so vulnerable in her white flowing gown. Yet even now he could feel her resistance to

216

him, a desire to be free of his hold. 'I thought perhaps I had hurt you the other night with what you considered to be my improper behaviour.' He tried to sound teasing, to coax a smile from her, but there was no such response.

'It is perfectly normal, I believe, for gentlemen to proposition actresses,' she said coldly. 'Fanny has warned me of it many times. However, you needn't worry, Sir James; you convinced her that there was nothing at all improper about your action. It was simply your kindly good nature. And I fully understand the reason for your behaviour.'

'What the hell are you talking about?'

'Ophelia,' called Peter in his off-stage whisper and Charlotte attempted to snatch her arm from James's hold.

'I have to go now,' she hissed as James held fast, his fingers curling about her arm like a vice, and his mouth came down close to her ear.

'Don't you dare accuse me of propositioning you when I have done no such thing. You would be in no doubt if that were the case. Nor am I quite so unselfishly sympathetic as you seem to think.'

'*Ophelia!*'

Charlotte became desperate. 'I must go.' But the more she struggled, the tighter James held her.

'Have I ever done anything the least bit offensive to you? Have I?' He looked so unlike himself in the false beard and long coat, yet so dignified, and still devastatingly attractive, that she didn't know whether to laugh or cry.

'N-no.'

'I'll speak with you later.' James released her at last and she fled to the wings, making a much more precipitate entry on stage than was strictly necessary.

James watched her performance, which was as graceful and professional as ever. But this time it afforded him little pleasure, for there was a cold ache about his heart which he found hard to eradicate. Charlotte was angry with him and, since he had admittedly behaved in an uncouth manner, was it any wonder? To steal a kiss was one thing; to steal it from a young girl in her bedroom was quite another. He had grown too used to Lady Susanna and her less than sensitive ways. But Charlotte was not Susanna. No wonder she had thought he was taking advantage simply because she was an actress. It was a notoriously popular pastime in some quarters. All the same, he had not expected her to be quite so upset by it. The question now was, how to convince her otherwise?

Throughout the rest of the performance James found it hard to concentrate and was heartily glad when Act Three came at last and he could relax. The character of Polonius having been done to death in typical Shakespearean fashion, James was only too glad to quickly divest himself of the heavy padded coat and beard, which were exceedingly hot and uncomfortable.

After supper he again sought out Charlotte where she sat quietly reading her lines in the green room, prettily dressed in the pink and mauve striped gown she had worn to run from home. He wished with a fervour that astonished him that she would give up this wandering life, stop chasing her dreams, abandon her quest to dig into the shadows of the past. And what could he offer in return? She looked startled for a moment when he took the book from her hand and sat down beside her.

'Listen to me, Charlotte. I realise that I have upset you and I am sorry for it. And you may as well know that apologies do not come easily to my lips.' He smiled at her and she only just resisted the impulse to smile back, for it was such a very human comment upon himself. 'Nevertheless I do so now, for I wish you to know that I would never demean your dignity to such an extent as to proposition you in the manner you describe. I am not, nor ever will be, a stage-door Johnny or whatever they call themselves.'

'I did not suggest that you were,' she said, trying not to weaken, though he looked so very fervent she found it difficult. Divested of the bulky costume, he was himself again, except that Sir James Caraddon would not normally have been dressed in such a bright red waistcoat or such a full-sleeved shirt lightly trimmed above the wrists with braiding to match.

'When this week is over I do intend to take you to my home.' He put a hand to her lips as she would have protested. 'No, say nothing. I shall have my way. I usually do, you know. You are tired, and have been under considerable strain since this whole thing blew up on that dratted birthday of yours. If you insist on attempting to find your mother you must at least be fit enough to face the ordeal. The way you are at present you have not the stamina. A week or two's proper care will make all the difference. And you need not fear your reputation will be compromised, for I have staff at my home who will take good care of you.'

As a strolling player looking for a bed for a night or two in someone's freezing garret? Or as mistress in James's bed? She dared not consider which she'd prefer. And even if his offer was made out of genuine friendship, how could she endure to sleep beneath his roof when he would be paying court to another lady – one he intended to marry?

She pushed aside his hand. 'I cannot. I cannot.'

'Yes, you can,' he insisted, giving her shoulders a gentle squeeze, his chin against her hair. And were it not for the fact that he had her back to his broad chest, he would have seen the look of tender sorrow upon her face.

The week continued to be successful. Fosdyke made an excuse of Fanny's needing to visit relatives which no one quite believed or questioned. Young Peter thrived in the part of Horatio despite his youth and proved a hit with the audience. James coped well enough with his own part but grew increasingly anxious for the week to end. He had had enough of the strolling players and had a sudden longing to return to his own civilised world, have a decent bed to sleep in and good food upon his table. But his anxieties over Charlotte were even greater. She had given up all pretence of attempting to be friendly with him. She barely glanced his way and never spoke a word if she could avoid it. Even Sally had noticed it and pulled a wry face at him from time to time. Tactfully she had not enquired the reason, for which James was grateful. His guilt was great enough, though it irritated him to feel so, for he felt it so unnecessary. He had apologised to Charlotte for his crass behaviour; what else could he do?

As for Charlotte, she performed her part with skill and sensitivity but she had no heart in it. The pleasure she had previously found in the theatre had somehow withered and died. Her one thought was to get through the week as quickly as possible; then she would be on her way and begin her real quest of searching for her mother.

When the last night of *Hamlet* came she told Fosdyke of her intention to leave the group the following day. He looked at her for a long moment before answering, then, to her utter surprise, informed her that she could not do so. 'Our tour does not end until we are in London, and you have agreed to accompany us there. I will not permit you to leave before that.'

'But we are less than a day's journey away,' she protested. 'All I am saying is that tonight will be my last performance with the Fosdyke Players. And when we arrive in London tomorrow and you pay the wages due to us, I intend to find a place to stay and then give full attention to the problem which brought me here.' She felt a reluctance to say more for she did not feel up to answering probing questions.

'There'll be time enough to decide on that tomorrow,' he said.

'I shan't change my mind.'

Fosdyke beamed at her, but Charlotte did

not notice that his blue eyes were cold as glass, her gaze being too abstracted and her mind on other things. 'If that is your wish, my dear, so be it. But we shall be sorry to lose you and I shall do my utmost to change your mind, I promise you.'

Finding herself swamped by a sudden, overwhelming weariness, Charlotte turned to make her way to the dressing-room and prepare for the final performance. Fosdyke followed her.

'You seem mightily troubled, dear Lottie, and it grieves me to see you so. Will you not tell me what it is that makes you cry?' Fosdyke tipped her chin upwards with one blunt finger. 'You know I would do anything to help you.'

She looked up at him with brimming eyes. 'It is kind of you to be so caring, but you have done enough for me already. It is simply that there is someone – someone whom I must find – in London. But you have no need to worry, for I shall be perfectly all right.'

'Is Sir James to accompany you on this expedition?'

Charlotte hesitated again. If she let Fosdyke think she was wandering the streets alone he would protest, she knew it, for he was surely a kindly man to have cared for her thus far. 'Sir James has offered me the use of his home.'

'Oh, my dear, is that wise?' Fosdyke frowned, and, lifting one of Charlotte's small hands between his own square bony ones, spoke to her in coaxing tones. 'You must not think that I shall cease to care or think about you simply because our tour is almost over. It is more important to me than you can possibly imagine that you should be well and happy. It would be most unsuitable for you to stay at the house of an unmarried gentleman, and he of the gentry and all. Nor necessary when Fanny and I will be only too pleased to have you stay with us.'

'Oh, but–'

'No buts. I will hear no more argument on the subject. We always rest up a bit before setting out on the road again come summer. Carry out your family business by all means, but stay among friends while you do it. Why, Sal herself will be no more than a step away in the next road where she lives with her mother and young Peter. We'll be your family in the future, dear little Lottie. You have a great future ahead of you,' he said, squeezing her hand with renewed enthusiasm. 'Now that I have the funds, I intend to start my own theatre, and shall be looking for just such a talent as your own to help me launch it.' His eyes glowed with the obsessive glint of the fanatic. 'You could be famous, Lottie; more famous than in your wildest dreams.'

Charlotte looked up to meet his gaze, and for a crazy moment she was tempted. To be a famous actress... Wasn't that what she had always wanted? A feeling of uncertainty was taking root. She had always appreciated Fosdyke's generosity in taking her on and allowing her to travel with the players. Apart from its having been much safer than travelling alone to London on the pittance she had thought to bring with her, she had enjoyed every minute of it. It had been fun and Fosdyke had taught her a great deal. Surely James's warnings not to be too trusting and keep her personal affairs secret were unnecessary. How could anyone help her if they did not understand her problems? James was clearly one who liked to follow that advice, while Charlotte's more open nature could not subscribe to what amounted almost to duplicity. Besides, she thought with a return of her stubborn independence, she had no wish to be dictated to by Sir James Caraddon. Added to which there was a strong possibility that Fosdyke might have contacts in the theatre world who could help her to trace her mother.

'What can I say?' she said, with a helpless little shrug of her so delightful shoulders, which Fosdyke had difficulty in keeping his hands from fondling. 'Perhaps I should explain it all to you. I would be glad of any help.'

Fosdyke almost purred with pleasure. 'I shall be most delighted to do so. You were intending to remain in the theatre, were you not? Your talent is too great to waste.'

Charlotte was struck momentarily speechless by this praise. Had James been free to love her openly she might well have been ready to subscribe her theatrical dreams to a period of fun and pleasure in her life that was now over and done with. But, since he was to marry another and cared not for her at all, there might be something to be said for forging a career for herself. Fresh tears spurted to her eyes even at the thought of James's apparent betrayal and she could bear it no longer. 'I'll think on it,' she mumbled and, spinning on her heel, fled into the dressing-room and shut fast the door.

Fosdyke stared at the blank panel of wood for some seconds before a slow smile spread across his square features. Matters were progressing very nicely his way. And, once his dual plan had been put into action, she would be in the bag. A pretty little pheasant flushed out from her keeper's hide.

CHAPTER ELEVEN

Meanwhile, at about the time that James was attempting to apologise to Charlotte, Lady Susanna Brimley sat in her boudoir on a cream brocade stool before her dressing-mirror as her maid powdered, brushed and curled her long golden hair.

'Do hurry, Clara,' complained Lady Susanna, wriggling irritably upon the small stool. 'Lady Berrisford does not like to be kept waiting.'

The young maid gave a barely perceptible sigh while struggling to hurry at her work. 'You've no need to fear, milady, for I'm nearly done.' Clara knew better than to dawdle. Her mistress was ever in a pet these days it seemed, a state of mind which was probably not unconnected with the long absence of Sir James. Not that Lady Susanna was one for sitting at home and moping. Oh, Lord, no.

'Out every night she is,' Clara was frequently inclined to inform the cook when they met for one of their regular cups of tea and gossip. 'Balls, soirées, card parties, operas... If it is deemed high enough in the social calendar then Lady Susanna will be there, you can count on it. But that's not to say that she don't miss Sir James, 'cause she does,' Clara would say, and the cook would sniff and look down her long nose and say she thought it a wonder, for didn't every young man in town come knocking on the mistress's door? Though indeed Sir James was mighty handsome, well set up, and a step above the rest.

'Too good for that madam, by far,' was Cook's opinion, and secretly Clara agreed with her though she always loyally defended her volatile and unpredictable mistress, outwardly at least.

'And now my hat. Pray do not fumble, Clara. No, no, the emerald green with the feather, you dolthead! I swear you grow more clumsy every day. Are you thinking of a lover, is that it?'

'No, madam,' said Clara huffily. She had a longstanding betrothal to the first footman which looked like staying that way unless he impressed his mistress sufficiently to deserve promotion. And Lady Susanna was not an easy lady to impress. Susanna fidgeted again upon the stool, and Clara dropped the brush. If only she wouldn't nag so much, Clara thought, then she wouldn't get half so flustered. 'I thought you would wish to wear the cream with this canary-yellow dress.'

'Nonsense, girl. If one wishes to be noticed one should always wear striking

228

colours. Now, reach me my new walking-cane with the ribbons which exactly match this hat, and the gloves. There, is that not perfect?' Lady Susanna strolled across the room, swirling from time to time to show off her new gown.

Stepping back to admire this display, Clara had to confess that Lady Susanna could wear bold colours exceedingly well. Perhaps it was due to her fair colouring. And indeed the gown was a particularly fine one, carefully copied from an engraving in *The Lady's Magazine*. Of stiff yellow silk, its hemline positively bristled with frills and ruching which were repeated on the tightly fitting elbow-length sleeves. The wide *décolletage* was unencumbered by lace or net, a style Lady Susanna much favoured. And now, with the addition of the tall, crowned, emerald silk hat with the most sweeping of ostrich feathers together with the other aforementioned accessories, there was no denying that here was a lady of quality.

'You look very nice, madam,' said Clara inadequately, and received a minor explosion in response.

'Tell John to bring the carriage round at once.' Susanna called all her grooms 'John'. It was considerably less trouble than having to remember their real names, so she never bothered to ask what they were. 'I do hope he has cleaned it, for I noticed a spot of mud on the wheel-hub yesterday and was obliged to point it out to him. Tell him I shall be leaving within the quarter-hour.'

'Very good, madam.' Clara moved to the door to do her mistress's bidding, adroitly concealing her irritation at having been so rushed and then informed that her ladyship was not leaving immediately after all. No doubt Jeremy was equally irritated at being called 'John' all the time and constantly blamed for the fact that there was mud on the road.

'Now, while I am away this afternoon you can clean my– Oh, no, who can that be? I supposed you'd best go and see.' The sound of the doorbell interrupted Susanna in her favourite task of allotting duties. She very much believed the dictum that the devil found work for idle hands to do, particularly in the lower classes, and so she deemed it her duty to ensure that no such danger lurked for her own servants. 'And bring me a light cordial. I've developed quite a thirst after all this fussing and shall need some sustenance before I face Lucinda's barrage of conversation.'

Left alone in her room while Clara hastened away to carry out these myriad duties before any further were added, Susanna paced restlessly back and forth. She dared not sit down for fear of creasing the silk.

Besides which, she did feel restless. It had been a long day, an even longer week, and Christmas the dullest she could remember. All the best people had abandoned town and gone off into some sort of rural bliss. Really, the King had a lot to answer for. George III's passion for farming seemed to have created a new fashion among those lesser mortals, in Susanna's opinion, who could think of nothing but to ape their betters.

Even James had deserted her, yet again, for Cornwall. She had hoped for an invitation herself this time, to meet his grandmother, who was said to be quite a character, and view the family home in Truro. They had others of course, not least a sprawling mansion in North Devon which was the family seat, but Lady Caraddon was individual enough to despise it, preferring the more civilised, warmer surroundings of her spacious, comfortable town-house in Truro. Susanna ached to go there, not simply to view the renowned collection of furniture and porcelain which was said to be housed there, but to gain a foothold in the family. She was sure that if she could be allowed sufficient time in James's presence she could bring him round to the subject of a firm agreement of marriage between them which to date he had skilfully avoided.

Susanna tapped her walking-cane thoughtfully upon the Persian rug. She bore him no real grudge over this reluctance he exhibited. It was the way of men. And the way of women was to overcome it with any means at their disposal. If she could but pin him down in one place long enough, thought Susanna with fresh exasperation, she would have him.

'There's a lady to see you, madam,' said Clara, bobbing a curtsy as she was expected to do every time she entered her mistress's room.

Susanna clicked her tongue with impatience. The girl was a noddle-head; why ever did she keep her? 'Haven't I just told you that I am going out to tea with Lady Berrisford?' Susanna said with strained patience, but Clara only smiled.

'She's a foreign-looking lady, madam, and says as how she thinks you'll be glad enough to see her. She has news of Sir James.'

Susanna stopped her pacing and became very still. 'Show her into the green drawing-room.' Perhaps fate had played into her hands. She very much hoped so.

Fanny had experienced no difficulty in locating Courtly Place. It turned out to be a five-storey, brand spanking new Georgian house with balconies and pillars set in a parade of similar properties, overlooking a green where nannies strolled with white-bonneted children.

'Very grand,' she muttered as she made her way up the white stone steps which led to the polished front door, an act of great temerity in itself. But she was well prepared.

She had raided her carefully acquired wardrobe of theatrical costume, having decided that it would be wise to disguise her identity as far as was reasonably possible. She'd chosen to wear a gown of black lace over tarlatan, deeply ruched at the hem. The neckline was low-cut but not excessively so and, in Fanny's opinion, showed off the smooth olive skin of her throat to perfection. The black hair was dressed high and covered with a mantilla of black lace and chiffon which completely concealed her head and shoulders. A lady of mystery indeed. The whole effect was strikingly continental, almost Spanish in appearance. Fanny judged that, by the time she had dispatched her message to the maid and she in turn had passed it on to her mistress together with a description of the person who offered it, Lady Susanna Brimley would certainly be unable to resist meeting her.

She proved to be quite correct in this, for in no time at all she found herself being shown most politely into a small drawing-room, charmingly decorated in pale green silk and furnished with spindly white furniture in the very latest style.

'Her ladyship will be down directly,' said Clara, stretching the truth a little as she found it necessary to do in this house. Lady Susanna, being a law unto herself, had been known to bid a gentleman to wait and then leave the house without giving the poor hopeful another thought.

But on this occasion Susanna was not in the least dilatory. Moments later, still clad in her outdoor clothes, for one never knew when a swift exit might be necessary with these unexpected callers, she swept in to confront Fanny with a polite, if insincere, smile upon her rosebud lips.

'You wished to see me? I'm afraid my maid did not tell me your name, which was remiss of her.' Susanna raised finely arched brows in mild enquiry, but Fanny remained seated and did not remove her veil. Let Lady Susanna wonder, she thought.

'My name is immaterial.'

Lady Susanna frowned. 'I do not make a habit of receiving people who are unknown to me.' She had moved to the door. 'Clearly you have made a mistake in thinking otherwise.'

'I think you will be ready enough to receive me when you hear what I have to say. I believe I am right in saying that you and a – a certain gentleman, now absent, have something of an understanding.'

Susanna swirled about to regard Fanny

with an expression which would have unnerved a less resolute heart. But Fanny held
her ground and waited.

'And who exactly would this gentleman be
with whom you claim I have a liaison?'

'Sir James Caraddon. I have news of him
which may interest you.'

Susanna became suddenly very still. After
a moment she said, 'I have an appointment
which I must keep. Pray feel free to speak
openly. I find it is usually the quickest
method of disclosing any gossip one is
bursting to mention.'

How very unpleasant she is, Fanny
thought, feeling a moment's sympathy for
Sir James. No wonder he'd been happy to
cast off the shackles of his political life for a
while if it contained such as this she-wolf.

'Well?' The voice was growing impatient
and more than a little frosty.

'Forgive me if I am wrong, but I was led to
believe that Sir James Caraddon and yourself were betrothed?'

Susanna drew in a sharp breath, not easy
with the restrictions of her corset, and
wished that it were indeed so. 'That is close
enough to the truth for you to have awak-
ened my interest; pray continue.'

'You'll have been wondering, I dare say,
where he's been to all these weeks,' said
Fanny – falling slightly into the vernacular
in her keenness to get the job done – to

grasp Lady Susanna's attention.

Susanna frowned. 'Not at all. He has been staying with his grandmother in Cornwall. He does so every year at this time.'

'Not so.' The small silence which followed told Fanny that she did indeed have her Ladyship's full attention. 'As a matter of fact he's been living with a company of strolling players.'

If Fanny had said that James had been living with thieves and vagabonds she would have got no greater reaction. Stark, appalled horror registered on the beautiful face, and the pretty, fashionably rouged mouth fell very slightly agape before snapping shut in a compressed line of outrage. 'I do not believe it.'

'It is true. And what is more he has found himself a new lady friend, a young girl in point of fact. I rather thought you might like to know of it.'

Now Lady Susanna did sit down. She positively sank on to the small round-backed chair opposite Fanny, dropping her cane with its bright emerald ribbons to the floor, followed one by one by her gloves. 'I think you had better start from the beginning. I wish to know *all*.'

And Fanny was only too happy to oblige while Lady Susanna stormed and raged about the iniquity and shallow-heartedness of common males. A point of view Fanny was only too willing to share. Later, with the black veil drawn back, the emerald hat nudging the gloves in equal abandonment upon the carpet, a degree of camaraderie formed between the two women. Cordial was sipped, ideas were aired, rejected and exchanged for new ones as the problem was tossed back and forth.

'The important point to remember,' said Fanny with emphasis, 'is that it ain't enough just to call Sir James home on some pretext or other. All the company will be in London by the end of the week, including Miss Pr ... Miss Charlotte Forbes. Sir James has already asked her to stay at his home and she could very well accept. He certainly don't intend to give her up, by the sound of it. He seemed quite smitten.' In point of fact, Fanny was more concerned with the possibility of Fosdyke's inviting Charlotte to stay with them at their own lodgings in Woodley Terrace. It would be typical of him. As long as the girl was in London Fosdyke would not abandon his scheming, and Fanny was certain there was much more to it than he had revealed to her thus far. Her best hope of success, therefore, was to emphasise the dangers to Lady Susanna's own schemes and gain her support.

'Then, what do you suggest?' For once Susanna was at a loss. Her need for James was greater even than she had been willing to own to herself until now. The very thought of him with another woman made her feel physically sick. She simply could not tolerate it.

'Well, I did have one or two suggestions which might suit,' said Fanny modestly. 'It is always possible to manufacture trouble which will help make her mind up to leaving.'

'One moment; why are you so concerned?' asked Susanna with a sudden sharpness. 'If it is money you are after–'

'Not at all,' put in Fanny hastily, rightly guessing that this would gain her little credibility. This woman, Fanny decided, would be more co-operative if she put her own cards on the table. Their natures were not dissimilar. 'To be honest with you, ma'am, Lottie Forbes is not content with one man. She's stolen mine as well as yours.'

'You mean she is the lover of both? The girl is a strumpet!'

Fanny had not meant quite that at all, but if her ladyship wanted to think Lottie was sleeping with all and sundry, why not let her? 'She'll not go willingly, but I think we might be able to persuade her to it.'

Susanna found herself leaning forward in her chair, breathless with excitement. There was nothing she liked more than a touch of intrigue. 'How?'

'Best way is to make life in London as

uncomfortable for her as possible. Now, Fosdyke wants rid of Sir James right enough, but he wants to keep little Lottie, which don't serve my purpose at all, nor yours for that matter. As long as Lottie is in London, Sir James could see her at any time.'

Susanna nodded, then flicked a hand impatiently. 'Go on, go on.'

'Nor is Fosdyke one to depend on a single course of action. He sent me to see you, to ask you to work out some way of bringing Sir James to heel, as he called it. But he won't rely on my being successful. He'll have other plans to back this one up.'

'And they are?'

'That I don't know, but I reckon it might have something to do with this production of *Hamlet*. Fosdyke ain't usually so fond to do it, it being so dismal. And the last performance is on Friday. I reckon it'd be as well for you to be there. You get Sir James in your grasp, then all we have to deal with is Miss Charlotte Forbes, nice as you please.'

Charlotte watched Act Three in bleak misery from the wings. Even Sal failed to cheer her as she passed by on her way on stage and went on with a worried frown creasing her brow. Fortunately it was in keeping with the scene as, after a few words with Polonius, Queen Gertrude was faced by Hamlet's accusations of offending his father. Charlotte paid no attention as James came off stage and even turned her back to him as he went behind the arras.

If only he had been honest about his betrothal with another she might have been able to bear loving him so much. But to flatter and tease and even kiss her in the way he had was quite unforgivable. He had used her, and she, poor fool that she was, had drunk it all in.

Hidden behind the curtain, Polonius was supposed to overhear the conversation between Hamlet and his mother. James had little to do except move the curtain a fraction at appropriate points in the dialogue and then when the Queen cried out for help, to join her cry.

'What, ho! Help, help, help!'

Her mind in a turmoil, Charlotte continued to watch Fosdyke strutting about the stage, raging at his mother. Barely concentrating upon the action, she watched his reaction to the swaying curtain, thinking what a fine actor he was; saw him stride over to the arras as he had done each evening, crying out which rat it was that hid from him. And, wrapped in her own wretched misery, she did not move as Hamlet's sword sliced through the curtain into the traitorous heart of his old friend Polonius. It was only when she heard a muffled cry and the thud of a falling body that the awful truth catapulted into her heart.

And, as Fosdyke thrust his sword through the arras with the deliberate intent of injuring Sir James, Lady Susanna was in the audience. Her finely attuned ears and highly strung disposition caused her at once to suspect foul play. She was on her feet in an instant, pushing her way through the crowds who quite appallingly did their best to stop her screaming and make her stay in her seat. But no one, save for Sir James himself, had ever bested Susanna yet and she forced her way through, causing pandemonium and uproar to break out in her wake.

She rushed on to the stage, knocking aside an astonished Queen Gertrude, and out through the wings. There she found exactly what she had feared: her darling James injured unto death, and his beloved head resting in the lap of a young girl who could only be the strumpet herself.

'My darling!' she squealed in high-pitched terror. 'Someone help. My beloved is dying!'

'A doctor has been sent for,' said Charlotte calmly, her voice sounding to her own ears as cold as stone. So this was the woman he preferred to herself. Evidently a woman of wealth as well as great beauty, Charlotte thought. Very tenderly she relinquished her place to Susanna. 'But he will not die. He has been struck in the chest but the heart is not pierced, bad enough but not fatal. Stay with him while I fetch a blanket.'

'Yes, do girl. He shall be leaving with me as soon as the doctor has tended the wound,' said Susanna authoritatively. 'My carriage is outside, be so good as to go and fetch my groom John.'

'Don't fuss, Susanna,' said a weakened James, teeth gritted against the pain. 'I shall be perfectly all right once the doctor is fetched.' He tried to sit up but was very firmly prevented from doing so.

'You will do as you are told, my beloved, for once in your life,' purred Susanna, for at last she had him exactly where she wanted him. 'Do hurry, girl, don't just stand there gawping.'

Obediently and without protest, casting only one lingering glance back at the pain-racked figure of Sir James cradled in the arms of his betrothed, Charlotte did as she was bid.

'It was an accident.' Fosdyke sat in the green room, head in his hands for all the world a man in the throes of anguish. 'How could it have come about? I cannot imagine. I was sure that area behind the curtain was empty. Did he change his position?' Fosdyke had not performed on stage for over thirty years and learnt nothing in the way of good acting. The small audience which gathered

242

about him was aghast, sympathetic and utterly convinced of his innocence. 'Thank God for that padded coat,' he said again. 'Undoubtedly it saved him from what could have proved a fatal blow.' In fact Fosdyke had banked upon it, for a dead Sir James would have proved a problem; an injured one got him very neatly out of Fosdyke's hair.

Charlotte sat listening to all this quite unmoved. She felt numb, as if she was incapable of feeling any emotion ever again. The only thought which rattled round and round in her head was that James had gone. He had been driven away in Lady Susanna's fine carriage, under protest admittedly, but with a rug firmly tucked about his long legs and the fervent admonishment that he must take greater care in future what kind of riff-raff he mixed with ringing in her ears.

'Are you listening to me, Lottie?'

Charlotte jumped. 'Oh, I'm sorry.'

'We were discussing our departure,' said Fosdyke in kindly tones. 'I would like to strike the set tonight and stow everything in the wagon right away. If you would have your bags packed and ready by seven in the morning, Lottie, we could be in Woodley Terrace by noon if we get a good road.'

'Woodley Terrace?'

'Our lodgings. You remember I told you of them.'

'Oh, yes. Of course.' A part of Charlotte wanted to protest, to say that she had other plans. But James had gone and he seemed to have taken all her will-power with him. 'Very well.'

And when they did arrive at the lodgings the next day in good time for the midday meal, Charlotte's depression had worsened if anything, and she could eat little of the game pie so carefully prepared by Mrs Barker, the landlady. The only bright spot was that Charlotte was to have a room to herself since Fanny had moved her things in with Fosdyke. Lying in the narrow bed that night, she felt the need to speak very firmly to herself. She would not be depressed or allow any self-pity. She had only herself to blame for her predicament. She should never have allowed Sir James to kiss her in the first place, for it was quite improper. Certainly he had meant nothing by it. Didn't all young gallants make free with actresses? He would not have expected her to fall in love with him, and would laugh fit to bust if he knew. She must turn her mind to more positive things.

Charlotte thumped her pillow, turned over and curled herself into a ball for comfort. She determinedly began to plan out her campaign. To find her mother – that was what mattered. To keep her mind very firmly upon her quest and not allow it to wander into less productive areas. Yet how was he? Had he recovered? And how could she find out? Certain she would not sleep a wink for the well of misery in her heart, Charlotte was surprised to find the sun streaming through the window and a loud banging on her door.

'Breakfast in ten minutes in the dining-room, Lottie,' That was Fanny, sounding unusually cheerful.

Charlotte quickly washed and dressed and ran downstairs to join Fosdyke and Fanny who were already at the table.

'And what do you plan today, Lottie? A long sleep no doubt, if you're as tired as us. Perhaps a walk in the park this afternoon?'

'As a matter of fact I planned to begin my tour of the theatres today.' Charlotte had since told Fosdyke just a little more about her purpose in coming to London, in the hope that he might be able to advise her.

'Today? Good heavens, is that wise? You must be quite worn out. Take a day or two to rest and recuperate, Lottie dear, before you start pounding the streets,' said Fosdyke, helping himself to a large portion of haddock.

'But I am anxious to find word of my mother. I have no time to spare.' Charlotte cleared her throat. 'I was wondering if you could see your way to settling with me this morning.'

'Settling?' Fosdyke looked blank though he understood well enough the question.

'I think Lottie's wanting her wages,' put in Fanny with a simper. 'Thought you were willing to work for your keep and transport, missy?'

Two bright spots of colour mounted Charlotte's cheekbones. 'I – I... Well it is only that I have no money left at all, and I understood that Sir James made some arrangement with you.'

There was a short silence and then Fosdyke was reaching in his pocket and drawing out a coin or two. 'Of course, of course. He said that I should take care of you and I will, Lottie, I will, do not doubt it. Here is five shillings which will see you through the next few days, I am sure.' He beamed at Charlotte, who felt a sickening thump as her heart plummeted.

'I'd much rather have the whole amount at once, if you don't mind,' she said bravely. 'So that I know exactly how I am placed.'

'How you are placed, my dear?' Fosdyke's habit of repeating what she said was beginning to irritate Charlotte. 'You are placed very safely and securely with us, as you can see, and need never worry again. Now, if you must visit these theatres then begin with the Haymarket and Drury Lane. And take a cab.' There was little chance of the mother being there, or anywhere else for that matter after all this time. She'd soon grow tired of looking. 'The city is not a fit place for a young lady to walk in alone, unless you would care for Fanny to accompany you?'

'No, no,' protested Charlotte hastily. 'I shall be perfectly all right on my own. As you say, I can always take a cab.'

In the event she did not. If five shillings was all the ready money she possessed for transport and food during the day, plus other incidentals – and who knew when Fosdyke would think to repeat this beneficent act? – she must spend it sparingly. This troubled Charlotte sorely, for she knew that until Fosdyke did pay her the wages due to her she was dependent upon him totally for food, lodging and even clothing. If James were here he would speak up for her, but he was not. Not any longer. Only then did it occur to Charlotte that she did not have his address, and she stood stock still on the pavement while the shock registered. Nor did he have any idea where she was residing either. For all she knew she might never set eyes on him in her life again. He had as good as vanished from the face of the earth. The thought filled her with utter despair.

After five days of trekking down countless streets, Charlotte lost count of the number of theatres, inns and even stable-yards where plays regularly took place, that she had visited. She asked questions till her voice was hoarse but always getting doleful shakes of the head or curt dismissals. No one could remember ever having worked with or seen an actress either by the name of Eleanor or Ella Forbes, or Pierce. Charlotte could think of no other possible names and as a description could only say that her mother was reputed to look very like herself, only with auburn hair. The five shillings was almost used up, and though she had twice ventured to ask for more Fosdyke had once complained of the number of outstanding bills he still had to pay following the season, and the second time as good as accused Charlotte of ingratitude since she was warmly lodged and well fed at Woodley Terrace and there were many in London who could not claim to be so.

'I do understand your difficulties,' Charlotte ventured. 'But if I do not receive my full pay then I am in dire difficulties. I have already asked about work at all these theatres and as yet have found none. I feel I must do all in my power to find my mother but in the event of there being no acting work at present I will look elsewhere for employment. I must pay my way,' she said, with the first show of spirit since the accident. 'I hate being beholden to you.'

'But of course you do, my dear,' purred Fosdyke, beginning to realise that perhaps he was mistaken in trying to control Charlotte by keeping her short of funds. Unlike Fanny, who clung to him like a limpet, Lottie would take herself off at a moment's notice if he did not watch out and that would never do. Reaching into his capacious pocket, he reluctantly pulled out a small pouch of coins. He did not miss the gleam in Fanny's eyes as he handed three golden guineas to Charlotte – still pitifully short of the amount he owed, but it mollified her a little. 'More than enough to see you safe, I should think.'

Charlotte breathed a sigh of relief. Now she could continue with her search. 'You are the very kindest of men,' she said, and Fosdyke beamed, well pleased, for his generosity had won him a smile from those enchanting lips. Now all he had to do was find a venue to establish the Fosdyke Theatre and, with Fanny suitably chastened and Sir James safely out of the way, he had only to choose his moment to put his proposition to Charlotte and his future would be settled. He saw no reason why she should not fall in with his plans. Was he not still a fine figure of a man? Excitement pounded in his veins at the mere thought.

CHAPTER TWELVE

'I swear I am better, Susanna, and will get up today no matter what you say,' declared James, pushing aside with distaste the breakfast-tray which she held out to him.

'How can I let you up if you will not eat?' Susanna said with almost equal firmness.

James drew a long sigh, though his patience was fast wearing thin after almost five days of Susanna's excessive ministrations. 'It is most considerate of you to nurse me yourself but there is really no more need of it. Bayley has looked after me for years and can continue to do so most efficiently.' James could well imagine his valet's opinion of Lady Susanna's commandeering his role of tending his master's needs.

'The man is a blunder-head,' declared Susanna, firmly setting back the tray on its four legs right over James's lap so that he could not move without spilling something. 'Whatever I ask for he maintains it is not available. If I say you must have beef broth, he makes chicken.'

'I do not like beef broth,' said James sourly, but Susanna was in her stride and did not listen.

'I vow the man has deliberately blocked and countermanded all my orders. Do you know that he will not even serve my afternoon tea in the library, saying it is your private sanctum? Yet absolutely no one could be expected to sit in your drawing-room. Have you seen the state of it recently, James? I vow the damask is quite peeling from the walls. You should do something about it.'

'I never use the drawing-room,' growled James. 'I do not entertain.'

'My darling James. It only proves how very badly you are served. Any household worth its salt would not have allowed such deterioration to take place. This place is in dire need of a woman's touch. Goodness knows what would have happened if I had not taken charge after your injury. I doubt you would have got even a fire in your bedroom and you would have taken weeks longer to recover.'

James very much doubted it. 'My staff have their routine. They know how I like things done. And I am well aware the drawing-room needs redecorating. That is why we do not use it.' But Susanna would have none of this and clicked her tongue dismissively.

'They have more idea how things are done now, I do assure you, for I have given those lazy housemaids. lessons in cleaning, of which they were in dire need.'

James bit back on the comments which all too readily sprang to his lips and attempted to thank Susanna for her efforts. Ever since she had insisted on moving in after the incident, even from his sick room he'd been well aware that the whole rhythm of his household had been thrown into uproar. It could not be permitted to continue. 'I am quite well again, Susanna, so there is no further necessity for you to remain,' he said, not for the first time.

'Oh, but I do not mind at all,' she purred, coming to sit on the edge of his bed.

James sighed and tried a different tack. 'I doubt it is seemly. Have you considered your reputation?'

She glanced at him archly. 'As a widow, one's reputation is not so easily tarnished as a young maid's might be. I am a woman of experience and maturity, James, so you need not trouble your head about such matters. Everyone knows I can take care of myself.'

James did not wonder at it. But he did wonder how he had ever allowed himself to become embroiled with her in the first place. She had once seemed such fun – witty and amusing and undoubtedly seductive. But now quite a different picture was emerging. She was revealing herself as no more than a harpy, and he did not much care for that.

He thought with longing of Charlotte's sweet nature and beguiling smiles. He remembered her enthusiasm, her courage when facing the hostility of an audience expecting to see quite another before them. He remembered the pretty sound of her laughter, the teasing expression in her jade-green eyes, and knew he would find no peace until he had found her again.

Picking up the breakfast tray, he almost thrust it into Susanna's hands in one smooth resolute gesture. 'If you do not vacate my room upon the instant you shall be the worse for it. I do intend to leave my bed and I assure you I have not a stitch on. And when Bayley comes in to retrieve my tray, which he is sure to do at any moment for he knows I cannot stomach fish at breakfast, what price your reputation then?' James made as if to fling back the bed-clothes and, with a tiny high-pitched squeal, Susanna abandoned the tray and fled to the door. But even here she paused for a final thrust.

'You can be so cruel, James, but I shall forgive you since you are ill. But do not think I am afraid for myself. It is your reputation I am thinking of.' Her eyes twinkled mischievously for a second before she continued, 'Were it not for Bayley, I might be tempted to stay and call your bluff. It could prove entertaining.'

'Out!' barked James, and Susanna hastily obeyed, deeming it wise not to argue further.

It was Fanny in the end who told Charlotte where James lived. And, unable to help herself, here she was standing outside the tall white stone town-house, wanting to know if he was well but not quite sure how to go about it. She had virtually abandoned her search, having visited every theatre and inn yard she could find, some of them not too salubrious, and Charlotte had almost hoped not to find her mother in any of them. The names had been given to her by Fanny, who was being especially helpful at the moment. She had even given Charlotte a pair of golden guineas to add to Fosdyke's three. But Charlotte was under no illusions over Fanny's sudden generosity. In fact she understood her perfectly. If she could pay Lady Susanna off with a pair of golden guineas, would she not do so?

As for dreams of fame on the London stage, these now seemed foolish and infantile, unconnected with the real world. Charlotte felt she had changed since leaving Caperley Farm where it was easy to fill one's head with fanciful longings in the secure knowledge that one was loved and cherished. Poor Uncle Nathan. What was he feeling at being so callously abandoned? She would write to him tomorrow and tell him she was safe.

She had come in the late afternoon to visit James's house at Fanny's suggestion, and Charlotte was glad now that she had taken the advice as she had no wish to be noticed. The sky was darkening and, gazing up at the brightly lit windows and the thick oak door, Charlotte knew she did not have the courage to knock upon it and ask after James's health however much she might long to do so. She had not expected it to be quite so splendid and, rubbing her palms gone damp with perspiration against her home-spun skirt, she guessed that even a parlour-maid in such an establishment would be better dressed than herself. If only she could see a glimpse of him through one of the tall windows she would be content. She would know that he was well again.

She stood so long in the street, half-hidden behind railings, that her feet and legs felt stiff with the frost that sparkled on the grass in the centre of the square. Plumes of her frozen breath steamed in the air but still she waited, her eyes fixed upon the lighted windows above. A cab came along the street, the clip-clopping of the horse's hooves echoing in the stillness of the gathering night. Charlotte shivered. She must go soon or she would not be able to move a limb. And then her patience was rewarded. There he was, outlined clearly against a first-floor window looking down on to the street, almost straight into her eyes. It sent the oddest tingle down her spine to see him look out so intently. Quickly she drew back into a bush. He must not see her. He must not know how she felt about him. It was then that the attack took place.

It took her completely off guard. One moment she was backing into the crisp fronds of the bush, the next she was on the ground, two street urchins robbing her of the last of her money. In her frantic efforts to protect herself and stop them taking her purse, Charlotte succeeded only in getting her dress torn, her nose bloodied and her head battered. The night seemed filled with sound as doors banged, footsteps pounded and a scream rang out eerily in the empty square, causing the horses to whinny with fright – her own voice, Charlotte realised. Then she was alone as the two youths ran off, pursued by shouts and whistles. But she did not move. She lay winded, hurting in every limb, but painfully conscious upon the spiky grass.

'Charlotte? I don't believe it! What in damnation are you doing here?'

'James.' She couldn't believe it either.

And then there was no more need of

words. She was in his arms and the tears were flowing unchecked, making a dreadful mess, she was sure, upon his silken cravat which had looked so very smart. He was lifting her in his arms and carrying her across the street into the lighted house.

'Your injury,' she murmured.

'Damn that,' he said, kicking the door closed behind him and calling out orders as he did so. Charlotte wound her arms more tightly about him and buried her small face into the warmth of his neck. It was like coming home. And she never wanted to leave his arms again.

However pleased Charlotte might feel to be with James again, and he to receive her, Lady Susanna was less than enchanted with the outcome of her scheming. Fanny had carried out her part of the bargain by procuring a couple of vagabonds ready enough to set upon anyone for a guinea or two. But James himself had overset Susanna's own part. He was meant to be still safely ensconced in his bedchamber while she, under the pretext of kindness, would have tended Charlotte's wounds and provided her with the transport to take her directly home – to Cornwall, where she would no doubt think twice before leaving those milder climes for the rougher streets of London ever again. And now here was James carrying the girl in his arms as if he would never let her go, and she clinging on to him with no sense of decorum at all. The situation had to be turned back to her own advantage without delay.

'James, really. You must think of your injury. No, not on the sofa she might bleed upon it. *Clara!* Why, the poor child is frozen,' cried Susanna effusively. 'We'll take her upstairs. Clara shall see that she is bathed at once before she catches a chill, and her wounds tended. What can she have been doing, prowling in those bushes, I wonder? Well, first things first. Give her to me.'

Reluctantly James abandoned his burden to the ministrations of Susanna and her maid and stood at the bottom of the stairs watching them go. What had Charlotte been doing out there in those bushes? As soon as she was recovered he would make it his business to ask. For the moment he felt a flood of relief that she was safely under his roof.

While Charlotte slept on the next morning, worn out by her anxieties and the results of her freezing vigil, James and Susanna seated themselves in the library with a fire blazing cheerfully in the grate and a tray of coffee and *petits fours* set before them. James was well strapped up and doing his utmost to hide any discomfort he felt, while Susanna poured coffee and considered how best to take her plan one step further. She was resolved to make herself indispensable to James's pleasure and comfort, but first of all she must rid herself of Charlotte. It would be less easy now that her plan had backfired upon her. If James had not been so stubbornly determined to leave his sick-bed, Susanna could have spirited the child away in the night without his even knowing. It had been agreed that Susanna was better able to do this than Fanny, since she had the resources of a carriage and servants at her disposal. Charlotte should have found herself well into the West Country before she'd even woken up. Instead of which she was upstairs, asleep, in the guest-room.

Handing him his coffee, milked and sugared just as he liked it, she said, 'I have arranged for John to drive Charlotte home as soon as she has breakfasted. And then, in view of your excellent progress into convalescence, I intend to dispatch Bayley to procure two seats for the theatre on Saturday night. There, are you not pleased? I thought an outing would cheer you.'

The last thing James wanted just now was to pay a visit to a play, to be reminded of the weeks he had spent with Charlotte and the way she had so mysteriously turned against him. Yet she was at this moment asleep upstairs, safe from the machinations of the

259

odious Fosdyke. A state of affairs he meant to maintain. 'Charlotte is perfectly all right where she is. She is certainly not returning to that Fosdyke character ever again.' His breath seemed to fill his chest at the mere thought of him touching Charlotte.

'Oh, my, no indeed!' cried Susanna, setting down her cup with a light clatter. 'I would not dream of suggesting such a thing. No, no. It was to Cornwall I meant.'

'Cornwall?'

Susanna adopted an air of flustered confusion. 'Cornwall is where she comes from, isn't it?' She made it sound as if it were the moon.

'Yes,' said James, beginning to feel irritated. 'Cornwall is Charlotte's home, but why on earth should she return just now?'

Susanna flicked out her wide skirts and pointed one foot so that James might notice how pretty and slender it was in the new yellow satin slippers. 'She told me herself that she had quite given up this ridiculous quest of finding her mother and was ready enough to return home to her uncle.' This at least was true, with some clever prompting from Susanna.

'I see.' James sounded subdued. It was not at all what he had expected, and he was disappointed. He'd judged Charlotte to have greater stamina than that. 'I will speak to her about it later,' he said dismissively.

'When she is fully recovered. As for the theatre, I confess I do not feel up to jolly jaunts yet, Susanna,' he said. 'Which play is it?'

Susanna shrugged slender shoulders, then adjusted the lace scarf draped so artlessly about them though not allowing it to conceal their fineness. 'I know not. Does it matter? Only you seemed so fond of the drama these days I thought it might cheer you. And afterwards we can take supper together. Monsieur Rochet shall prepare a delicious meal for us, to celebrate your recovery. And there will be no Bayley to interrupt us at my house,' she finished, with no attempt at subtlety.

'Monsieur who?'

'My new chef,' she said. Really, how James did so fuss about trivialities. 'French cooks are quite the rage now, you know.'

'No, I did not know.'

All James's instincts cried out against tête-à-tête supper parties at Susanna's home. Yet he had no wish to be unfeeling. It was largely his own fault that he was so embroiled with Lady Susanna Brimley, though he had valiantly tried not to allow it to become serious. He must take care to let her down gently, for he was under no illusion that she could do him immeasurable harm. 'I shall be poor company, I fear. If you are set on this evening out, why not ask a few friends to accompany us, then at least you will have someone to entertain you.' His face suddenly brightened as he remembered something. 'And I am sure Charlotte would love a trip to the theatre. She expressed that wish when I first met her at Caperley Farm.'

Susanna's lips set in an uncompromising line. How very unlucky she was. Everything was turning quite topple-tail against her. 'I have already told you that Charlotte wished to return home.'

'I think she could be persuaded to postpone that desire in return for a night at the Drury Lane.'

At the sound of a small gasp from the door, James jumped to his feet. 'Ah, there you are. Now you can ask her to choose,' said James mildly, smiling from one to the other of them with a touch of asperity in his voice.

'Did you say Drury Lane?' asked Charlotte, coming slowly into the room. She felt rather shy about intruding since it was such a grand room, lined with books from floor to ceiling. And the two of them had looked so intense that she had been struggling to find the courage to knock for some moments upon the open door, when she'd overheard this snippet of conversation. Her green eyes sparkled up at James as they had once done long, long ago, and he could not fail but smile back in response.

262

'I did indeed. You would still like to see it, I trust.'

'Oh,' Charlotte breathed, so stunned that she could find no other words, and James laughed. Then, turning to Susanna with no apparent sign that he had noticed how white and pinched she had become, he said softly,

'I believe that matter is settled.'

Charlotte was nervously excited in any case about this, her first visit to a live theatre. To attend with James himself was more than she dared contemplate.

'But what can I wear?' had been her first thought, for she had brought nothing with her from Cornwall fit for such an occasion, and what she had thought to bring was in her room at Woodley Terrace.

'I shall find you something, never fear,' Lady Susanna had promised, and so she had; but, studying herself now in the mirror, Charlotte could not help but feel acute disappointment at the picture she presented. The dress was fine enough in its way, she supposed, made of silk and in the very latest style. But it was simply too much. It was just too big, too long, too full at the waist, too colourful, too *loud* for Charlotte's comfort. In bright tangerine and yellow, it did nothing for her whatsoever. Even Clara agreed when she saw the final picture.

'Heavens above, they'll see you coming in

that a mile off!' she clucked, then slapped one hand over her mouth as if wishing she could bite her tongue off.

'My sentiments exactly,' mourned Charlotte. 'But what am I to do, Clara? I have no clothes or money of my own at present, and no way to get any. At least...' For the first time Charlotte began to understand the folly of her rash decision not to touch a penny of her father's money. She had to have clothes, didn't she? And independence, she had also discovered, was hard to establish without adequate funds. It was a galling revelation.

Clara was thoughtful. 'I'd lend you my own best frock since we are of a size, but it wouldn't be half so grand as this one.'

Charlotte seized upon the offer with relief. 'Oh, Clara. I have no wish to look grand, only not to be laughed at.'

Clara glanced at the much-plumed tangerine turban she held in her hand and burst out laughing. 'Oh, I do see what you mean, miss! Wait there.'

Moments later Charlotte again confronted the looking-glass and this time the reflection brought a smile of relief. True, it was a simple frock, as Clara had said, of cream spotted muslin with full elbow-length sleeves and a neat square neck.

'If you wear this blue sash about your waist and a matching shawl you'll look as pretty as a picture,' announced Clara, well pleased. 'And I'll dress your lovely hair so you won't need a hat.'

'Where did you find this?' cried Charlotte. She had heard stories of maids being better dressed than their mistresses, but the blue shawl was made of the finest silk and not likely to belong in such a wardrobe.

'I borrowed it,' mumbled Clara. 'But don't worry, it'll be all right.' She hoped it would anyway, since it belonged to Lady Susanna herself. But it had quite fired Clara up to see how her ladyship had been prepared to let the innocent Charlotte take her first visit to the theatre looking like an over-ripe piece of fruit. It would serve her right, for she dared say nothing if Sir James liked the effect, as Clara meant him to do.

And Sir James was indeed appreciative. His gaze roved over Charlotte's slender figure in her simple cream gown, at the curve of her dark lashes that lay so beguiling upon her flushed cheeks as she cast her shy gaze floorwards, and at the soft fall of brown ringlets, lit with golden lights, that nestled against her bare neck. He could recall kissing that neck and it was with immense strength of will that he restrained himself from repeating the action.

'You look quite enchanting.'

Charlotte risked a glance into his eyes and as her insides melted to water wished she had not. For long moments she was held by his gaze and nothing else seemed to exist for her until a loud voice cried out.

'Well, there's gratitude for you! Did I not leave one of my own gowns for your use?'

Swirling about, Charlotte faced the outraged Lady Susanna. 'I'm sorry; it simply didn't fit. Clara was kind enough to lend me hers. I do hope it will be suitable.'

'A trifle provincial for the Drury Lane, I think. Go and put on the silk.'

Charlotte turned back to James, a pleading look in her eyes, to find him still smiling at her. 'It is absolutely suitable. And the blue shawl sets it off quite perfectly, I think.'

Susanna opened her mouth to protest for she recognised it at once as her own, and a favourite too, but closed it again at the warning light in James's eye. She would never feel able to wear it again of course. But then, if this child liked it, it was clearly unsuitable for herself. Clara would hear the edge of her tongue later on the matter.

At the theatre Charlotte gazed about her, entranced. Never had she seen anything quite so grand in her life before. It was bigger than she had imagined with three tiers of seats seeming to reach right up to the circular crested ceiling, each supported by fluted pillars. The whole was lit by hundreds of candelabra, giving a luminous, magical glow. Even the smell of the place thrilled her: a mixture of warm mustiness, floor-polish, gin and candle-fat which was not altogether unpleasant. She stared at the gallants with their quizzing glasses; a young woman in a most horrendous yellow dress and wig with huge blue beads hung about her scrawny neck; a man all in black and white in one of the side-boxes with his feet upon the cushions, cracking nuts in his palms, tossing them into his cavernous red mouth and throwing the empty shells upon the poor unsuspecting folk occupying the benches in the pit below.

To be in Drury Lane, waiting to see the fabled Sarah Siddons appear, was excitement enough. But to sit beside James, so darkly handsome, in one of the side-boxes she felt almost like a queen. Nothing could dampen her delight, not even the frosty glances coming from the direction of Lady Susanna. She felt quite breathless with the joy of it all. It was only too apparent that Lady Susanna did not like her, which was not to be wondered at, but Charlotte was so grateful to James for bringing her that she meant not to worry over it. She had made it so abundantly plain in those last few days that she wanted nothing to do with him that it was a wonder he had permitted her this favour. And Charlotte hoped she was adult enough not to embarrass herself, or him, by revealing how she felt about him.

Lady Susanna had no such reticence and clung to James's arm, pressing her supple body against his as she gazed adoringly up into his face. Charlotte turned her own face away, for she could not bear to see his response, which was unfortunate, for she missed seeing James set Lady Susanna very firmly in her place and measure a good arm's length between their two chairs.

But now the orchestra was playing the opening bars, the play was about to begin and, as Charlotte gave her attention to the stage and to the players who entertained with such consummate skill, she was ashamed to find her cheeks wet with tears. Under cover of darkness, she brushed them angrily away with the back of her hand.

The play was certainly no masterpiece and would have failed to impress utterly had it not been for the skilful acting of Sarah Siddons, who proved to be every bit as charismatic as Charlotte had been led to believe. She was a fine figure of a woman with her noble straight nose, full shapely lips and mass of curly hair. Handsome rather than beautiful, her great skill lay in the sincerity of her acting. Despite herself, Charlotte was transported beyond her own problems, held captive by the actress's brilliant performance. Siddons seemed to float across the stage, her simplest utterances reaching every spellbound corner of that great theatre and she evinced such power in the portrayal of the character that Charlotte felt humbled at her own earlier efforts. Here was the very height of dramatic interpretation. Here was pathos, passion and such intensity that Charlotte could only marvel at it as she experienced with the actress every mood, every nuance of meaning she was intended to feel. It was an episode in her life she knew she would never forget.

But this great performance taught her much more. It showed Charlotte that she could never reach such a height of creative emotion in her own acting, such natural skill as was displayed on this stage tonight. It was a sobering thought, but Charlotte realised that much of the pleasure she had experienced from performing with the Fosdyke Players had been simply from the fun of it. And, even more telling, the presence of James Caraddon in the wings. For it was for him she had given her best performances. It was because of him she had made the audience cry and laugh, for James was the one she had wished to impress, not herself, not her own vanity at all. And yet she could not have him, for he belonged to another.

Charlotte glanced across the box to Lady Susanna and recognised the look of triumph in her face. She had seen Charlotte's tears and guessed her thoughts. But Charlotte saw no help for it. Delighted as she had been to be rescued from those unseen attackers by James himself, it did not refute the fact that Lady Susanna was not only present in his house, but living there, and had evidently been so for some time.

'Did you find that a moving scene?' whispered James, wiping a tear from her cheek at the first interval, and Charlotte shivered, wishing he would keep his distance or how could she control her traitorous emotions? 'You seemed so sad and it is meant to be a comedy.' James's feeling of unease about Charlotte had deepened and he regarded her now with some degree of anxiety, which he did his best to hide. 'Were you remembering our own days on the road? We had some fun, did we not? Remember when Fosdyke died and Phil forgot his lines, so Fosdyke miraculously came to life again long enough to prompt him? I thought *I* would die from laughing,' said James. 'It was the funniest thing I ever saw, though the play was supposed to be a tragedy. Yes, we had some fun,' he said again, a hint of regret in his voice. Charlotte had seemed different then. Not cold as she had been those last few days, or withdrawn as she was tonight. He wished he could understand her behaviour. Women were indeed creatures of mystery, and since he had always avoided becoming embroiled in their emotional problems how could he hope to understand Charlotte's now?

She met his gaze at last, with reluctance. and smiled. 'Yes, we did have fun.'

Susanna was edging forward, trying to overhear their conversation and failing, much to her chagrin.

'I suspect you could play Siddons's part,' James told her. 'For all the play is a froth of nonsense, I hope your first taste of this great theatre is not a disappointment to you.'

'I am loving every moment,' said Charlotte, 'but I shall never act again.'

'Never?'

'I shall go home to Cornwall as soon as it can be arranged. You were right about my mother. It was a foolish quest to start and one impossible to finish.' As soon as she had spoken, a deep sense of despair descended on her, but not for the loss of her quest; from the knowledge that once she had returned to Cornwall it was doubtful whether she would ever see James Caraddon again.

James stared at her, his brow creased in a thoughtful frown as the second act commenced. Had it come to such a state between them that she'd sooner return to the farm and the simple Dickon?

Overhearing this latter exchange, Lady Susanna settled back with a sigh of satisfaction to enjoy the rest of the performance, or at least to enjoy her favourite occupation of viewing who was here and allowing them to have a good view of herself. It looked as if Fanny's little scheme might be working after all.

CHAPTER THIRTEEN

But if Charlotte thought that she could quietly disappear, she had reckoned without James. He took quite a different view. Realising something was seriously troubling Charlotte, by the time they had left the theatre that night he was determined not to allow her to return to Cornwall until he had discovered the cause.

It was much more urgent to persuade Susanna to return to her home.

The next morning over coffee the question of Charlotte's return to Caperley was once more broached, by Susanna.

'Since tomorrow is Monday and usually a quiet day for travelling, I thought it would be ideal for Charlotte's journey, don't you think so, James? I have arranged for ample provisions to be packed for the journey and Clara has agreed to accompany her.' Clara was only too pleased to offer. Life with the

Lady Susanna had grown decidedly prickly since the incident of the shawl.

Both Charlotte and James stared at Susanna for a moment without speaking. Then Charlotte quietly nodded. 'Whatever you say. I have no wish to be a nuisance, nor to rob you of your maid.'

'Think nothing of it. She was becoming tiresome in any case.' Susanna smoothed out the silken folds of her blue-green shot-silk gown. She had chosen it specially today to look beautiful for James, but he seemed scarcely to glance at her. His eyes would keep constantly straying across to Charlotte's. It was most vexing. She got up and started to parade about the room, to allow him ample opportunity to admire it and, of course, its wearer. But since it had the opposite effect she gave up and came to sit on the sofa beside him. 'Fortunately the weather is perfectly clement at the moment with no sign of fog or ice, so I see no reason for delay.'

'Except that Charlotte has seen so little of London,' put in James in a voice so quiet that had Susanna possessed any sensitivity at all she would have recognised the danger in it. But her head was filled with her own needs, and that made her clumsy.

'I see no reason why she should, even if she had the clothes for it, which she does not.'

'Nevertheless,' said James, 'I would like her to stay a little longer. Will you do so, Charlotte?'

Before Charlotte could frame a reply there came a rap upon the door and a footman entered, bearing a card upon a silver tray, announcing a caller.

James glanced at the card. 'George Bletherington? Tell him I'm not at home.'

Susanna was horrified. 'You cannot refuse to see Lord Bletherington! He is a very important politician.'

'He is an old gossip and will have come to discover what I've been up to. I'm surprised it's taken him so long to realise I am home. He loves nothing better than to slander anyone with his razor-sharp tongue – me in particular since we do not agree on the question of government reform.'

'Then we must win him round, not rebuff him,' declared Susanna anxiously. 'He will poison Pitt against you, make no mistake about it, and then where will you be? Show him in, John,' said Susanna to the footman.

Hot fury surged through James and the tension of it caused a fresh spurt of pain to shoot across his chest. 'His name is David.' Then, speaking directly to the young footman, said, 'Pray tell Lord Bletherington, if you will, David, that I am indisposed and will call upon him next week when I am more myself.'

'Very good, sir.' Knowing when best to make a speedy departure, the young foot-man did so, not daring to glance at Lady Susanna's scarlet face. He heard her voice though as he softly closed the door.

'How dare you show me up in front of the servants?' she cried, jumping up and stamp-ing a foot in temper. 'How *dare* you em-barrass me so?'

James gazed up at her dispassionately for some seconds before answering. 'I believe they are *my* servants, ma'am.'

In the appalling silence which followed, Susanna realised that she'd gone too far, but it was too late now to retreat. Pride must be saved and her only salvation was to throw herself upon James's good nature. She well knew he possessed a soft heart beneath the gritty exterior. It was this very softness which made him such an effective, if un-usual politician since he was far too caring of people to fob them off with bland non-answers. Yet his outspokenness would keep him on the back-benches unless he per-mitted her to help him. Sending away the powerful Lord Bletherington was typical of his blindness.

Susanna flung herself on to her knees before him, her eyes suffused with ready tears. 'James, my darling, forgive my lack of tact. It is only that I care so much for your well-being, for your political future, that I cannot bear to see you endanger it. You know I would do nothing to hurt you.' Susanna stroked a fingertip over his cheek, tracing the outline of his lips. James took away her hand and held it for a moment in his own before getting up from the sofa and walking away from her.

It was a bitter blow to her pride. 'I do understand; none better,' James said quietly. 'But you must allow me to arrange my own affairs, Susanna.'

Very quietly, not daring to fracture the evident fragility of their relationship, Charlotte slipped from the room. Susanna, seeing the tactful withdrawal, was fired with a new fury. Were it not for that irresponsible child gallivanting half across the country, James would have married her by now, she was sure of it. She had come to believe this fiction so firmly that to Susanna it was as real as the truth.

Turning to James, she met his coldly assessing stare with fire in her own eyes. 'I thought you would enjoy being looked after while you were laid low,' she said. 'You and I were once close and I thought it might bring you a pleasure. Instead of which I have received nothing but ingratitude and criticism.'

'I'm sorry; I never meant to hurt you.'

How she wanted him. He had never looked so desirable as he did at this moment, so strong, so imperious, so much latent passion in his glorious powerful body. Far too much for that little fish of a child. Surely he would soften towards her, and as she leaned closer, wanting him to fully appreciate the intoxicating delicacy of her highly expensive perfume, Susanna put on her most seductive smile which had never failed her before. 'You can leave me to deal with Lord Bletherington since he is an old friend of mine,' she said. 'I will see he starts no nasty rumours about you.' Then she kissed him full upon the lips. It was a kiss full of promised passion; soft, teasing, meant to awaken the darker reaches of his mind. It left James quite unmoved.

His lack of response finally penetrated and she stepped back, away from him, a small gasp upon her lips. 'It is *her*, isn't it? That chit of a harlot.'

James took Susanna's wrist in a grip so strong she knew that if she tried to escape it would break. 'Don't ever let me hear you call her that again.'

But Susanna was beyond caring now. James had not only deserted her at Christmastide, but spent it with some foolish chit with doe-eyes. She wanted only to inflict as much hurt as she could. 'She *is* a harlot!' she spat at him. 'Lottie Forbes, an actress who travelled half across the West Country with a group of strolling players – and yourself,

277

for no good reason that I can think of. Are you trying to tell me that your relationship with her was entirely innocent? That her relationship with this Fosdyke was entirely innocent? I do not believe it.'

'Believe what you will, but Charlotte is innocent, and I'll not have you make suggestions to the contrary. Be quiet, woman!'

'*You'll* not have?' Susanna was enraged. No one spoke to her in that manner, the daughter of an earl. 'How dare you tell me what to do? You have no rights over me. I'll say what I like. Charlotte Forbes is a harlot, like many an actress before her. Have her as a mistress if you will, but you'll not have me as a wife if you do!' There was triumph in her voice.

'So be it,' said James quietly, and his words rode like a death knell into Susanna's heart. Once more her fiery tongue had betrayed her, and this time she had sealed her own coffin. She had lost him, and who else would marry her now if Sir James Caraddon cast her off for a mere actress?

Susanna stormed to the door, skirts hissing angrily over the polished boards. Not for a moment would she allow James to see how much she cared. Let him think it was but injured pride. But before she left she gave her parting shot; with all the venom of a witch from *Macbeth* she offered up her curse. 'But if you think you can find happiness with that whore *and* power in politics, you are mistaken, James Caraddon. For I shall see that you do not.'

James found Charlotte in the garden. She was sitting in the summer house, a small forlorn figure of abject misery. As soon as she saw James striding towards her she was on her feet, hands clasped in supplication before her.

'I am so sorry, James. It is all my fault that your relationship with Lady Susanna is fractured. She was so angry. Has she gone? Will she forgive you, do you think? I shall go at once and assure her that she will soon be rid of me.'

James stopped her words with one finger upon her lips. Such soft lips. 'You will do no such thing. So many questions, so many worries. I am not in the least concerned about Lady Susanna.'

Charlotte's green eyes were wide with shock at the scene she had witnessed for which she held herself entirely to blame. No wonder Lady Susanna was alarmed, for having an actress who had roamed the countryside with a group of strolling players in his house could do little for James's reputation as an up-and-coming politician. 'Oh, but I do understand how she must feel. I am the intruder and I do realise now that I have, well – compromised you. But I never

279

meant to do so. I didn't think. It was only that—'

But she never did finish that sentence. She never did explain how impulsive and stubborn she could be at times, for, sighing deeply, James pulled her into his arms and stopped any further words with a kiss that robbed her of the last atom of strength in her trembling body.

'I repeat,' he said, his grey eyes laughing down into her own, which were so dazed with delight they could scarce focus upon him, 'I am not in the least concerned about Lady Susanna. She always took our relationship more seriously than it deserved.' Then he quite startled Charlotte by bursting into laughter, his arms still comfortably linked about her waist so that she had no alternative but to rest her own upon them. She found she didn't mind that in the least, but his laughter was unnerving.

'Have I amused you in some way?' she asked in a tight little voice, but he only laughed all the more. Then he saw her expression and stopped. Pulling her closer into the warmth of his embrace, he kissed her lightly on the nose.

'*You* have done me a great favour. Because of you Lady Susanna has been driven to release me from this half-hearted relationship. If I hadn't been such a coward I would have rid myself of the woman long ago.'

'I see.' In truth Charlotte did not see. So the kiss had been out of gratitude? The disappointment she felt by this revelation was keen. She had rid James of a shrew-voiced woman and so he kissed and hugged her out of thankfulness and laughed with relief that he no longer had to marry her. Charlotte had never known misery so deep. But still James did not release her. Instead he took her hands in each of his own and stepped back so that he could better view her.

'Susanna was, however, right in one respect. You do not have a fit wardrobe for life in the capital, not in the circles I move in, I'm afraid. We shall have to do something about that.'

'We?'

'Since you are staying.'

'Am I?'

The smile faded from James's lips. 'You will stay, won't you, Charlotte? At least for a little while. Have we not become friends? You must know—' James stopped, biting back the words which had sprung so thoughtlessly, almost automatically, to his lips. He had wanted to reveal how he felt about her, but how did he feel? In the infinitesimal moment of time which stretched out between them, he gazed at her dear, sweet face, saw how her eyes moved over his, knew that life without her would be a dull, drab affair. Yet there was still a reticence about her, a shyness that he had no wish to startle, for he guessed that she would flee his presence as swiftly and easily as she had done the farm. And, even more important in view of the way she had been rejected so callously in the past, and had had her trust in human love so cruelly shattered, he had to be sure in his own mind that what he felt for her was genuine and would last. He offered her a warm smile now and, seeing how it caused her to relax, knew his judgement to be correct. Gaining her trust and confidence would take time. 'I have no wish to rush you into any decisions about your future, Charlotte. But, if nothing else, know that I am your friend, that I would never knowingly hurt you and that you are welcome to stay here for as long as you wish. We may find your mother yet. And even if we do not, I shall not regret having you in my house for one moment.'

'But the gossipmongers–'

'Will wag their tongues and shake their heads,' he moaned, and now it was her turn to laugh. 'And I'll tell you this, Charlotte Forbes; I don't care. I do not care a jot what they say or do. I want you here, with me.' Then he was holding her hands to his lips and kissing the back of each one and Charlotte thought she would die with the pleasure of it. 'Are we agreed?' His eyes were serious now, probing, questioning, sparking with his demands and, dared she imagine, almost pleading. Charlotte dropped her gaze and gave a tiny nod of her head which he could interpret as he might, for she could find no words to speak.

James was jubilant, delight plainly writ on his face, like a young boy at Christmastide. 'I shall show you everything,' he said. Then his arms were round her again and he was sweeping her off her feet, swirling her round and round and they were both laughing with the joy of this as yet unspoken realisation that something very special had sprung up between them over these last weeks, and neither had the wish to end it.

The next few days passed by in a whirl of activity and heady emotion. And Charlotte found herself agreeing to many things that once would have horrified her. Now she had no time to think, no time to judge anything rationally. She was in love, and as each day passed began to hope with a growing tingle inside her that her feelings might very well be reciprocated.

James took her on a tour of the city, showing her all the sights, including the Palace of Westminster where he spent a good deal of his time. 'Though I've neglected it somewhat lately,' he said with a wry smile.

'Because of me?'

'A charming reason. I'm not complaining. But I must return soon for there is much work to be done, and though I am not in the Cabinet I sit on several committees.'

They were strolling along the Embankment, a soft breeze coming in off the water, bringing with it the promise of an early spring. There was a hint of birdsong and Charlotte was poignantly reminded of her country home which she had so abruptly left. But, watching James's face, she saw how deeply satisfied he was with his life in the great city of London and for an instant she felt a stab of pain which was almost physical in her middle chest. How much harm had she done to his career by taking him from the House these long weeks, and why had he never complained? 'Would you like to be in the Cabinet?' she asked.

For answer he took her small gloved hand and rested it in the crook of his arm. It sat remarkably comfortably there. 'There have been times when that has been the last thing I've wanted and I've dreamed of nothing more than to retire to Brampton and play the country gentleman. But then again I do not deny the prospect of high office is enticing. Pitt goes from strength to strength. He is strong, energetic, masterful, a man of vision. And not a man who gives up easily once he has set his mind on something.'

Charlotte gave a little giggle. 'He sounds

rather like yourself.'

James squeezed her hand. 'You flatter me. Pitt will bring stability, without doubt, for he is an able man bent on improving the efficiency of government without resorting to the corruption which has so often taken place in the past. It is a stony path to tread but I believe he can succeed. He is not content to accept what has always gone before and is already making moves to dispose of sinecures by not handing them on automatically when the holder dies. I applaud that.'

Charlotte had been watching his expression, for he had come alive as he talked, and she saw that his job was important to him. 'Yet he must make many enemies.'

James acknowledged this with a wry smile. 'It is the way of politics. I too have enemies who would much rather not see me get into Cabinet. They would be pleased to see my news-sheet fail, or to buy it from me, as some have already tried to do, in order to silence the uncomfortable comments it insists upon making.' James smiled as if he was pleased, but Charlotte was startled. She could imagine no one setting himself against James Caraddon; he seemed so strong, so impregnable.

'But, why?' she asked.

James looked down at her and the smile deepened. 'No other reason but personal ambition. In politics it is very much a case of every man for himself. If in furthering one's own career it is at the expense of the next man, so be it. That is his bad luck.'

'Even if you are on the same side?' Charlotte was appalled at this new insight into the leaders of her land. 'Why, I think that quite dreadful. There are surely more important matters than personal ambition?'

James laughed. 'I'm sure you are right, but I'm afraid that working as a team is a hard lesson for many to learn in politics. The driving force of ambition is too strong in most men. That is probably the reason why I am still on the back benches.'

'Why? Are you not ambitious?' She was puzzled, for he seemed so to her. His lips tightened in anger for a moment and then he laughed.

'We are getting very serious here, are we not?' he countered.

'I want to know. I am interested,' she said, waiting for his answer. 'For if you love politics and are indeed ambitious you will surely reach your goal in the end.'

'Ah, but there is the crux of it,' said James quietly. 'Perhaps I am not prepared to stand upon enough heads to reach it.'

She looked into his eyes and understood. For all his strength and confident assurance that he could choose his own path, there was no streak of ruthlessness in his charac-

286

ter. Not for Sir James Caraddon that all-enveloping ambition which could destroy its holder as easily as those it attempted to usurp. He was a man of principle. She found she was glad of that. Yet he was a skilled and caring politician, and any prime minister worth his salt would surely recognise his worth eventually. Perhaps the breeze from the river had changed, for she shivered. And, as James thoughtfully turned them homeward, the thought that echoed round and round her head was that if he was to succeed without that streak of ruthlessness and without corruption then he must remain steadfast to his honour. And she could not help but wonder if she had tarnished that image.

The next day James informed Charlotte that she was to attend her first function.

'It is not a political function, so you need have no fears of succumbing to boredom,' he told her with a smile. They seemed to laugh a good deal these days and they grew easy together. 'Do you like music?'

'Of course.'

'Splendid. Then, put on one of these fine gowns we have procured and be ready by six. We are to attend a piano recital at Lady Alsager's. But first I must go to the House today, so I shall leave you to entertain yourself.' At the door he turned and smiled at

287

her. 'Do you know, Charlotte, I enjoy coming home to this drab house so much more knowing you are here?'

'But I cannot stay here forever,' she said, going towards him. 'I must go home soon. Uncle Nathan will expect me to. I've been thinking that I shall soon have to make up my mind to accepting this inheritance of mine, or how shall I live?'

'There is no hurry,' he said. 'You must do only what you feel is right.'

'But I cannot live on your generosity indefinitely,' she protested, and their eyes met and held. After a long moment James gave something like a shrug.

'If you say so. I shall see you at six, then.' And he was gone, leaving Charlotte with a distinct feeling of unease. So often these days she seemed to say the wrong thing. She found it hard to judge his mood for he was increasingly unpredictable. Surely he did not mean them to go on in this fashion. For what purpose? He had not even asked her to become his mistress. Nor could she clarify what her own reaction would be if he did so. She'd been most careful to observe the proprieties as far as was possible in their situation. She spent very little time alone with him and then only outside of the house, never in it. And there was the housekeeper, and Clara, who had now left Lady Susanna's service, and Bayley of course, besides several other servants. Even so, she must leave soon or tongues really would start to wag and she had no more desire for her own reputation to be besmirched than James's. If only she could make up her mind to it. Sighing, she went slowly back upstairs. The truth was that she had no wish to leave at all. A happiness had grown between them and these last two weeks in James's house had only intensified it. To part from him now would be like amputating a limb. Yet, despite his occasional kind words, as now, James had not for a moment attempted to take advantage of the situation. In fact the last time he had kissed her had been on the day Susanna had left in her storm of rage and vowing a vengeance that could be heard all over the house. Since then they had lived in complete decorum, as brother and sister, as perfect friends.

Charlotte stopped and, sitting down upon the top step of the long staircase, rested her chin upon her hand, and her eyes grew misty as she wondered if that state of affairs might ever change.

The dress she chose to wear was of ivory silk taffeta, the hemline garlanded with pink roses and the neck cut low and square with no kerchief since the occasion was a formal one. Yet, pretty though the dress undoubtedly was, Charlotte was unprepared for the effect of her entry into the music-room of Lady Alsager's house, upon James's arm. A silence so complete and awesome in its implications seemed to crystallise in Charlotte's head like the pricking of sharp needles and, had it not been for the light pressure of James's hand upon hers, she was sure she would have turned tail and run for shelter.

As it was, she smiled and nodded and walked with him to their seats, set near to the back of a dozen rows. She felt strange and unsure of herself, and something of this must have communicated itself to him for he gave her hand a little squeeze and whispered in her ear.

'Don't worry. You are quite the most beautiful person present, and I promise you will enjoy this evening. He is a brilliant pianist. And afterwards we will taste one of Lady Alsager's famous suppers and mingle with her noted guests, who will adore you, as I do.'

Faced with such assured confidence, Charlotte could do no other than ignore her misgivings, which she could not have named in any case, and, folding her hands neatly upon the stiff silk of her lap, prepared to be entertained.

It was only as everyone settled into their places and the pianist started his recital that Charlotte dared move her head to look about her. And the first face she saw, directly across the aisle from her, was that of Lady Susanna.

Charlotte's heart froze. There was something in the glint of triumph in the other woman's eyes that made her want to look as quickly away, but something held her, like a hypnosis, and it was Lady Susanna who smilingly broke the hold. It seemed to be a victory of sorts, and Charlotte feared it would not be the only one that evening.

CHAPTER FOURTEEN

She was unfortunately proved correct in this, for as soon as the recital was over and everyone filed into the supper-room it became only too apparent to Charlotte that she was the subject of much speculation. She saw the heads bob, the lips snap together when she approached, skirts drawn away as she passed and eyes raking her over from head to toe. If James noticed anything amiss he made no comment. He found them a pair of chairs and brought her a plate full of tempting morsels to savour. But, though she obediently ate to please him, she neither knew nor cared what it was that she ate. And never had she heard him talk so much in all of their acquaintance. Can he be as nervous as I? she wondered. Surely not. Nor simply embarrassed by the fact that not a single person approached them throughout the meal. Finally, however, someone did approach – Lord Bletherington himself, and he seemed far from pleased to see them.

'So there you are, James, m'boy. Heard you were out of sorts, but you look well enough to me so why have you been hiding yourself away?' He did not even glance in Charlotte's direction and she felt snubbed.

James rose from his seat, nodded an acknowledgement and assured Lord Bletherington that the tale was true. 'Suffered a minor injury but I'm better now, thanks,' he said.

'Not swords, what? Dangerous toys, swords. Been neglecting that news-sheet of yours too, I hear. Why don't you sell it to me and have done with it? I'd make more money out of it than you, m'boy.'

'I shouldn't wonder,' said James drily. 'Allow me to introduce to you Miss Charlotte Forbes,' he said, reaching out a hand to include Charlotte, but before she had got to her feet Lord Bletherington had given a brief nod in her direction and, turning abruptly back to James, proceeded to speak at length about the latest Parliamentary business. Charlotte was obliged to remain trapped in her seat and, though James cast her a sympathetic, long-suffering look, there was nothing he could do when moments later Bletherington took his arm and started to lead him off.

'Come and meet him yourself, Caraddon. You'll see what I mean exactly. The man has some excellent theories.'

James mouthed to Charlotte that he would not be long and she smiled and flapped a hand at him as if to say, get on with it, I shall be fine. James had his work to do. She was only too keenly aware how she had stood in his way long enough. What possible harm could come to her, sitting here sipping white wine?

James still had not returned by the time supper was over, and the servants began to clear away the tables for cards. Charlotte had no alternative but to move back into the music-room along with everyone else. The chairs were now arranged around the walls so that dancing could take place but they were already all filled, and some of them by gentlemen. Not one stood to offer his place though she could be clearly seen hovering uncertainly by the big double doors.

Where *was* James?

Her glass was empty and, uncertain how to dispose of it, she glanced about her for a footman or a handy table. She found herself instead face to face with Lady Susanna.

'Not deserted you already, has he? How very uncivilised.' Her eyes were mocking, sharp with amusement.

Charlotte stiffened. 'Not at all,' she said with commendable dignity. 'He is merely speaking with Lord Bletherington, as you wished him to, if I recall. I am quite content to wait until James has concluded his business.'

If there was one thing Lady Susanna disliked intensely it was to be met with a calm confidence in response to her taunts, particularly from this chit. How dared the girl stand there and smilingly preach the edict of patient femininity, so certain James would return to her? And look so delightfully young and appetising with it. Susanna cut the thought off at birth. It would not do at all to show her jealousy. Yet it was there. If she had to lose him, Susanna would much rather it were to anyone than this untutored child from the country, with her big dark innocent eyes and slender curves. How Susanna hated her. 'It is very hot in here,' she said, fluttering her fan. 'Would you care for a turn about the garden?'

Charlotte politely declined. 'I had better wait here or James will not know where to find me.'

'Lord above, he'll not look for you in an age. He will be at the card tables for hours. He and George Bletherington and their other cronies love nothing better than to gamble the night away.' It was a gross exaggeration of the truth but Charlotte was not to know that.

'O-oh. I didn't realise. I thought when he said he wouldn't be long–'

'That he meant minutes, and not half the night?' Lady Susanna gave a pretty, tinkling laugh. 'What an innocent you are.'

And miserably Charlotte knew this to be true. She had trusted people all her life and they had lied to her, for whatever noble reason. And if she hadn't been so trusting of Fosdyke perhaps James would never have been injured, for she was almost certain that it had not been entirely an accident. Even now she wasn't sure of the reason. She had perhaps been wrong to trust Fanny. Knowing that Fanny wanted her to return to Cornwall, she had taken her advice and the loan of her money and received a beating from a couple of thugs as a result. Was that truly a coincidence? Could Fanny be totally innocent? And now she was trusting James. Perhaps that was a mistake too. But Charlotte told herself she was not an entire nincompoop and would likewise not make the mistake of trusting Lady Susanna either, for all her smiling charm. If that she-dragon wished to lure Charlotte into the garden there must be a purpose behind it. 'I think I had better wait here. I am sure James will not be long,' Charlotte stubbornly insisted.

The smile slipped just a little. 'Of course,

darling. For who else does he have, now that his friends have deserted him?'

Charlotte's heart gave a tiny lurch. 'Deserted him? What are you talking about?'

Susanna waved a prettily manicured hand airily about her. 'Do you see anyone eager to make the acquaintance of James's new conquest, that is yourself, my dear? Odd, don't you think? Did they rush to greet you when you arrived? Have the young gallants been queuing up to dance with you, pretty though you undoubtedly are? Is your card quite full? Have you not noticed a decided chill in the air?'

Charlotte had gone quite cold. 'I – I hadn't really thought. I didn't notice any...' But she had.

Now that Susanna had the advantage she stroked her white-powdered curls like a cat quietly grooming itself before swallowing the mouse. 'The truth is, my dear, though it saddens me deeply to have to say it, that you are the very worst thing that has happened to James in his entire career. You do realise he was about to be offered high office in Government? And, being a man of scruples, his honour is of paramount importance to him.'

'I – I know that.'

Susanna's wide, smiling mouth formed a soft pout. 'What a pity, then, that he should take up with an actress, a strolling player, a vagabond of the streets as a mistress. And, as if that were not enough, take her to live with him in his own house.' Charlotte attempted to interrupt but Susanna rolled inexorably onward. 'It is not so unusual for a minister of His Majesty's Government to place his mistress in a house of her own of course, somewhere convenient for him to visit after a late-night sitting. But in his own home, darling...' Susanna let the sentence hang in the air unfinished.

Charlotte felt herself shaking from head to foot. 'It is not at all like that. You are quite wrong.'

'Of course James is ever gallant, and his failing is his soft heart, that is very true. And I'm sure he was concerned about your homeless state. However, you must realise, my dear, the effect your presence has upon his prospects. And certainly marriage is not even to be considered. You had not expected it, had you? A man in his position does not marry with his mistress, particularly one with a dubious past. The scandal would quite ruin him, do you not agree?' Susanna raised perfect brows in query and Charlotte felt sick.

'I had never hoped for any such thing.' But she had, she had.

Susanna patted her hand. 'Very sensible of you. A politician's wife has to be a very special kind of person. She must come from the right social sphere for a start, with an impeccable lineage, and be able to entertain her husband's colleagues properly. She must know the right people and how to aid his advancement. And, though he and I may have our spats from time to time, nothing in the end will keep us apart, for I am exactly what he needs in a wife, don't you see? And he is not indifferent towards me, I do assure you. Our relationship goes back a long way.' Again the tinkling laugh which crashed against Charlotte's nerves like the waves on her Cornish rocks. She longed to shut out the taunting voice but could not. She could not even move to run away.

Lady Susanna rested a slim white hand upon Charlotte's. 'I know you and I have not been the best of friends. I understand how you feel about him; none better. But I feel bound to say that if you truly love James this is not the way to help him. Be his mistress if you will; it is not uncommon, and I'd as soon it was you than some more scheming hussy. But have him buy you an apartment of your own. Be discreet, my dear. That way, you and I can become tolerably good friends and James's career will be safe. Now, I cannot say fairer than that, can I?'

The lilting music swirled merrily about Charlotte, a kaleidoscope of dancing colours spun before her eyes; but inside her head was a dark, numbing silence.

Susanna lightly tapped Charlotte's wrist with her closed fan. 'Think about what I have said. But do not take too long about it or you could lose James altogether. It is you he will blame if he is castigated completely by his colleagues and his brilliant future torn into tatters.' Susanna lifted her skirts with a flourish, already smiling a greeting to a breathless young gallant who was bowing before her. 'And that would be most unpleasant,' she said over one shoulder as, placing her hand upon the young man's arm, she swept away.

James found Charlotte sitting on a seat tucked away behind the fountain in the very depths of the garden. She had been crying, just a little, but fortunately it was so dark that he did not notice.

'What are you doing out here? I've been searching high and low. Were you hot?'

'It was rather stuffy in there, yes,' agreed Charlotte in a small voice. 'But I'm perfectly all right. Were you playing cards? There was no need to leave your friends on my account.'

'Cards? Good Lord, no. Whatever makes you think so? And I wish to be with you, not those old sots.' He was smiling down at her, his wide lips curved into that bewitching smile which quite turned her heart. She tried desperately not to look at him, not to

299

respond. But he was leaning closer, slipping his arm around the back of the seat above her shoulders and she could smell the fresh male aroma of clean soap, of the brandy he had drunk at supper. 'Are you not happy, Charlotte? You look suddenly sad.' In truth he was worried about her. Was she still hankering after that long-lost mother, or was it Fosdyke and his crew she missed? The latter was a grim thought.

Charlotte drew a deep, quivering breath. It was now or never. However much she might dislike Lady Susanna Brimley, the woman had a point. And the situation was even worse than Lady Susanna imagined. Heaven knew what would happen once the full story of Charlotte's background were known. She must be out of James's life long before that scandal broke. And hadn't it done enough damage already by ruining her mother's life? Even that of her uncle to a degree, by exiling him to the country when, Charlotte was quite sure, he would be much happier living in a small city flat in close proximity to a large lending-library and dozens of intriguing bookshops. She made herself look up at James. 'I have decided to go home.'

'But the night is young, and I have not yet danced with you,' James protested teasingly, not understanding.

Charlotte tried to swallow the hard knot of

emotion in her throat and failed. 'No, I meant home to Cornwall.'

She thought the silence would go on forever. Why did he not speak? His hand at last fell away from her shoulder and he sat back from her, his eyes searching her face, the set of his lips tight and grim. Never had she felt so miserable in all her life.

'Why?'

A single word but powerfully presented, and not for a moment dared she ignore it. 'Because it is what I wish,' she prevaricated, then, seeing his expression, bumbled on, 'I never meant to stay forever. You know I did not. I have failed in my quest; so be it. I must return to where I belong.'

'You could just as easily belong here.' He had spoken so softly, the faintest movement of sound on the night breeze, that she wondered it she had heard correctly. 'You must know that I want you.'

It was what she had so longed to hear. But it was too late. She knew it. Lady Susanna's words still rattled in her mind. An hour ago, even a moment ago, she might have interpreted James's statement with hope for their future; now she was filled with despair. She stood up, hands clasped tightly so he would not see them tremble, desperate not to break down before him. 'I must go.'

'You surely do not *want* to go back to Cornwall, to Dickon?'

A small sob caught in her throat as she shook her head. 'I'm sorry, but I don't think I'd make a very good mistress.'

'What are you talking about?' For an instant his eyes sparkled with a new hope and he was on his feet beside her, taking her in his arms and she was trying, not very successfully, to fend him off. 'You little goose. If that is all that troubles you, you need worry no more.' James was unused to the feelings of inadequacies which now beset him so badly. What had he said to give her such an impression? This was a whole new scenario for him. How could he right it without risking the humiliation of rejection? He tried to lighten the tension with a touch of humour. 'Here am I, the confirmed bachelor, attempting to make up my mind to marry at last, to take a wife into my all-male stronghold, and you decide to abandon me without even giving me the chance to come to terms with it. How can you be so cruel?'

Charlotte was gazing at him, transfixed. What was he saying? Could he truly wish to marry her? For an instant her heart leapt in response to him, her eyes met his and her lips almost smiled and accepted his glorious, wonderful offer. But then she considered his exact words – 'attempting to make up my mind to marry at last'. How could that be called an offer from the heart? It was nothing more than pity, coupled perhaps with a need that was more physical than emotional. Had Lord Bletherington made it clear to James what everyone thought of her? Had she compromised him? Charlotte recalled too Lady Susanna's words, that James's wife 'must come from the right social sphere for a start, with an impeccable lineage'. Hardly so in her own case. She had to put an end to this agony at once. 'I cannot be your wife either, James. It is kind of you to ask but you must know that I cannot.'

'Why not, for God's sake? And I wasn't intending to be kind.' He was reaching for her again but she slapped his hands away. The tears burned the backs of her eyes and she longed to be anywhere but right here in this beautiful moonlit garden with the man she loved. She had to escape.

'I am wrong for you, you know that I am. You need a wife who meets very particular requirements, which I do not. Lady Susanna is the one for you.'

'*Lady Susanna?*' He almost shouted the name and Charlotte, much flustered, hushed him and put her fingers to his lips as she glanced back anxiously over one shoulder. 'Has she been talking to you?' James demanded, snatching the hand away and, keeping a firm hold upon it, grasped her other one as well for good measure.

Charlotte stubbornly shook her head. It

would not do for James to think that she and Lady Susanna had discussed him in any way. He deserved to keep his pride at least. 'No, of course not. But I can work things out for myself,' she said. At last I can, she thought. Now that the stars have been drawn from my eyes. 'You know very well that I can never marry anyone until I have established beyond question the nature of my birth. That I am not – not...' she had to say it, now, here, to impress upon him how strongly she felt about the situation '...that I am not a child of incest.' There; it was done. She turned to go but he still had hold of her hands and she could not escape.

'Damn you! You know I don't care about all that nonsense.'

Charlotte swirled to face him, her eyes blurred with tears. 'But I do!' she cried. 'I do! Can't you see that?'

'I see that you have led me to believe there was more in our relationship these past weeks than you actually feel,' he said coldly. 'Was it only the stage you cared for, after all? Your dreams of fame?'

It was too much, the look in his eyes, the touch of his hands, the memory of those happy weeks together; in another moment the tears would spill over and run down her cheeks. She had to do something, anything, to break the power of his hold. And he had given her the cue. She tossed her head and

304

met his gaze boldly. 'You are right in that I have no wish for marriage. I do intend to go on the stage as I have so many times told you. It is what I most want above everything. It is my heritage. I need nothing but that. I will consider becoming your mistress if that is what you wish, but in my own house where you can call upon me discreetly. Are not actresses famous for their discretion in such things? But never your wife. I dare say I should find politics vastly boring.' Her heart was breaking.

For answer James made some indistinguishable noise deep in his throat then pulled her angrily into his arms. His lips came down to crush hers with a new fierceness, hard, unyielding, demanding, cruel almost. He cared not how he hurt her. He wanted to hurt her as much as she had hurt him. With one hand he held her small face in a vice-like grip, while the other he fastened about her waist and, lifting her in his arms, forced her down among the soft, sweet-smelling grasses. She might have cried out but he did not hear her. The blood pounded in his head so that he doubted his own sanity. He made his desire for her painfully evident and in doing so extinguished her own. She lay cold and unmoving beneath him, her heart like stone in her breast. And after a moment he became aware of her lack of response, of their situation, and he too froze. Then he snatched himself from her and was standing, legs astride, looking down at her with open contempt on his face.

'Get up. Tidy yourself. You may indeed go home, for I want none of a woman who thinks she can buy her future with her virtue.' Taking her elbow in an icy grip, he propelled her back to the house.

And, as he led her through the crowd of dancers out to the hall, Charlotte felt the daggers of their curious stares follow her. Lady Susanna stood smilingly by as a footman handed Charlotte her wrap and James made an attempt at a polite if clipped farewell to Lady Alsager. But as they went out into the night Charlotte knew that the scandalmongers had won and there wasn't a thing she could do about it.

They sat in silence during the drive home, and it was only when Charlotte started to mount the stairs to her room that James spoke to her again in a voice as cold as the night itself.

'I shall no doubt be out by the time you wake up in the morning. The carriage will be at your disposal as usual. Perhaps tomorrow night, when you have time to think, we can discuss your future plans more rationally.'

She stared at him for a split second, tracing his image in her mind for all time.

He was disappointed in her; she could read it in the bleakness of the grey eyes, as chilling and flat as the sea after a storm. Their whole relationship had been a terrible mistake. Forced together by circumstances and duty, they had had their judgement clouded by the undeniable physical attraction between them. He no doubt regretted ever considering marriage, for all it had been mentioned with precious little enthusiasm. Now she could see that James thought the shades had been drawn back from his eyes as she had presented a picture of herself as a woman of easy virtue – was that the term? And all along he had attempted to deny it, despite that very first meeting when he had caught her apparently frolicking in the hay with her cousin. Now she could see all his doubts return. Well, he had no need to fear; she would never again embarrass him, any more than she would ruin his career. Without a word she turned and walked steadily up the stairs.

Charlotte had her bags packed before she climbed into bed. Nor did it take long, since she put in only those items which were strictly hers and nothing which Sir James had bought for her. She did not even trouble to remove all her clothes and lay in her shift, unmoving beneath the quilt. And before the dawn had broken she was creeping down the stairs, dressed in her simple striped dress and old cloak, and scurrying out of the kitchen door, praying that none of the servants were about yet on their morning chores.

She knew what she must do: what she should have done at the very beginning. If she had, she would surely have saved herself a good deal of heartache, which was strange, considering how she had been sure she was taking the best course to avoid it.

Fortunately she remembered the name of her father's solicitors and did not expect to experience any difficulty in locating them. They would provide her with the necessary funds to see her safely back to Cornwall, where she would buy herself a small house some distance from Truro so that she need never run the risk of meeting Sir James Caraddon again. She could not bear that. Perhaps somewhere overlooking the sea, and Uncle Nathan could move in with her and leave the farm entirely to Dickon. She would devote herself to his care as he had done to hers throughout the years. So taken was Charlotte with this idea that it kept her mind fully occupied as she made her way through the early-morning mists; and, though it helped her to bear with the parting from James, it caused her to miss the fact that she was followed by a stealthy figure whose patience at last had been rewarded.

Her presence was not missed until Clara took in a dish of chocolate shortly before noon. Knowing that her new mistress had spent last evening at a late function, she had let her sleep soundly on. Or so Clara had thought. But, after pulling back the curtains and setting the chocolate on the bedside cabinet, she saw not only that her mistress was up and about but that the bed had scarcely been slept in. The obvious answer was the first to present itself and a knowing look came into the maid's eye. 'It must have been a good night, my lady,' said she, and, picking up the chocolate, made her way to the master's bedchamber where she stopped to listen carefully at the door, her ear pressed hard against the door panel. She could make out no sounds. Still, best to be on the safe side. Jobs were hard to come by and she'd been lucky to get this one after the affair of the shawl. Deciding that discretion was the better part of valour, Clara drank the chocolate herself and trotted back to the kitchen. Who was she to spoil the fun?

But at two o'clock when still no bell had sounded to call her to help Charlotte to dress, Clara decided to take action. The poor lady had to eat, after all. How selfish some men were! Laying a tray of a suitably dainty repast, bearing in mind that it might well have been a hectic night, Clara set off again up the stairs and moments later was knocking on James's door.

'And what do you think you are doing?' boomed Bayley, coming suddenly up behind her.

'Taking breakfast, or rather lunch – well, anyway...' Clara said, flustered.

Bayley then took great pleasure in informing this new maidservant that it was his task to furnish his master with breakfast, that he had done so at a quarter after seven as usual this morning, whereupon Sir had gone out. As usual. Clara took all this in with few protests, a gaping jaw and finally a conviction that her mistress must have been murdered in the scoundrel's bed at the very least. Nothing would satisfy her but to have the door opened immediately and Bayley present her with a room, neat as the proverbial new pin and completely empty, he was glad to say, of any female whatsoever.

And so the hue and cry began.

No one dared fetch James from the House of course, not until every corner of his home had been investigated, from cellars to attics. Clara, with the help of David, the footman, retraced James's and Charlotte's steps to the house of Lady Alsager, and, on the pretence of looking for a pair of embroidered gloves, ascertained from the butler that there had been something of a hullabaloo last night, though no one could guess quite what. For certainly Sir James had looked like thunder as they had left, rather early, if he recalled correctly.

'And no one saw Miss Charlotte arrive,' mourned Clara as they made their way back to James's townhouse.

'Are you suggesting some sort of foul play?' asked Bayley, much miffed, for no one was allowed to criticise his beloved master, other than himself of course.

'Perhaps they were set upon,' cried Clara, and indeed when they came to question the servants in the neighbouring houses – of whom there were a number who enjoyed keeping a close watch on what passed in the street below, for one never knew what Lord and Lady might be going in or out of which door – they discovered that there had been strangers about during the night. But a woman, not a man. And just before dawn.

'I saw her walk off with your young lady with my own eyes,' said next door's Martha, who was always up to light the fires early. 'I thought at the time it was odd. Your lady being so young and smart, and this other one, well, no better than she ought to be I'd say. Bit brash she was, and dark, too. Gypsy, I shouldn't wonder,' and Clara felt a chill run down her spine. Hadn't she met one who answered such a description, not so very long ago? She'd not liked the look of her then, and now her fears had been proved correct. Poor little Charlotte had been abducted by the gypsies; there was no doubt about it.

And when James was finally called it was after seven in the evening, and, far from being with the gypsies, Charlotte was half-way to France.

CHAPTER FIFTEEN

James scoured the entire area. He visited every park, every street, every shop in the vain hope that Charlotte had merely gone off on some expedition or other. But as the hours passed with still no sign this seemed unlikely, apart from the fact that even in their present state of disagreement she was hardly likely to be so inconsiderate. It was Clara in the end who found the note.

James had sent her to Charlotte's room to go through her mistress's clothes and ascertain what she might be wearing. There, propped upon the mantelshelf as nice as you please, was a square white envelope addressed to Sir James Carradon in Charlotte's round, flowing hand.

Clara watched in breathless anticipation as James devoured the contents, and saw at once that the news was bad.

'She has gone home, after all,' said James, deflated, then frowned. 'Yet how could that be if next door's housekeeper saw her with a gypsy-woman outside the house at dawn? Who on earth could she have been?'

Clara shuffled her feet and cleared her throat. 'Well, I didn't like to tell you, but I reckon I might have seen her before, though I don't know her name.'

'What are you talking about, girl?' Then, seeing Clara's nervousness, added more kindly, 'There is nothing for you to fear, Clara. This is none of your doing and I assure you your job is perfectly safe. But I am most concerned about Miss Charlotte and if there is anything you know which might cast any light on the subject I would be most grateful, for I am at my wits' end where to look next. Two sheep's heads, as they say, are better than one.'

Clara grinned and, thus encouraged, not only described in surprisingly accurate detail Fanny's appearance in her Spanish disguise but related almost word for word the conversation which had taken place that day behind locked doors in Lady Susanna's parlour. Had James not been so riveted by it, he would have been hard put to it not to smile at the picture thus presented of an eavesdropping maid. In the circumstances, however, he saw all and more of what had occurred: plot and counter-plot to outrun

313

any Shakespeare, and there was the greatest danger that this time their plan would not backfire, for James still had not the first idea where to look for Charlotte. Fosdyke would have made off with his prize long since, if James was any judge.

'Though I do know now where to take my first question, thanks to you, Clara. You must come with me, for Charlotte may be in need of as many friends as we can muster by the time we find her. Dear God, I pray we are in time, for I trust Fosdyke not a scrap.' James was halfway to the hall even as he spoke, snatching up his greatcoat, hat and gloves and calling for the carriage in a voice that had lost all vestige of his usual mannerliness. Round-eyed, Clara grabbed her best red cape and scurried along beside him. She could guess where their first stop would be and not for the world would she miss it.

Charlotte felt sick. It was not so much the boat journey, though that had been difficult enough, pitching and tossing on a choppy sea with a stiff north-westerly breeze. Nor was it particularly the overcrowded lodgings, where they now found themselves, somewhere in the heart of Paris. But her life seemed to have spun out of control, with James left far behind her in England, and Fosdyke not quite himself but different in some inexplicable way.

When Charlotte had come out of James's house only two mornings ago, she had been almost glad to find Fanny waiting. Here at least was a friendly face. Together they easily traced the location of Grisedale and Henning, her father's solicitors. She needed money if she was to get safely home and she could think of no other source. It was on her way out from the solicitor's office, having been granted a small sum from her inheritance on presentation of identification in the form of the letter she had thankfully brought with her, that they met Fosdyke. Without Charlotte's knowledge he had waited patiently for days, for just such an opportunity.

'Well, well, well. Ain't this a surprise to find Lottie again? You must tell us all about your adventures later. Fanny, you go back to Woodley Terrace. Pack everything up and meet us you know where.'

Without a word, Fanny did as she was bid.

And equally obediently, since she had no heart left in her with which to protest, Charlotte allowed herself to be led to a park seat where she briefly related the attack she'd suffered and how Sir James had taken pity on her. She made no mention of Lady Susanna's intervention nor of her quarrel with James, but Fosdyke was shrewd enough to guess that something of the sort had taken place.

'And what are your plans now, little Lottie?' he asked with excessive courtesy, and Charlotte explained her desire to return home, hence her need of money.

She told him then about the inheritance, not realising that he already knew, of course. 'I had not wished to touch it and now that I have I feel besmirched by it,' Charlotte said, tears thick in her voice. 'But I swear it is only temporary until I am on my feet. I shall repay every last penny. What kind of a father would leave money to a child in order to be rid of her?'

'A coward and a heartless cur,' said Fosdyke dramatically. 'It is fortunate that you have friends.' He must tread softly. If he took care not to startle this little filly she might come sweetly into his stable, after all. 'And were you to ask a friend's advice I would give it unstintingly.'

Charlotte glanced up at him, noting his square, cheerful face with its thatch of brown hair and sparkling blue eyes; the only welcome sight left in the whole of London. She gave a wry little smile. 'I dare say I am in need of some.'

'Then cut loose. Leave these shores and start afresh along with Fanny and me. There are jobs aplenty on the continent. You have great talent, little Lottie, and I have the contacts. I can find you all the work you need to make your fortune, and you know

316

that you can trust me, do you not, for have I not been a friend to you?' And, as an afterthought, added, 'We might even discover this relative you seek.' Though Fosdyke, for the life of him, could not remember who it was.

Charlotte could feel relief flowing into her. To return to Cornwall, to Dickon, even to Uncle Nathan without having achieved anything had pressed upon her mind. And what then? What kind of life could she build for herself there in that quiet backwater without being forced to resort to this odious fortune? She had often enough expressed a desire to go on stage for a living; well, here was her chance. If she could not have James, she could at least have that. It might serve to make life relatively tolerable. She turned to Fosdyke. 'Very well. I shall come.'

Fosdyke insisted that she take the precaution of returning to the solicitors to inform them of her whereabouts in the coming months. He gave them the address of the lodging-house he usually used when in Paris and they in turn promised to make arrangements for Charlotte to draw upon a bank there. Fosdyke did not share Charlotte's romantic desire for poverty and in no time at all the necessary letters and papers were drawn up.

They took the first sailing that afternoon from Dover, after first being met by Fanny, complete with hired chaise and baggage.

Charlotte had suggested that she ask Clara to accompany her, since she would have liked female company of her own, not being a close friend of Fanny; but Fosdyke had assured her that there were maids galore in Paris.

And so here they were. The rooms were cheap and, though the ceilings looked in danger of collapsing at any moment, the beds were clean and the food plentiful and good.

'This is but temporary. We shall soar to great heights, the three of us, and will soon have the money to buy our own fine house,' Fosdyke kept repeating. Charlotte laughed at this but a small kernel of unease was born. His constant references to *we* and *our* disturbed her. If she was ever to purchase her own house it would not be with her father's money, nor would she wish to share it with Fanny and Fosdyke, for all his goodness to her in the past. But she did not intend to wait so long for a place of her own. Once she was established she would rent her own rooms and cut loose from them altogether. Yet it would be churlish just now to say so.

The very first morning, Fosdyke went out and left his card at all the likely theatres, including the Paris Opera House which Charlotte considered somewhat presumptuous; they were thus informed that very shortly they would be receiving a call from a 'Mr Wilfred Clement Fosdyke and his protégée, a Miss Lottie Forbes, who would have the honour of displaying her skills in the arts of acting, singing and suchlike delectable arts.' Charlotte trembled at the very prospect of an audition before strangers, but she assumed Fosdyke knew what he was doing.

'And now we must fit ourselves out in proper fashion before facing Paris, this finest capital of Europe, if not the world,' said Fosdyke expansively.

'Will it cost a good deal?' queried Charlotte, conscious of the leanness of her purse, for she had insisted on the absolute minimum of funds to be paid to her.

'You must not think of it as an expense but an investment, my dear,' said Fosdyke. 'No one is likely to offer work to a drab.' This sounded sensible enough and so Charlotte permitted Fosdyke to take her around all the very finest dress establishments. They also visited tailors, for he too must look presentable; perruquiers, milliners, hatters and shoemakers, not to mention all the necessary little items which must accompany these numerous and splendid outfits. And everything had to be of the finest-quality workmanship. Brussels lace, silver buckles, red-heeled pumps, frills, bows, ruffles and furbelows till Charlotte was dizzy with it all. But she was not quite such the innocent. The number of promissory notes she was signing on her new bank account was considerable, covering not only her own expenses but those of Fanny and Fosdyke too.

'Is it quite necessary for you to have four velvet suits, Mr Fosdyke? And at fifteen guineas a time? We never had so many outfits in England. And I am sure I can manage with two ballgowns.'

'But this is not England, Lottie. This is Paris. And the last thing we must look is provincial.'

Certainly, if the ladies who paraded the boulevards were anything to go by, fashion here was indeed considerably different to that in London. Never had Charlotte seen so many fantastical rig-outs in all her life. With their gaudy colours and wide skirts, hair cut short and curly about their heads and as loaded with powder as their faces were with paint and patches, they looked for all the world as if they had just stepped out of one of Harlequin's pantomimes.

She found too that Fosdyke was un-accountably short of funds to pay their full month's rent, required in advance of course, and it was Charlotte again who paid. She made a vow to find work as quickly as possible.

Dressed in a pale rose gown of shot silk which showed off her complexion to perfection, Charlotte prepared for her first audition. Fosdyke schooled her in what to say and how to present herself. It seemed very little to Charlotte, being only a line or two from *Romeo and Juliet*, which she knew anyway, but Fosdyke assured her it would be sufficient. He also made her pay particular attention to way she walked, used her fan and did her hair, and refused to allow her to cover the considerable décolletage of her new dress with a kerchief, however fine the workmanship of the Brussels lace.

'This is not the time for shyness,' asserted Fosdyke.

And so, leaving Fanny languishing in her room drinking wine and nibbling crumbly cake in a new silk nightgown, Fosdyke led the way to the first establishment on his list. The theatre was smaller and darker than Charlotte had expected, but the manager was interested in her from the outset and offered her a position before she had even opened her mouth. If there had not been still so much of the country girl in her make-up she might have realised then that all was not well. Instead of which, she was delighted to have found work so quickly and at such a princely sum each week. He and Fosdyke appeared to be old friends and went off to the local hostelry for a glass of wine while she sat sipping a cup of coffee, watching a rehearsal of an incomprehensible French farce and feeling more relaxed than she had in a long time.

And to think that she had worried over the audition! The only part she had not liked was when Monsieur Cartelet had asked her to lift her skirts and show her legs. Charlotte had at once cast an anguished look at Fosdyke, who had motioned irritably for her to obey. Pink-cheeked, she had granted the briefest glimpse of her ankles and calves, which were not uncomely, and this seemed to settle the matter.

Studying the performance now being so ruthlessly rehearsed, Charlotte realised that language was evidently going to be a problem, and she gave much thought to it. Nothing had been said about her inability to speak French. She had rather assumed, foolishly as it turned out, that the plays would be in English, perhaps played to the many English tourists who crowded into the theatres each night in their expensive silks and satins. Could she learn French? Was it difficult? And who could teach her? Fosdyke seemed to know none at all. It was late afternoon when he returned and when she asked him he merely laughed loudly and said she would find no difficulty in making herself understood, and neither would her customers.

'You mean I'll be taught sufficient French for the audience to understand me?' she asked.

Fosdyke's blue eyes glowed in the light from one of the candle-lanterns which lit the dark narrow streets along which they hurried away from the theatre, and he smiled. 'You will be taught all you need to know,' he said.

And so she was. Fortunately Charlotte had little to say in her first part. Her main function seemed to require her merely to express suitable astonishment at the antics which took place around her and look bemused, which was not at all difficult. A young girl of the name of Arabella taught her three lines in slow, careful French; showed her how to stand and where to move, and dressed her in a cheap, tawdry, blue silk dress which scarcely covered Charlotte's breasts and caused her to flush with embarrassment. When Charlotte mentioned it, Arabella laughed and said she should be glad she had something to show; many hadn't.

'And how did that go?' asked Fosdyke when Charlotte came off stage at the end of the first performance.

'I believe I was the oddest French maid this theatre has ever seen,' she said. 'And I still have not a clue what the play was all about, but I suspect it is just as well. It seems just a little – well...'

'Risqué?'

Charlotte laughingly conceded that she had meant something of the sort.

'And now for supper to celebrate your first night's success,' said Fosdyke. 'Fanny is meeting us at the Globe. I thought the audience most appreciative. They applauded splendidly when you came on.'

'Then it could hardly have been the quality of my acting, could it,' said Charlotte wryly, 'since I had not at that stage spoken a word?'

Charlotte soon discovered that although she was well paid she had to work hard for the money. There were two performances a night plus several matinées. But by the end of the first week she felt her confidence begin to return and was able to add a little more feeling to her performance. As a consequence her audience rating soared.

Fosdyke had watched her with close, though guarded, attention, as had the manager, Monsieur Cartelet. Each night after the performance had ended Fosdyke took Charlotte and Fanny to a supper-house. Many of the girls stayed behind at the theatre while others went to similar establishments, or so Charlotte assumed.

After the last performance on the Saturday evening Monsieur Cartelet came over to them as they were preparing to leave.

'That was a good first week,' he said, in perfect English. 'Next week, Lottie, I'll put you on to full pay.' He gave a lopsided smile. 'For which I'll expect full return on my investment.'

'You shall have it,' agreed Charlotte, eyes shining. 'And, Monsieur Cartelet, I would like you to know that I have bought myself a book and am starting to learn French. I mean to go far in the theatre and I appreciate your giving me a start.'

He went off, laughing as if she had said something exceptionally amusing. Which, in a way, she had, though Charlotte could hardly be expected to know that. By the time the performance ended on the following Monday evening, however, it would be a different story.

'You must know where she is.' James was visiting Lady Susanna for the sixth time that week. On the first two occasions she had been out, or so her maid had said. On the third she had refused point blank to see him.

But, driven by his need to find Charlotte, he had thrust aside the new maid and footman and, guided by Clara, had found his way to the inner sanctum of Susanna's bedchamber, a room she would gladly have taken him to herself in earlier days, and burst in, unannounced.

Susanna had taken a fainting fit, of course. It was her usual recourse in ticklish situations. Unmoved by this show of hysteria, James had bullied and cajoled her, but to no avail. Susanna had clung to the harts-horn which she held to her delicate nose, turned her face away and refused to utter a word. When this had not succeeded in making James leave, she had crumpled limply to the ground, albeit with exquisite delicacy, into absolute if feigned unconsciousness. The uncomfortable interview; as far as she was concerned, was over.

And so, grimly determined, he had returned every day until now, when, wearied by his persistence and knowing it would continue indefinitely, Susanna faced him, bleary-eyed and unusually subdued across the green parlour.

'Well, where is she?'

'I cannot say. I have not the least idea. I do not know. I do not *care*. I have told you a dozen, a thousand times already.' Susanna took a steadying sip of her cordial, for with James in his present mood she doubted that any sign of hysteria or fainting fit would work. He had bludgeoned his way in yet again and there was nothing else for it but to see it through. Ironically enough on this occasion she was telling the truth when she said she had no idea where Charlotte was, but could she make James believe that? She was vastly weary of him, and wished he would go away and stop pacing her oriental carpet in this agitated manner. He would quite wear it out. Yet there were things she could tell him, even now, should she choose to help. But she did not.

'Do stay calm, James. Charlotte Forbes is a grown woman and can surely be allowed to arrange her own life. Frankly I heartily wish I had never set eyes on the chit. The last I saw of her was at Lady Alsager's musical soirée when you and she left early.'

James stopped his pacing to pay closer attention and force his mind back to that night. Before he'd been called away by that silly fool Bletherington, Charlotte had been her usual cheerful self. There had even been a particular awareness between them that night, when they had both seemed sweetly conscious of every touch and scent of skin and hair; a delightful intimacy which might well have developed. But when he had joined her later in the garden he'd been almost sure she'd been crying, though she made no mention of it. And in the ensuing quarrel his disappointment in her had made him vent his anger. Something he found difficult to forgive in himself.

'What did you say to her on that night?' James asked the question softly, but Susanna was not fooled. He had never been a man to be ignored, and now he was like a terrier with the smell of a rat in his nostrils. He would not let up until he had the whole tale out of her. She knew it and she feared it. And he looked so threatening, so huge, towering over her in her tiny parlour.

Tears trembled becomingly on her lower lids as Susanna gazed up at him, but James felt not the slightest stirring of pity, for despite her beauty he knew Lady Susanna Brimley to be more than capable of callous acts of heartlessness. 'Well?' he said sharply, a cutting quality to the single word that made her wince.

'I suggested merely that it would be better for everyone if she were to go home.'

There was a long silence. Unconvinced that this was all, James waited for more. And finally, in nervous distraught whispers, it came.

'I wanted you for myself, James. I love you. I have always loved you. You know that.' The words and the tears tumbled out. 'I wanted her to go away so that you and I could be as we once were.'

'There was never anything beyond friendship between you and I, Susanna, and you know it,' James said, but kinder now as he saw her genuine distress. 'You only imagine you love me. I doubt you are capable of loving anyone beyond yourself. But there must have been more to it than that. What did you say that upset Charlotte so much that she refused my admittedly clumsy offer of marriage and fled my house the very next day?'

The eyes snapped wide. *'Marriage?* You offered her marriage? Why, for God's sake?'

Silence.

Susanna flung back her head and brushed the tears from her doll-like blue eyes and the veneer of charm from her sulky, rosebud lips. She knew when she was beaten. 'Oh, very well. I told her no one would speak to you or to her if she stayed, that your career would be ruined. That no politician should marry his mistress, particularly one who was an actress without any sign of breeding whatsoever.' James winced, imagining all too clearly the effect this would have had on Charlotte. 'And no one did speak to her that night. I made sure of it.' Then Susanna was on her feet, clinging to James with clutching, clawing fingers. 'She is wrong for you, my darling. She can bring you nothing but trouble, while I can bring advancement, riches, glories you've never dreamed possible.'

With commendable self-possession, James took a punishing grip upon Susanna's arms and placed her firmly and abruptly back in her chair. Speaking slowly so that she did not miss a word, nor possibly misunderstand him, he said, 'Can you not see that it is Charlotte I want, not power, not riches, not any advancement you can procure for me? Clara has told me of your earlier attempts to tamper with my life, and with Charlotte's. Now I am telling you to leave us alone, or you'll be sorry for it. It might then be you whom no one speaks to. Do I make myself clear?'

Susanna could do nothing but collapse in her chair and sob.

As James strode to the door she called after him one last time. 'If I help you is there still hope – for us?'

The expression upon his face was everything, but she had admitted too much now to withdraw. Knotting her fingers in her lace handkerchief, Susanna told him through her sobs of a visit from Fanny only the day before, informing her how Charlotte had gone at last to the lawyers to accept her inheritance, preparatory to going abroad. It was all James needed.

Fosdyke's original intention had been to marry Charlotte. Now he pondered on the necessity for this, for it seemed that he could have access to her fortune without resorting to such drastic measures. And there was really no reason why it should be necessary. Hadn't he kept Fanny dangling for years? Once the rustic innocence had been finally eradicated from Charlotte he doubted she would complain. What was it the French called it? *Ménage à trois?* The French had a name for everything! And it should prove most interesting.

But first must come the unburdening of Charlotte's maidenly inhibitions. He wouldn't mind deflowering her himself. But the first time was worth a considerable sum of money, and he was never one to turn away a good business prospect. There would be other opportunities.

'Have you prepared her?' asked Cartelet as soon as they met at the theatre that Monday evening.

Fosdyke shrugged expressively. 'What is there to prepare?'

'Is she willing?'

'Willing or not, the arrangements will go ahead,' said Fosdyke, and there was no sign now of the gleaming smile, only a certain twist of the thick lips. 'Have you found a suitable client?'

Monsieur Cartelet's small eyes gleamed. 'A count. A rich one.'

'Excellent.' It took but moments to make the arrangements which would seal Charlotte's future, and the two men walked away, content.

Meanwhile Charlotte dressed unhurriedly, her mind on her future plans, in the somewhat cramped conditions of the dressing-room. One day she would play at the finest theatres in Paris, London and

Rome. She would make a
huge house and a small
happily away from grasping,
for the rest of her life. She h
covered that life in a Parisia
not at all as much fun as thos
road with the strolling playe
girls were not so friendly, or
understand what they said to
them were none too clean
missed Sally and Peter, even
in their various roles of hero an
most of all she missed James. So
pain of her need was so great it
heart had been scoured clean
body and had left a raw gaping
place. Yet desperately she foug
she dreamed her dreams, thoug
them to be nonsense, it helped
mind from dwelling on James
and on the life they might hav
gether.

'I hear you are coming with us to
house tonight,' whispered Arabel
were about to go on stage.

'Am I?'

Arabella's smile faded slightly
shrugged. 'Funny, I thought you
different, more class than the rest. I
wish to be one of us, why not, eh?'

Charlotte smiled a response and
trying to puzzle out why not going

332

other girls for supper had put her in a higher class. She was delighted to be going with them. Perhaps it meant that she would at last start to make some friends.

There was something about the whole performance that night which was different. It was the same part. She had the same inconsequential lines to say. She smiled and postured in exactly the same way as every other performance, but somehow it was different. Charlotte felt vibrant with energy, filled with an unquenchable optimism. She bounced, and giggled, and flew from bedroom to hall, from hall to bedroom, on and off the stage in a dizzying delight of confusion, and the audience loved it. And she loved them. She could almost feel their presence. For all her part was a small one, Charlotte made the most of it, and received a most satisfying applause at the end of it.

Hot and breathless with her efforts, she stripped off her gown to change into a fresh one. Not tonight one of the many silk and satin gowns she now had in plenty. Fosdyke had insisted that she wear a dress as simple as a milkmaid's, in pink and white striped muslin with a lacy shawl to drape demurely about her shoulders. She rather liked it, for it reminded her of the Charlotte she had once been before this new, more money-conscious one had happened along, whose one thought was how many guineas she could save in a week.

'Come, we must hurry,' urged Arabella, and led Charlotte from the dressing-room only moments before her visitor arrived.

The noise at Babette's was astounding, the atmosphere stuffy, the rabble around the gaming-tables decidedly seedy. Charlotte wished, very fervently, that she had not come at all and admitted as much to Arabella.

'Can you find a chaise to take me home? You were right; this is not for me.'

'And what is it that is not for you, my cherub?' asked Fosdyke, coming up behind her. Charlotte turned to him with relief.

'Oh, thank heavens. I am so tired, and this place seems a trifle – well – disreputable for my taste, Mr Fosdyke. Would you mind very much taking me home?'

The last thing she had expected was for him to refuse. 'What nonsense. The entertainments have scarcely begun. Come, let us find a booth and we can sup. You will feel more yourself then.'

Taking her hand, he led her to a small square booth, completely empty and curtained on three sides by a dingy threadbare fabric that had never seen the inside of a washtub. Charlotte felt quite light-headed. The very smell of the place was making her queasy. Placing her within, Fosdyke called for food, and great bowls of steaming chicken broth were brought. The smell of it almost made her faint, but Charlotte drank what she could, hoping it would make her feel better. The stinking atmosphere ate into any flavour there might have been in the soup and at last she set it aside, the dish still more than half-full. Fosdyke gave her a sharp look, eyes narrowing with speculation.

'Are you unwell, my dear? Have we been working you too hard?'

'I do feel rather giddy,' Charlotte admitted. 'It is so hot and steamy in here. And the smell, so oddly sweet, yet sour; what is it?'

Fosdyke was on his feet in an instant, ushering her from the booth. 'What you require is a little lie-down, my dear. I'd take you home at once, only I have business to attend to and that must come first as I am sure you will understand.'

Charlotte felt worse than she had done before the soup, so made little protest as Fosdyke led her upstairs to a small room and, thrusting her within, begged her to lie down and close her eyes.

'When you wake you will feel a new woman,' he promised. 'And I shall then be ready to take us all home.'

'Thank you,' whispered Charlotte, giddy with tiredness. She felt so very sleepy, her eyes were heavy and her head was beginning to ache.

Much pleased with the simplicity with which he had carried out his plan, Fosdyke withdrew back downstairs to the gaming-tables where, as far as he was concerned, the real action took place. He had no more need to worry about Charlotte for several hours. The Count would take care of her.

CHAPTER SIXTEEN

James entered Babette's establishment just as Fosdyke disappeared upstairs with Charlotte. It took him only a moment to discover that she was not present, at least not in sight, and less than that to ascertain the exact nature of the place.

Not a man to waste time, he went straight to Madame herself, his mind sharpening in preparation for rapid changes in plan. As a politician, he was adept at thinking on his feet.

'*Madame.*' He bowed over the podgy hand as he kissed it and then addressed her in perfect French. 'Sir James Caraddon, if you please. I have heard much of your establishment, of your–' he glanced significantly about him '–excellent service.'

'Nothing but the best quality here,' she said, much flattered.

James smiled, and Madame Babette whimpered. What a man! How she would have made him dance to her tune once upon a day. She heaved a great sigh into her pounds of flesh that flopped in their usual state of exhaustion in the wide, cushioned chair. Once her body had been voluptuous, captivating; if not a hand-span waist then at least a bosom never to be forgotten. Time had played its cruel tricks and her games must be played outside the bedchamber now. But she had done well, brought up several 'nieces' and 'nephews' who now owned vast mansions in the more affluent areas of Paris, denying all knowledge of their 'aunt', which quite delighted her. To Babette it was a mark of her success to lift even a part of her family from the gutter into the fringes of the French aristocracy.

She smiled at James, revealing blackened stubs of teeth. 'And what is to your taste, good sir? Name it and it is yours.'

James was thinking fast. If Charlotte was here, then he may already be too late. His heart felt as if it would burst in his chest at the thought. But he must keep calm. For Charlotte's sake he must keep his head. The girls in the theatre dressing-room had assured him that she would be here with Fosdyke. He dared not think what had gone on this last week. He could only pray that he was in time. And if not...? 'I seek something very special.' James smiled again, his fine brows quirking with speculative enquiry, and Madame Babette sighed nostalgically.

'I may be able to help,' she said, her low tone throbbing with promise. 'Name your fancy.'

'I am most particular who I sport with,' James said, deciding to take the risk. If it did not work he could make his excuses and try another way. 'Pristine merchandise is what I favour. Untouched, unflawed, and beautiful, naturally.'

'Naturally, *monsieur*.' Madame's eyes gleamed, and then the bushy brows came down in a frown. 'A virgin? Difficult to find. I had one, but...' Madame Babette grunted and lifted her shoulders in an expressive shrug. They were almost impossible to find in her experience, but she had one or two who could pass for it.

'I can pay.' Madame lifted her eyebrows as she viewed the pouch of coins he showered into her lap. 'And there is more if I am satisfied with the goods.'

There was a small silence.

'Cartelet,' she called, her voice as demanding and musical as a crow's.

'Madame?'

In a few blunt sentences James's requirements were outlined, the money having been swiftly pocketed and a minimum portion, just enough to capture his interest, handed over to Cartelet. Madame jerked her head in the direction of the stairs. 'I believe we did have a new girl tonight?'

'She is taken, *madame.*'

Madame Babette, unused to being crossed, stamped her great foot upon the floor and the room trembled. 'Give the Count Marguerite. He'll never know the difference.'

'He'll not be pleased. I think he's already gone up.'

The hand lashed out, rattling Cartelet's teeth in his jaw. 'I never asked your opinion. Get on with it.' Turning to James, the black teeth once more revealed in a grimace that passed for her smile, she said, 'You'll not be disappointed, I think. But go gently with her; she's a young maid, unbroken, fresh from the country. A gentleman like yourself should set her nicely on the daisy path to dalliance. We don't want to spoil her at the start, eh?'

She was still cackling as James mounted the stairs behind Cartelet, his heart in his throat. Never had he prayed so fervently as he did now. He only wished the man would not dawdle so. James longed to knock him to one side, to bound up the stairs and tear open every door until he found Charlotte. But that would be lunatic and, in the end, time-consuming for it was not a small establishment and he might miss her. After climbing several flights of stairs they turned at last into a landing. Outside a door Cartelet stopped and tapped lightly upon it. Nothing happened.

James stepped nearer to the door. Was that a sound? A cry rang out and he could wait no longer. Heart pounding fit to burst, he could no longer restrain the molten energy that flowed through his limbs. Thrusting the astonished Cartelet to one side, James burst open the locked door, splintering the ancient wood with his wide shoulders.

He stood riveted to the spot. 'Charlotte!' She was indeed there, standing on the bed, legs astride, her muslin dress torn to the waist revealing the pretty, almost school-girlish lace of her shift and the soft bloom of half one breast. She had her hands raised, and in them was a bedpost. 'Dear Lord, she must have ripped it off with her bare hands,' murmured James. Sprawled senseless upon the bed lay the half-clothed body of the Count, or so James presumed. That gentleman had clearly been in the process of taking off his shirt when Charlotte must have felled him with a mighty blow. He had the lump upon his regal head to prove it and would doubtless not forget this visit to Madame Babette's in a hurry.

With a cry Charlotte leapt from the bed

and ran straight into James's arms. And there was really nothing more he wanted to do than to hold her safe and to kiss her. Then, lifting her in his arms, ignoring the protests of the astonished Monsieur Cartelet, James carried her out of the room and down the stairs. Charlotte buried her face into his shoulder and clung fast.

They were met by the furious anger of Fosdyke, who almost growled and snapped at them from the foot of the staircase like a demented wolf.

'You've lost her, Fosdyke. I'm taking her home with me and if you come near her again I'll whip you to within an inch of your life, not to mention having you flung into gaol for abduction.'

'But I–'

'Did you hear me? Oh, yes; as for our little business arrangement. You will be hearing from my lawyers next week, terminating our agreement. I do not do business with rogues.'

Fosdyke glared at James for a long moment before finally offering a sweeping, mocking bow. '*Touch*é, good sir. May you enjoy her as much as I would have done. You'll forgive me if I do not return the loans she made to me. My situation is a little stretched just at present.'

James told him he would have great pleasure in sending his account to the devil and, kicking open the door, swept out with Charlotte clasped firmly against his breast.

'But how did you know that I was there?'

They were on the deck of the ship bound for London and James was outlining his search to Charlotte, but he kept getting side-tracked, for it was far too beautiful a day for serious talk and she was much too delicious not to kiss.

When James had filled in all the details to Charlotte's satisfaction she had to have one or two portions repeated, just to be sure that he had truly needed to find her as much as he had said.

'I dare say you guessed what Fosdyke really had in mind, being far more worldly than I,' Charlotte said, then ruefully added, 'Is there anyone at all that I can trust?'

The answer to that was so obvious that James had difficulty not spanking her, so he kissed her again, just for good measure. 'When we get home, do you know the very first thing I shall do?'

Charlotte gazed at him, wide-eyed, and shook her head, a sudden fear in her voice. 'Send me home to Cornwall?'

James threw back his head and laughed, squeezing her close in his arms at the same time. The sea breezes had burnished her cheeks to copper, and wisps of her hair curled and danced about her face. How could he resist such vibrant, loving beauty? 'No, my sweet. From now on your home is with me. I shall waste not a moment in making you my wife before you have the chance to run away again.'

Charlotte opened her mouth to protest, her heart leaping and sinking, burning and going cold by turn at his words. If only she could. His fingers closed her lips and her protests. 'Listen to me before you speak, my little love. I intend to reduce my political commitments. No, do not interrupt. I'd grown tired of the corruption, the cheating, the personal favours and back-stabbing that goes on. I shall do my duty, but I have discovered other interests now. I have also sold my paper.'

'Then the scandalmongers have won.'

James laughed. 'Not at all. I have not sold it to Bletherington but to a new man who will develop it in a way I approve of. Instead I have bought a plot of land where I intend to build the finest theatre London has ever seen. No, not for you to act in it, my love, though I dare say you might from time to time when you are not too busy looking after me and our future family.'

Charlotte flushed bright scarlet. What was he saying?

'But I certainly hope that you will help me to run it. The theatre is yet in its infancy and I believe its prime may well be both interesting and profitable.'

'Oh, James,' was all she could manage as she looked up at him with adoring eyes, even as hope died in her breast. 'But I still cannot marry you. You have forgotten. There is the question of my birth.'

Again the fingers came down, stroking and tracing the beloved line of her lips which he wanted to kiss and kiss again till she begged for mercy. But first things first. Taking Charlotte's hand, he led her to a quiet corner of the ship where they were not observed. Seating her gently on a coil of ropes, he took her cold hands between his own.

'I have not forgotten, Charlotte. As I have so often told you, the particulars of your birth are of no importance to me. I love you for what you are, not for who you are. Do you understand?'

She scarcely dared believe the evidence of her own ears.

'I have also found your mother.'

A gasp of astonishment, of delight, of fear.

James smiled. 'She sends her love and looks forward to seeing you. While searching for you, I left my card all over town at every theatre and every establishment with theatrical connections I could find. She has changed her name of course, so that is probably why you could not find her. But she recognised your name and, out of concern for you, called upon me. She asked that when I did find you, which thank God I have, I tell you the story of your birth so it would be less painful for her. I shall do my best, though it is a sorry tale and I shall make it brief.'

'Go on. I am ready.' Charlotte withdrew her hands from his and clasped them tightly together. She must face whatever it was with courage.

'Your mother, Eleanor, was courted by two brothers, Jeffrey and Justin Forbes. She fell in love with and secretly married the younger son, Jeffrey. Out of fear of Justin's jealousy, they dared not risk discovery. They were right to fear him, for, driven mad by his jealousy and desire for Eleanor, Justin challenged his brother to a mock duel which turned deadly serious. Justin used it to kill his brother as if by accident.'

Charlotte had turned deathly pale, and James put out a hand in case she should fall, but she shook her head and sat up very straight. 'Continue. I am fine.'

'After her husband's death, Eleanor stayed on at the family home and married Justin.'

Charlotte gasped. 'Just as happened in *Hamlet*.'

James frowned for a moment. 'I suppose there may be a similarity. Except that Eleanor was already carrying you, so when Justin begged her to stay and marry him she decided it would be better than trying to bear a child alone with no means of support. She admits she should have found the courage to tell Justin that she and his brother had been legally married, and that she was pregnant. But she failed to do so. Understandably in the circumstances.'

'I see.' For the first time Charlotte began to view her mother as a real person, with an insurmountable problem. 'Then, my father was Jeffrey, not Justin, Forbes?'

James nodded. 'Eleanor realised her mistake in marrying Justin almost at once. Justin's violent, possessive nature constantly got the better of him and when he discovered that his wife was with child by his dead brother his rage knew no bounds. To her credit, Eleanor stayed for almost two years, long enough to wean you and see you safely on a healthy path. So many infants die in those first two years that she felt she owed you that at least. But she could take no more, and left one dark morning in January, leaving you a letter expressing her love and hoping that as you grew you would find it in your heart to forgive her.'

'I never got it.'

'No doubt your father destroyed it. Eleanor believed Justin would continue to care for you, and you had a nurse who adored you. She believed she had nothing to offer you.'

'Except her love,' said Charlotte softly, tears shining in her eyes.

James gently inclined his head. 'I think she realises that now, and it is hard for her to live with. Particularly since Justin at once dismissed your beloved nurse, and all the other servants you knew, then left you in the care of a total stranger while he went abroad. Though, by the time Eleanor had learned all this, Nathan had long since taken you under his capable wing and she decided to leave well alone. Besides which the vicious rumours had started and the last thing she could do in the circumstances was to go to her brother's house. It would have only made matters worse for you.'

'Yes, I see that.'

'But perhaps Justin's guilt did get the better of him in the end and that is why he left you his fortune – to compensate for killing your father.'

Charlotte hung her head for a moment, too moved to speak.

'Your mother too was ashamed.'

'But it was not my mother's fault that I was abandoned.'

James smiled with relief. 'I am glad to hear you say so. You will like your mother. She is a lovely lady. No longer an actress, she runs an establishment which makes costumes for such as the Drury Lane, the Haymarket and the Opera, the very best theatres. She made a good life for herself and a successful business, but I suspect she is lonely and would more than welcome a prodigal daughter.'

'Oh, James, I cannot thank you enough for finding her.' And now the tears were running, and James was kissing each one away, his arms cradling her soft body against his own.

'I did promise her that she would find her daughter again, and that one day, not too far distant, she might well have grandchildren at her knee as well.'

And, before Charlotte was able to repeat his name on a sigh yet again, now becoming a trifle monotonous in James's opinion, he concentrated her attentions entirely upon his kisses, which she was more than willing to do.

The publishers hope that this book has given you enjoyable reading. Large Print Books are especially designed to be as easy to see and hold as possible. If you wish a complete list of our books please ask at your local library or write directly to:

Magna Large Print Books
Magna House, Long Preston,
Skipton, North Yorkshire.
BD23 4ND